AF753814

A HARD LEFT

ALSO BY PAUL MCGRATH

The Terran Incognita Series

Left (Book 1)

Left is Right (Book 2)

A HARD LEFT

THE TERRAN INCOGNITA SERIES
BOOK 3

PAUL MCGRATH

Stoney Creek Publishing

Stoney Creek Publishing
A Member of the Texas Book Consortium

Published by
Stoney Creek Publishing Group
StoneyCreekPublishing.com

Copyright © 2026 by Paul McGrath. All rights reserved.

ISBN: 978-1-965766-81-1
ISBN (ebook): 978-1-965766-82-8
Library of Congress Control Number: 2026905893

No part of this book may be reproduced in any form or by any electronic or mechanical means, including information storage and retrieval systems, without written permission from the author, except for the use of brief quotations in a book review.

This book is a work of fiction. Names, characters, places, and incidents are either the product of the author's imagination or are used fictitiously, and any resemblance to actual persons, living or dead, business establishments, events or locales is entirely coincidental.

Cover design by Ken Ellis

Printed in the United States

Dedicated to the memory of Jim Bouton, whose words seldom failed to cross the heart of the plate. You opened a young boy's eyes to the frailties of heroes. I hope you are still able to "smoke 'em on the inside."

CHAPTER 1

The Aurus Senat came to a stop in a blue plume of smoke outside the dreary beige, monolithic building that took up nearly a full block of 55 Savushkina Street in St. Petersburg. There was no address number on the nondescript four-story building; that was by design. Heavy-coated guards, wearing camouflage and armed with Kalashnikovs, patrolled the perimeter sidewalks, and the outcropped brickwork marking the roofline shielded security cameras placed at twenty-foot increments.

The structure was the very definition of paranoia. When a building is too big to hide, fear can be used to keep eyes from prying—or mouths from talking.

The mid-February snowfall was beginning to produce faster and heavier salvos, and the flurries were forming piles in the street. The driver of the Aurus leapt from the vehicle and moved quickly to open the rear passenger door. Nikolai Ivanov, fearing for his handmade alligator shoes, dodged the slushy curb as he stepped out of the vehicle and put his black beaver Cossack hat atop his head for the short walk to the door. He pulled his overcoat tight, waved an arm at the driver, and trudged toward the entrance and into the building's intimidating security antechamber. His status afforded him no protection from this room. His credentials, like those of anyone else who entered, were checked thoroughly.

Ivanov, who had just turned fifty-five, was the newly promoted director of the Glavset, the Russian name for the innocuous Internet Research Agency (IRA). In the West, the site was given a label with a darker connotation: the "Propaganda Kitchen." The stew of zeroes and ones that emerged from this building had been creating mischief, mayhem, and malevolence for decades. One former IRA employee, a journalism student who became a pseudo-mole, described his work there as "a merry-go-round of lies." Its political influence and disinformation "active measures"—a term that originated in the 1950s—had ensnared countries across the globe. For those in the game, "active measures" are intended to be covert and offer a veneer of deniability for the perpetrators.

The IRA typically saw 400 or so employees working day and night in twelve-hour shifts in vast open floor plans, manufacturing disinformation and pro-Kremlin propaganda (among other mischief). The so-called "troll farm" is a quasi-private company believed to have been created by businessman-turned-oligarch-turned-warlord Yevgeny Prighozin, the future founder of the Wagner Group, a private military organization. Prighozin and the Wagner Group were often used to perform the "bloodwork" of the Russian president, at least until the two had a falling-out over Russia's conduct in the Ukraine war. The spat turned into a short-lived coup that eventually saw Prighozin banished to Belorussia. A plane crash—or was it an assassination attempt?—in August 2023 killed Prighozin and nine others, ending the dispute for good.

The Russians were far from being the only world actors partaking in cyber warfare and information theft. The North Koreans were credited—blamed?—for a bold assault against Sony Pictures in 2014, one that proved quite embarrassing to certain movie moguls. The Chinese launched Salt Typhoon in late 2024, gaining remote control over targeted servers and then penetrating nine U.S. telecommunications companies. The Chinese purloined access to the metadata of millions of cellphone users in the Washington, D.C., area, including devices belonging to both presidential candidates and the Republican running mate.

Moscow was now feeling the pressure to stay in the race with Beijing.

Ivanov paused to look over what he had become steward of. It was a sea of computers and data storage devices with blinking lights and whirring disc drives. All was silent except for the click-clacking of keyboards across the chamber. He smiled as he took in the vastness of his cyber kingdom, and his smile widened a bit as his thoughts turned briefly to the woman he'd had just a half-hour before.

Before Ivanov could enter his windowless office—what windows existed were covered by thick curtains or deeply darkened—he was stopped by his executive assistant, Olga Alexandrova, who handed him a hot cup of tea. She was also the wife of Ivanov's second-in-command, Dmitri Alexandrov, who had been interim head of "the farm."

"Thank you, Olga. That will be all for now," Ivanov said, carefully sipping the tea to counter the outside chill. He took a quick glance at Olga's backside as he entered his office. He removed his hat and overcoat and sat at his desk to review the latest reports, sticky notes flagging the most urgent. His gray-brown hair touched his shoulders in the back, and his mustache was upturned with a telltale bit of wax on each end.

Ivanov leaned back in his chair and interlocked his fingers on the vest of his suit. He thought about how he got his start in this "troll" business in an equally nondescript building in another part of St. Petersburg. He had been part of a small team of hackers who had stolen thousands, if not millions, from Citibank in 1994. Citibank officials had contacted the FBI after several corporate customers reported some $400,000 missing from their accounts. The Russian hackers, working for themselves then rather than the Kremlin, used valid user identifications and passwords to infiltrate telecom networks and thus gain access to the bank's cash-management computer system. That was the system corporate clients used to transfer funds globally to other banks.

The FBI pinpointed some 40 transactions between June and October

1994 that resulted in more than $10 million being sent to overseas accounts—the first online bank robbery. Citibank managed to get those assets frozen, narrowing the pursuit trail to a "live" account in San Francisco. An attempt to withdraw funds there led first to the arrest of a Russian, then to the arrest of her husband. The pair guided the FBI to a third Russian, Vladimir Levin, who was arrested in 1995 after being lured to London. He pleaded guilty in 1998.

Or was it Levin at all? A St. Petersburg hacker who went by the name "Megazoid" claimed it was he who did the actual cyber-burgling of the Citibank system using only a 2400-baud modem and a second-hand PC. Braggadocio in the hacker ranks is not unheard of, so could Ivanov have been this "Megazoid"? Or someone else? It remains unknown.

Ivanov managed to escape without being charged, and the caper established his bona fides in the hacker world and with Moscow. In the decades after the Citibank heist, he went on to hold a number of computer "consultant" positions, including a few with the Internet Research Agency.

When Glavset was established is somewhat murky; it was reportedly first exposed by an American journalist in 2015. Reports indicate that it had grown in darkness to having more than 1,000 employees. The agency's task list expanded from cybercrime to promoting the Kremlin's foreign and domestic policies and interests on social networks, online newspaper sites, and digital discussion boards through thousands of false accounts, often called bots. The Russian president was particularly pleased with Glavset's success in influencing the recent U.S. presidential election, especially in getting nearly half of the American electorate to believe no meddling had occurred. In 2016, when the Republican candidate dared the agency to uncover the missing emails of Hillary Clinton, the Democratic candidate, it did just that. Glavset turned the emails over to online provocateur WikiLeaks to do with as it pleased. In February 2018, 13 Russians, all believed to be members of the Main Directorate of the General Staff of the Armed Forces of the Russian Federation (GRU for short), and three Russian entities, including Glavset, were indicted by a U.S. federal grand jury on election interference charges.

The agency attempted more election shenanigans in 2020, and in 2024, the FBI discovered a Russian network of fake news sites pumping out thousands of bogus stories, including one about the Ukrainian first lady purchasing a Bugatti Tourbillon sports car. Social mediums in the U.S. took the axe to hundreds of fraudulent sites and bots, although it appears to have been the proverbial too-little-too-late effort.

France has frequently been another favorite target, becoming the subject of Moscow's cyber hornets in its elections in 2017 and 2024. Russian interference took the form of disinformation campaigns and hacking attempts aimed at undermining candidate Emmanuel Macron. The French successfully countered these efforts by proactively informing political parties about the threats and maintaining strict media regulations during the election period.

More recently, Moscow's "Matryoshka" propaganda operation targeted Moldova, with its contested Transnistria region, with 39 false claims, including that the Moldovan president was addicted to psychotropic drugs and had embezzled $24 million. Despite these efforts, the pro-European ruling party won decisively, retaining power and giving an embarrassing black eye to Matryoshka's masters.

This was the agency Ivanov was now directed to lead. *At least I do not have to partake in the brutish activities of my GRU colleagues,* Ivanov told himself. *Those actions are below a man of my caliber.* The Kremlin had recently taken to hiring street thugs and other criminals to perform sabotage in Western nations, such as the March 2024 arson fire that consumed a London warehouse containing supplies for Ukraine. These "contractors" were often paid using cryptocurrency.

Ivanov tweaked the ends of his mustache, then buzzed Olga on his intercom. "Please send Dmitri...your husband...in as soon as he is free. *Spasibo* (thank you)."

Dmitri Alexandrov, heavyset and unkempt, soon appeared, out of breath, at Ivanov's door. "Come in, Dmitri," the new chief said. "Have a seat."

Alexandrov did as was requested, his face reddening when the seat cushion emitted an embarrassing sound.

Ivanov smiled at his comrade's discomfort. "Tell me, Dmitri, what are our most promising operations at the moment?"

"First, comrade director, let me express my congratulations to you for securing this position. I know your reputation, and it is quite an honor to work with you."

"Thank you, Dmitri. But please continue."

"*Da*. Despite our earlier failures, we have had great success at stirring up trouble for the French president. Thanks greatly to our efforts in inciting the French people, the president has had to order early parliamentary elections. It may result in the fall of the French government."

"Yes. That has made for some intriguing reading," Ivanov said. "What else is ongoing?"

"We continue to tweak the noses of the Americans by spreading a variety of stories—some true, some not—about the Cabinet selections of the incoming president. They are being besmirched and compromised almost as soon as he names them. And we have had great success in our initial tests with artificial intelligence, particularly in the creation of videos using fake celebrities and political figures. I recommend that we direct more resources to that team."

"Good. Very good, Dmitri. Continue your efforts on those fronts," said Ivanov, who now leaned forward in his chair. "I want to give you a heads-up on a possible bigger operation."

"Bigger operation, sir?"

"I can't say any more at the moment. Let's just say that we have our harpoon stuck deeply into a huge American whale. This could be the capture that changes everything."

"Outstanding, sir. Can you tell me the name of this American whale?"

"Not as yet," replied Ivanov, enjoying yet another opportunity to leave a secret dangling. "For now, let's just call him 'The Benefactor.' "

CHAPTER 2

It had been months since Isabella Muñoz had driven a panel truck for hours and hours to escape a life as a sex slave at a white supremacist encampment hidden in the woods near Coeur d'Alene, Idaho. Isabella, now twenty-two, had brought fifteen other captives, all of them much younger, with her on the multistate journey back to El Paso, the city where they all had entered the U.S. They had been smuggled into the city through a tunnel that connected to the Mexican side, but their quest for a new life had turned into a trek into an old terror. The smugglers and a Texas motorcycle gang had sold Isabella and the other girls to an alliance of American Aryans.

The Aryans had hoped to turn their female captives into a revenue stream. An American girl, Kristi Fleming, had been added to the Aryan harem, but, as Isabella learned later, fears over the growing national search had persuaded the supremacists to release Kristi in California. Most of the others were, like Isabella, of Mexican origin, but some were from Venezuela or Ecuador. The girls were housed together and were not touched. "Save them for the paying customers" was the standing order. The only exception was Isabella; she was used repeatedly in the "sex rooms" despite the command. Threats of harm to the others coerced her acquiescence. Although now free,

Isabella had been unable to scrape away memories of those horrible nights. She wondered if she would still be able to bear children someday.

At the end of the drive from Coeur d'Alene, Isabella had found an area of El Paso where day laborers gathered. It was the safest place she could think of to release her fifteen passengers; none of them knew where their parents were. Isabella was one of the lucky ones; she borrowed a cellphone and was able to reach her father, who was still in El Paso with the rest of Isabella's family. They were reunited, and Isabella spent weeks recovering from her ordeal. Because she spoke English rather well, she was quickly able to join her mother as a domestic worker and later became a waitress at her aunt's restaurant.

Isabella often thought of the two Americans who had rescued her and the others. They had given her only their first names—Anton and Ellie. She felt the pair must have been heaven sent; they used some devices to keep the Aryan guards standing in place and put them under their control. It was like the guards had become hypnotized, which was how she explained it to those who asked. Isabella smiled at the memory of being allowed to kick her chief abuser in the *cojones*.

Time passed, but thoughts of Coeur d'Alene still haunted her. Isabella became curious to learn if justice—retribution?—had been obtained. Despite the possible consequences of exposing herself, she approached an El Paso police officer breakfasting at a café. The patrolman was dubious of her story, so she offered to lead police to the warehouse where the U.S. side of the tunnel was located. Fearful of a trap, the officer called for backup, and a sergeant and a second patrolman, a rookie cop, soon appeared. The kidnapped girls had not been able to see much of the building, but Isabella's father—too fearful of American police to join her—had given a good description of the warehouse. Still, it took more than an hour before Isabella shouted, "That's the one."

The sergeant and his partner cautiously approached the warehouse; Isabella and the other officer remained with the vehicle. The warehouse appeared abandoned; boards and sheeting secured a gaping hole where garage doors had been. The sergeant drew his weapon and tore away enough of the sheeting to allow entry. He radioed to the officer with Isabella, "Going in. Keep your eyes open out here." Then he and his partner disappeared into the dark interior.

After a few minutes, the novice officer signaled for the two outside to enter. The sergeant was probing the large room with his flashlight, and the two patrolmen began chattering with one another. Isabella moved to where the tunnel entrance should have been—but it had been filled in with a large amount of concrete. *What happened here?* she wondered. The top of the concrete did not align with the warehouse floor, but it was enough to make the tunnel forever unusable. The sergeant rejoined them and pointed his flashlight at the tire marks on the warehouse floor. It appeared that a large vehicle—a cement truck?—had sped out of the warehouse. The sergeant noted that the damage to the door was likely made by a vehicle that was exiting, not one entering. "That's strange," he said, and then he began talking excitedly on his radio.

"Am I free to go?" Isabella asked the first officer.

"You'd better wait for a bit, ma'am. You aren't in custody, but I bet there are some folks who are going to have questions about all this," the officer said.

"I don't know too much. But I will help in any way I can. These *bastardos* should pay for what they did."

Within twenty minutes, a platoon of squad cars poured down the alleyway that led to the warehouse. Detectives began consulting with the patrol sergeant as forensics team members attempted to ferret out what evidence they could. Using a detailed map of Juarez, one of the detectives was able to provide a good guess as to location of the tunnel entrance on the Mexican side. "This warehouse here is the most direct path. We'll need to get approval from Juarez before we can go over and make certain though," he said.

Another detective asked Isabella to give her account of what had happened. She began by describing the smugglers as best she could and how the exchange went down. Then she mentioned how she and the other captives had been transported to Idaho and that some group called the Patriot Boyz had held them in a compound in the woods.

"Wait. Did you say Patriot Boyz?" asked the detective. "Oh, shit. Fuck me running."

The detective then went to another officer, this one better dressed—Isabella presumed it was his superior—and told him what he had learned. "This could be connected to the kidnapping of that Albuquerque girl," the superior said. "We're going to have to get the FBI in on this."

"Fucking feds," said the other detective. "They are going to parachute in here to grab all the glory on this."

"We don't have much choice, do we?" said the superior. "Besides, they can deal with Juarez better than we can. Call up your favorite or least favorite feeb, and let's make an appointment."

Isabella stood watching the fervent activity inside and out of the warehouse. The detectives were incredulous over her description of the tunnel. Headroom. Lights. Air-conditioning. She did not know the full name of the smugglers' *jefe;* she recalled that she heard one of his men call him Ernesto. Before she could continue, the lead detective received a call.

"Right. Right. That's right," he said. "Now is a good time? OK, we are on our way. Be there in fifteen or so."

The detective pocketed the phone. "Isabella, we'd like for you to come with us. The almighty Federal Bureau of Investigation would like a word," he said. "You are not in any trouble. Far from it. I'm thinking you've paved your way into *Estados Unidos* for good."

On the drive over to the federal building in El Paso, the lead detective shared what he knew, which was little more than what Isabella knew from watching the news. Close to 200 members of various white supremacist groups and a dozen or so members of a Texas motorcycle gang had been arrested on human smuggling charges and/or their roles in the kidnapping of Kristi Fleming. A variety of other charges were thrown in for good measure.

"Funny thing was, these guys all turned themselves in. Even provided some of the evidence to put their necks in the noose," he said. "It made national news. Some of them fixed up a Black church, and some of them sang tunes outside a cop station before they fessed up. Talk about wild."

Isabella smiled to herself but said nothing. From what she saw during her rescue, she had a good idea who was responsible for the supremacists' actions before her surrender.

They arrived at the federal building and were quickly ushered into the office of Special Agent in Charge Damian Cruz. The officers shook hands, and Isabella was offered a seat. Beverage requests were soon filled.

"Isabella...can I call you Isabella?" Cruz asked. She nodded.

"It looks like you can help us fill in some pieces of a very large puzzle," he continued. "Thanks to their own admissions, we have brought some serious charges against the leaders of some pretty nasty folks. Duke Kuhn of the Patriot Boyz, 'Boogie' Thorne of the White Hammers. Silas Vance of the New Confederacy. Zephyr Reed of the Wrathkeepers. Lady Justice has already had her way with a couple of others. Nikolai Petrov of the Pioneer Guard and Romero Martinez, head honcho of the Bandoleros motorcycle gang. There was an Albuquerque deputy involved as well. He's in custody."

Isabella's eyes widened. "Might I ask what happened to Mr. Petrov?"

"No need to be so formal with that piece of shit," Cruz said. "His nickname was 'The Bear,' and you might say he met a fitting end. He got eaten by a polar bear at a Michigan zoo."

Isabella said nothing but thought it odd that Petrov was at a zoo. He didn't seem the zoo type. The detectives couldn't stop from chuckling.

"Martinez drove his bike into the Gulf of Mexico. Found his body two days later," Cruz said. "Isabella, do you mind if I record this conversation?"

She wondered if she had any choice, but she agreed.

"I want you to know that this will have no negative bearing on your immigration status. We greatly appreciate your help. What can you tell us about the smuggling operation and the camp in Idaho?"

Isabella repeated what she had told the detectives about coming to the border, entering the tunnel, and being separated afterward. She related how they were driven for hours, fed chips and sodas occasionally, and given bathroom breaks. She described being handed over to a new group somewhere in Wyoming. Isabella did not include being assaulted by Petrov at the handoff site. The man was dead; it would be her secret.

She then described how the original handful of girls grew to sixteen, including Kristi Fleming once she arrived. Isabella knew little more about Kristi's kidnapping than what the teen had told authorities. "She said one of her kidnappers had like a Russian accent. I would guess that it might have been this Petrov," she said.

"You are probably right, but we will likely never know," said Cruz. "We showed Kristi Fleming a photo array of all the group leaders and the members we arrested. She wasn't able to positively identify any of them. Apparently, they kept her blindfolded. Did they blindfold you?"

"No, they wanted me to keep the other girls under control."

"Can you look at some pictures and tell us if you recognize anyone?" Cruz called up a display on his computer and turned the screen toward Isabella.

She was able to identify Theo Davies, a co-leader of the Patriot Boyz, and a few other members of the Patriot Boyz and Pioneer Guard who drove them to the Idaho camp. She was kept blindfolded after that, even during the rapes, except when in the cabin with the other girls. Isabella then related what she remembered of the camp routines, the food they were given, the types of guns the guards had, and what conversations she could pick up.

"This is great information, Isabella. You are being very helpful," Cruz said. "Now, what can you tell us about your rescue? You told the detectives that there were only two people involved?"

"There may have been more, but I could only see two."

"What kind of weapons were they carrying?"

"That was very odd. They didn't have any weapons, but all of the guards seemed to be frozen in their place. They didn't move the whole time we were loading up in the truck to get away."

"Frozen? Frozen how?" Cruz inquired.

"I don't know, sir. They just couldn't move."

"Did they identify themselves in any way?"

Isabella felt she had to reply. "They said their names were Anton, he was the man, and Ellie, the woman," she said. "But I had a feeling those were not their real names. Just what they wanted me to hear."

"How do you know that?"

"I'm not sure, sir. It's just a feeling," she said.

"What did they look like? Would you be able to pick them out in a lineup if there was one?"

"I don't think so. All I can remember is blond hair on the man and dark hair on the woman. But they were very confident and very brave. Being outnumbered did not seem to bother them."

"Interesting," said Cruz. "Well, let's take a little break. We've arranged a little something special for you. There's someone eager to talk to you. I hope you don't mind that we told her you would be here."

Cruz clicked on the Zoom application on his computer and soon the blond-framed visage of Kristi Fleming appeared.

"ISABELLA! It really is you. I'm so glad to see you," Kristi said rapid-fire.

Isabella couldn't speak. Tears streamed down her face.

"Thankyouthankyouthankyou for everything you did for me," Kristi said. "You kept me alive and kept me from being...you know. I can never thank you enough."

Isabella choked, then regained a bit of her composure. "We never knew what happened to you after the guards took you away. Are YOU OK?"

"Yes, I'm fine. Back home and back in school." Kristi described how the guards bound her on the floorboard of a car and took her to a California hospital after misleading her that she was being taken north. "I'm so glad those men got arrested. But I'm still afraid to go out after dark by myself."

"That's very understandable," Isabella said. She then told Kristi about her escape and what happened to the other girls.

The three law enforcement officers just let them talk, and Cruz jotted down notes from time to time.

The two talked for a bit longer, then exchanged cellphone numbers. Kristi ended the Zoom call with, "Please come see me sometime. I'd love to show you around Albuquerque."

Then her face disappeared.

Cruz turned the screen around. "Isabella, we would like for you to help us locate the other girls if possible. If you young ladies are willing to help us, I believe we can expedite things to help you and your families stay here," he said. "I'm sure we can offer more if you and your friends are willing to testify."

"Can you keep us safe?"

"We can do that."

Isabella couldn't see the skeptical looks cross the faces of the two detectives.

"It's called witness protection. Also, some judges might allow you to testify remotely so you won't have to face those men in the courtroom."

"That would be the best option. I want to see those men punished, so I will do all I can to help. Yes, I will try to find the others," she said.

The special agent in charge called for a federal prosecutor to come down, and Isabella had to repeat most of her story, which made the El Paso detectives even less enamored of their federal colleagues. She then began signing a thick batch of preliminary documents to become a protected witness for the government. He wasn't looking forward to the extensive report he was going to have to write on this interview, a report that would then be forwarded to Washington for dissemination to the other FBI field offices.

Cruz sat silently for the most part, offering guidance and encouragement when needed, as Isabella signed the forms. *Sometimes you can look a gift horse in the mouth, especially when that gift horse just walks into your office,* he thought.

CHAPTER 3

It turns out lug nuts can freeze.

Anton struggled mightily with the tire iron, but it would no longer budge.

"*Girgach gradakh ma'ch!* Fuckshit and shitfuck," Anton grumbled as he stepped away in frustration from the vehicle in the driveway.

Gator, a chiweenie rescue dog—literally—clambered atop the sofa and peered between the curtains, whimpering over his owner's travails.

Ellie sipped her coffee and came over to the window to pet Gator's head. "Oh, Daddy's not happy, is he?" She gave the concerned dog another scritch.

Anton-7—now in his human form and using the pseudonym of Michael Gort, a name he had borrowed from a character in a 1950s science fiction movie—wiped his sweaty hands with a work rag. Ellie had taken her Tesla on some errands and then, as was her habit, detoured to inspect the area's new home construction. In the process, she picked up a nail or screw. Again. The rear driver's side tire was now completely flat. He had the spare and jack ready if he could win the battle against one rusted lug nut.

Anton was now married to Ellie, or by her Xylodonian birth name,

Juleetha-6. They were both Centurion Guardians for Xylodon's Security Corps. Anton often reminded himself, *At least I'm a third brevet, so I still outrank her.* For what little that mattered in their Hernando, Mississippi, household. Both of them were now using the cover of being teachers at Hernando Elementary School.

Xylodon was a highly advanced planet just beyond the Milky Way system, and its leaders had looked upon Earth's space advances with growing trepidation. Additionally, Xylodon was an exceedingly dry planet—unlike Earth—and the same leaders coveted that planet's ability to produce water. The development of "artificial water" some two centuries ago had helped prevent a crisis, but still the shortage was a concern. For those reasons and others, teams of Centurion Guardians had been dispatched to nearly all parts of Earth to conduct surveillance and uncover scientific data that might assist Xylodon with water preservation, procurement, and production. The endeavor was named Operation Silent Vigilance. Anton, who had had multiple earlier tours on Earth, had been sent to Mississippi for his next assignment; a panicked colleague ended up stranding him there. Juleetha had been ordered to Colorado to observe the North American Aerospace Defense Command. While Anton had assumed the role of a U.S. government biologist, Juleetha debuted the teaching credentials she brought to Hernando.

Nearly two years ago, Anton and Juleetha had stepped away from Operation Silent Vigilance—Anton because of need, Juleetha because of choice. As retribution for the tragic death of a human friend, Anton—then using the personas of Roy McDonald and Radley Duvall—had used his planet's technology to remove nearly all the guns in America. That action, a severe violation of Xylodonian security protocols regarding interaction or interference with planet inhabitants, made him the target of a two-planet manhunt. He was forced to come up with some chicanery to remain free from Xylodonian custody. And after the guns were eventually returned, he was able to stay clear of Earth authorities thanks to a smokescreen created by Juleetha—now Ellen Atkinson. The Security Corps thought that she had disappeared—accidental deaths did occur. The truth was, she had chosen to leave her post in Colorado because of a tragedy not unsimilar to the one

Anton experienced. In truth, they both had experienced the gut punch of the latter incident.

Anton's subsequent actions—healing six cancer patients and then topping that by removing the guns—had sounded many alarm bells among the human authorities, such as the FBI. To avoid them, "Roy McDonald" had to disappear; and so "Michael Gort" was born.

A few months after Michael and Ellie had settled into living together, they put themselves on the path to exposure once again. They had answered a friend's request to resolve a dangerous matter on the Earth—the abduction of a human girl—not knowing they been uncovered by Xylodonian authorities. Their mission to save the girl was almost unraveled by their Xylodonian compatriots, but again they were able to turn tragedy into something fruitful. With the aid of that aforementioned colleague, Anton and Juleetha thwarted a human-trafficking ring and freed its victims. At the conclusion of that adventure, they were married in a shipboard ceremony presided over by that colleague. Citing a plethora of reasons, including gaining justice for two slain Guardians, this same Security Corps compatriot had decided to return to Xylodon without them in custody. In exchange for his display of compassion, Anton and Juleetha ("I prefer Ellie, thank you") agreed to rejoin Operation Silent Vigilance.

Life in Hernando for Anton and Ellie had returned to the mundane tasks of teaching pre-teen humans and walking Gator—just the way they liked it. At one point, they had feared that increased human scrutiny in the wake of the Kristi Fleming mission might precipitate a move away from Hernando. But in the end, they decided the pluses were just too plentiful. To satisfy their vow to Termas-3, that jittery colleague, they began sending in reports and updates from the hidden comm room in Ellie's garage, which they had started calling "Hernando's Hideaway."

The couple had told some of their co-workers and neighbors about their marital status, but not all—"For now, just let them keep thinking we're living in sin," Ellie advised.

On this warm Saturday morning, instead of enjoying that delicious Earth beverage known as coffee, Anton/Michael found himself battling with an extremely stingy lug nut. He had left the four-way tire iron attached to the nut when he stepped away to dry his hands.

"Are we having fun yet?" asked Ellie, who had emerged from their house in denim cutoffs and a sleeveless T-shirt. Anton noticed she wasn't wearing a bra.

"You are going to excite the neighbors if you keep dressing like that," he said.

"Ha. You are going to excite them if you keep spouting profanities in Xylodonian," she replied. "Besides, I don't think you mind how I dress."

"Nope. And even if I did, I know better than to say anything. No fool I," he countered. "I do have a question though."

"Yes, dear. What is it?"

"How come you have to pick up a nail every time you go look at what new houses are on the menu?"

"Pppffffttt. It's not every time, you ol' grouch." She then tossed the cold coffee in her cup at him. He dodged it. "Who knows? We may need more space someday."

Anton knew better than to venture down that conversational road.

"Well, it appears that the Mississippi climate has played havoc with one of the nuts holding this tire on. That, and I wonder who tightened it. Butkyz-51?" The latter was a Xylodonian athlete from decades ago who was famed for his temper and aggressiveness. "This baby ain't coming off."

He tried stepping on one prong of the tire iron, hoping his weight might make it turn. No luck.

"Are you turning it the right way?" Ellie asked.

The question earned a foul look from Anton.

"OK, cowboy. Don't get upset. But I bet you I can get that lug nut off in about two seconds."

"Oh, really? I'll take that bet. What are we wagering?" he asked.

"Not what you have in mind, you perv. How about lunch?"

"You're on. Go for it, wenchlet."

"Wenchlet now, is it? OK, I want you to stand over here." Ellie guided him to a spot on the driveway just near the rear of the car and the miscreant tire. After Anton was positioned to her satisfaction, she stood away from the car.

"Don't move. Watch this." She turned a dial on her watch.

The tire iron spun counterclockwise until the nut came off. It took about two seconds. Ellie had used her holo-biometrometer, a watchlike device that had a variety of offensive, defensive, stealth, and medical capabilities. They both had one. The device—a "holo" in shortened Xylodonian vernacular—emits various light frequencies that impact the brain to halt or limit motor functions, ensure compliance, and elicit truthfulness. Holos could emit a wide beam, allowing the operator to affect an entire movie theater, for example, or a narrow beam to impact an individual. Improved versions affected animal species as well as humanoids. The holos have other utilitarian functions as well: communication, image capture...and being able to turn a rusted lug nut. Humans have their Swiss army knives, Xylodonians have their holos.

"You cheated," Anton said.

"No, I didn't. We didn't set any ground rules. That's lunch on you, fella."

"Uh-huh. Why did you want me back here?"

"So, the neighbors couldn't see me cheat...I mean get the nut off. You were my shield."

"Aren't I always?" Anton said.

"Pppffffttt."

Anton jacked up the car and replaced the tire; the original indeed had a nail. "I guess going to the tire shop is now on our agenda today."

"But first, let's have some more coffee."

Anton wiped his hands again and placed the tool in the trunk of the Tesla. "Wonderful idea."

With fresh brew—Texas pecan from Buc-ee's—in their mugs, they sat down at the small kitchen table. Gator was soon on Anton's lap.

"Hey, I have a question," Anton said.

"Shoot."

"When we first met, you told me you had been married for a short time and ended up with this house. And then you said that wasn't true. So, which is it Juleetha Sue?"

"Uuuggghh. You know I hate that name. No, I've never been

married. I did have to create a husband (she pointed to her watch) to get these judgmental Mississippi humans to give me a home loan. Did you know that it wasn't until the 1970s that an unmarried woman could get a home loan in America? Or a credit card?"

Anton felt a rant coming on, so he quickly crossed that particular T.

"I'd like to say I'm surprised, but I've seen too much of late to dispute you. So, no husband. Not even on Xylodon?"

Ellie wondered why he was curious about this topic but played along. "If you must know, I did have a serious boyfriend, but he got orders to go to Neptune Station while I was in the Academy. He was still working in Neptune engineering when I was sent to Earth. We drifted apart after that."

"His loss, my gain," Anton said, taking her hand across the table.

Ellie said, "Now, it's my turn. You don't talk about your parents much. What were they like?"

"My paternal was an adviser to a member of the Presidium (Xylodon's ruling body), and my maternal dabbled in art and architecture. They both passed before I graduated from the Protectorate Academy. Perhaps that is why I was drawn to Ezra so easily." Ezra "Gator" Hopkins, a former U.S. Navy salt, professional wiseass, and the unofficial mayor of Eudora, Mississippi, had befriended both covert Xylodonians. Ezra was murdered in the Waffle Barn mass shooting, becoming the impetus for Anton's removal of America's guns and the namesake for their rescued chiweenie.. "What about your family?"

"My paternal and maternal are gone as well. They had worked for many years in Xylos (the Xylodonian capital) for the water conservation agency," Ellie said. "I have a younger sister, but I have lost track of her."

"No idea where she is? That's too bad. I never had siblings. What is her name?" Anton asked.

Ellie's head went to the tabletop. "Julista-5."

"Julista. That's not so bad."

With her head still down, Ellie replied, "Yes, it is. Not as bad as Juleetha, but it is bad. I don't know what our parentals were drinking at our namings."

Anton chuckled and bolted down what remained of his coffee. "I

That misstep earned him the task of writing guidelines for the Guardian training manual. On his latest visit, Termas not only failed to return with Anton and Juleetha after their arrest, but he also joined them in their attempt to gain justice for their two slain comrades. Then he followed that by conducting an act of retribution against a human criminal. After that, he not only granted the two fugitives their freedom, but he presided over their marriage ceremony.

He had a long time during the flight back to deliberate over what he had done. *My career is over. I'm headed to our prison moon,* he had decided. *What will I tell Zephyra? Our son?*

Termas neared the hangar exit, hoping to catch an air taxi to his domicile. *I want to see my family one more time before Protectorate security puts me in binds.* But then the hangar public address system squawked: "Termas-3, please report to the office of the sub-protector immediately. Termas-3, please report to the office of the sub-protector immediately."

Termas pulled out his communicator and reached the sub-protector's executive assistant. "Please tell Sub-Protector Korphan I am on my way."

Dread briefly anchored him in place. Then, Termas sighed and signaled for transport to the Protectorate building. It was time to meet his fate.

It took about ten minutes to reach the Protectorate, which oversaw Xylodon's Security Corps, the planet's military and law enforcement organizations. Members of the Protectorate answered to the fifty members of the Presidium, which elects the Praetor, Xylodon's supreme leader. The Praetor also carried the title of Supreme Protector, although it was less often used.

Sub-Protector Korphan-2 was second in command of the Protectorate, and he ran the day-to-day operations of the military intelligence branch of the organization. The military operations and law enforcement branches had their own sub-protectors. They all fell under the umbrella of the Chief Protector, but her office was in the Presidium; thus, it was the sub-protectors who had the most responsibility—and accountability—for overseeing the Centurion Guardians.

Korphan's executive assistant did not look up when Termas entered the outer office; he simply pointed toward the door. Termas paused at the door and knocked.

"Enter."

Termas shut the door behind him and strode cautiously into the room. He stood at attention. Korphan sat at his desk signing documents, saying nothing. To say that the atmosphere was frosty is to say water is wet. Termas maintained his position at attention for several uncomfortable minutes while Korphan futzed with the paperwork.

At last, the sub-protector spoke without looking up. "You *GRADAKH GIRGACH NIMNULE!*" Then he paused, taking a breath. "No, I promised myself I would not get angry." But then he bellowed: *"MA'CH SHEEROK GRADAKH ZUNGIN!"* This was followed by thirty seconds of more silence before he put down his pen and looked at Termas. "I've never been good with promises."

Termas felt it was best to remain quiet.

"You know, Termas, I look at you, and now I know why the Presidium wants to drop the word 'intelligence' from the name of our agency," he said, shaking his head. "Your last two missions have been remarkable. They will go down in the annals of Protectorate history. You couldn't keep your *glorg* in your pants on one, and on the next one, two Guardians were killed and you let another two get away. I will say this: You have managed to make Centurion Guardian history in both cases. *Gradakh! Gradakh! Gradakh!"*

Korphan paused. "How is Zephyra, by the way?"

"She is doing very well, sir, and the baby is ..."

"Silence!"

"Yes, sir."

"Gradakh nimnule. So, before I become so consumed with rage that I can no longer think, how about you explain yourself. You can keep standing there."

Termas cleared his throat and stared at a spot about a foot above Korphan's head. Even for a fervent gambler like Termas, there was no chance he would look Korphan in the eye.

Termas summarized the last mission as best he could. Their surveillance had paid off, and the team had located Anton living with an Earth woman in Hernando, Mississippi. They later determined that the Earth woman was Juleetha-6, the missing Guardian. "At that point, we thought fortune was smiling on us." He continued. Before they could execute an arrest, the two fugitives headed west in Juleetha's Earth vehicle. They opted to follow their quarry until an opportune moment to arrest them presented itself.

Korphan interrupted. "That was in Colorado, correct? Near where Juleetha had been stationed?"

"Yes, sir." Termas described how Aethal and Zylbrad took the fugitives by surprise before they, too, were ambushed by two human criminals. The two humans were about to terminate Anton and Juleetha, but he arrived just in time. Using her holo, Juleetha eliminated the two humans by thought-controlling a large Earth predator.

"So, why didn't you arrest them and bring them back?" said Korphan, thinking, *I bet this is going to be good.*

"Sir, they explained to me why they were on this journey. They both had given their word to complete it. They said a criminal consortium was kidnapping young human females for illicit purposes. Members of this consortium were responsible for the deaths of Aethal and Zylbrad," Termas said. "I could not face telling their families what happened to them without stating that their killers had met justice."

"Justice. Uh-huh. Go on."

"We located the criminal encampment in the state of Idaho," he said, then he described how they incapacitated the guards and rescued the female captives. Termas quickly let his eyes drop and was pleased to find Korphan intrigued. At least, it appeared that way.

"Juleetha then came up with a clever idea to use thought control on the criminals and have them perform a variety of useful tasks and then turn themselves in."

"Useful tasks?"

"She forced one of these racist criminal groups to paint and repair a church where Black humans worshipped. She also made another group sing and dance in front of a police station. Other groups were made to perform similar beneficial actions."

Korphan put a hand over his mouth to hide a smile. *Who ever knew you could use a holo for that?*

Termas continued. "Our interrogation of the criminal leaders led us to perhaps the most heinous member of the consortium, a human who was running a legal drug operation in Michigan. This human's nickname was 'The Bear,' so Anton came up with a plan that resulted in this human being terminated by a polar bear."

"You do realize that killing is a violation of one of Xylodon's most sacred protocols, don't you?" asked Korphan.

"Technically, the bear did it," said Termas.

"Technically, the...SILENCE! *Nimnule!*" shouted Korphan. *Technically, the bear did it. Not bad,* he thought.

"Yes, sir."

There was a lingering pause. Korphan looked out his window, then looked back at Termas. "So?"

"So, sir?"

"So, what was the rationalization that caused you, a second-brevet Centurion Guardian, to go along with this *xlarthflarp* plan?"

"As I indicated, sir, it was to obtain justice for Aethal and Zylbrad. Partly, anyway."

"And the other part?"

"Anton and Juleetha showed me images of what happens to these human children in the hands of these criminals. It's terrible to behold, and it's not just females they abuse. I thought of what I would do if someone abducted my son. I agreed with Anton that these *sheerok* humans had to be stopped."

"But there's more, isn't there?" said Korphan.

"Sir?"

"After you were finished playing judge and jury on Earth, you then let Anton and Juleetha go. Why?"

"I supposed you could call it guilt, sir. And shame. Guilt because I had left Anton behind in the first place. Shame because Anton is perhaps the best Guardian ever produced by the Academy, and I couldn't live with myself if I was the one who brought him back to be prosecuted."

"You do realize that his rogue actions with the sick children and the guns have threatened to expose our operation on Earth?"

"Yes, sir. But it is my observation that the ruse you orchestrated has thrown the humans completely off the scent," Termas said. "Anton and

Juleetha have covered their tracks, and they have agreed to rejoin Operation Silent Vigilance."

"Oh, they have, have they? Well, that makes it all better," Korphan snapped.

"Sir, I know I have strayed from Xylodonian regulations, but our field training also calls upon Guardians to improvise when necessary. I did what I thought was right under the circumstances. I am ready to accept whatever punishment you or the Protectorate prescribes."

Korphan silently ruminated. *Termas is right. There are no signs our operations are in jeopardy. Yet. But be that as it may...*Korphan finally spoke. "There is improvisation, and then there is recklessness. And bad judgment. I am going to have to refer this matter to the Chief Prosecutor, and she will likely have to bring it before the Presidium. The...entire...Presidium!"

The blood drained from Termas' face.

"For now, Guardian, you are confined to your domicile. You are not to speak to anyone about what happened, is that clear? Anyone."

"Yes, sir. Understood. But might I ask a favor, sir?"

"That is pretty bold of you," Korphan replied. "What is it?"

"Might I be allowed to visit the families of Aethal and Zylbrad to offer my condolences and answer any questions they might have?"

Korphan conceded. "Yes, doing so remotely would be too impersonal and would be an insult to their sacrifice. You may do so. But that is to be the extent of your movements until you receive further orders."

"Yes, sir."

"Guardian dismissed."

As Termas left, he knew his career was on the thinnest of ice. *But my conscience is clear.*

About three months later, the Presidium rendered its judgment (bureaucracy takes its time, no matter the planet). Termas was suspended with reduced pay for six months. He was also restricted to duties on Xylodon for the next three years.

Plenty of time to watch a son grow up.

CHAPTER 5

Maxim Everson sat at his desk, using a stiletto letter opener to clean under his fingernails. Scrape. Scrape. Scrape.

The flabby, almost pallid multibillionaire was ensconced in his protected comm room at the bottom of his Central Texas mansion. Everson was wearing his trademark black T-shirt and black cargo pants; he paused his grooming to run his right hand through the bristle-short dark hair atop his head. The dark hair gave way to a blond mullet that curled at his shoulders. "Business in the front, party in the back," he often said. He was impatiently waiting for an overseas call—perhaps the most important call of his life—but time zones could be frustratingly mercurial.

Nearly everyone knew the Maxim Everson story; he certainly had told it enough to all the media that would listen. And then there was the vainglorious "autobiography" written by a paid fanboy. Everson, now fifty-three, had been born in Estonia and was raised by a single mother. He never knew his father. After college, he began making a fortune in cryptocurrency—he eventually became known as the "Crypto King" to his many supporters or the "Crypto Creep" to his equally plentiful detractors. Not that he paid any heed to the latter; Everson respected only one view, and that was Everson's.

He emigrated to the United States in 1992, changing his birth surname of Kukk to Everson ("Kukk is too close to cuck, and there's no way I'm using that," he once told reporters.) He envisioned himself becoming the next great Silicon Valley entrepreneur and in many ways achieved that status. His road to fortune was not without bumps; he was fired from one of his early jobs because of insubordination. He considered himself several planes above his supervisor, a central Mississippi native, and told him so. For some reason, "fucking Mississippi hillbilly" didn't go over well.

But he recovered from that setback. His first company, Everson Technologies, dabbled in a variety of gaming applications in its formative years, turning a modest but steady profit. He and his company then created an app that allowed users to summon transport to and from airports but also have food and beverages delivered to their airport location. No waiting in lines, no airport stress. Everson went from millionaire status to billionaire.

His next venture was cheaper energy via solar panels and windmills; the latter quickly earned major profits as California, by 1995, was producing thirty percent of the world's wind-produced energy. But while Everson was sharing in the wind-powered booty, he began running afoul of California's environmental regulations and grew less than enamored with the state's tax structure. In 2008, his company mantra became, "Go east, young man." And that's what he did, bringing his company to Texas, which had surpassed California in the production of wind energy and boasted mightily of its lax business laws. Cha-ching became CHA-CHING with boots on. Taking advantage of state and local tax abatements, he established a massive manufacturing operation in South Texas, becoming a global leader in solar and wind energy products. Everson put his headquarters in the Austin area, the Silicon Valley of Texas.

With the profits came international fame and notoriety. There were magazine covers and television appearances. His surname became a synonym for success and entrepreneurship. But then came the social media whispers. Everson was never a handsome man, but a wallet filled with platinum credit cards carries its own attractions. By 2022, he found himself with a half dozen children (that he was told about) from four different women, none of whom he had married but all of whom were being supported. But, not desiring to be an absentee father as his own was, Everson built a luxury complex outside Austin for this "family" to live in all together. He even arranged for his mother to vacate Estonia and move to the compound. It was almost as if his "family" had formed its own company.

At about the same time, Everson ventured into the business of space, partnering with a cloister of other billionaires to launch a satellite internet service called Sky-Link. Some likened it to "broadband in the stars." Sky-Link became a useful tool for Ukraine in its war against the encroachments of Russia, although Everson declined to extend Sky-Link services over Russian-occupied Crimea, contending that doing so would violate U.S. sanctions against Moscow. At the same time, perhaps because of his Estonian roots, Everson maintained a collegial relationship with the Russian leader. When the Russian dictator asked him to perform a favor for China—an ally of Moscow—by not providing Sky-Link to Taiwan, Everson listened, leaving Taiwan to attempt to fashion its own version.

He had become a political power player as well, donating almost $15 million to the winning candidate in the last Texas gubernatorial election. In return, his largesse earned him an advisory position of sorts with the governor's administration.

Everson was now ready to play the next card in his coziness deck with the Russians. To continue his communications with Russian officials, Everson had created a bunkerlike room that was equipped with the latest in sound-masking protection. He employed an array of signal-detection devices to foil any attempts to pierce the cyber walls of his below-ground sanctorum. The defenses had worked marvelously thus far, and they would be needed again. That overseas call that he was expecting? It was coming from the interim head of the Internet Research Agency.

At last, the phone with the encrypted line buzzed to life. Everson dropped the letter opener and picked up the receiver.

"Well, hello, Nikolai. How are things in St. Petersburg?"

"Maxim, Maxim, Maxim. So good to hear your voice again, my

friend," said Nikolai Ivanov. "It is very cold today, my friend. You would need more than a black T-shirt to go out today."

"That's one of the reasons I prefer to stay in Texas," Everson replied. "How is the transition coming? Settling in OK?"

"Yes, yes, my friend. I appreciate your concern. But please tell me, why did you have me call today? My superiors are very eager to know."

"I'm sure they are," said the billionaire. "My company is in the final phases of something we have developed that your organization might find very useful. And it could be mutually profitable to us both."

"Oh, that sounds very intriguing, my friend. Can you tell me more about it?"

"It has a multiplicity of functions. But primarily it retrieves data. You might call it a 'data vacuum cleaner,' " Everson replied.

"A data vacuum cleaner. Now, that is something," remarked Ivanov. "Is there something else? You did say it has 'a multiplicity of functions.' "

"Indeed, I did, and you might appreciate this function most of all, given your history. This software will have the ability to penetrate the security apparatus of any financial institution," Everson said. "That little ten million dollar heist you pulled back in the '90? Kid stuff."

"Kid stuff, you say. Indeed, that would be most interesting. Most interesting," the Russian said. "But why do you need us? Why split the profits with a partner?"

"Let's just say that your agency gives me a way of keeping my fingerprints off of this. You folks can keep me behind the curtain."

"I see. I see. Like that wizard in Oz. Can you give me and my superiors a rough timeline? When will this vacuum-cleaner software will be ready to use?"

"My team thinks we are a few weeks away from application launch. And then I think we should conduct a test before moving forward to more expansive usage," said Everson.

"Yes, yes. Please keep me apprised of your progress. I will inform Moscow of this technological wonder. I'm sure they will want to assist in any way you might need," said Ivanov.

"I appreciate that, Nikolai," Everson said. "If this works the way I think it will, you will be a very rich man."

"And now I know again why they call you 'The Benefactor.' "

CHAPTER 6

"What the holy fuck?"

Memphis FBI Agent David Broadscale had barely warmed his computer when the first email he opened hit like a thunderclap. The email was a summary of the interview conducted by Damian Cruz, special agent in charge of the El Paso field office, with Isabella Muñoz, who had escaped a human-smuggling ring operated by some of America's pro-Nazi patriots. Cruz's report first went to Washington to be converted into the proper language and spun before being disseminated to the nation's 54 other field offices—sans El Paso, of course. The SACs at the field offices could decide whether the information was valuable enough to forward to their attached satellite offices.

Broadscale had mostly skimmed the report; he found the references to the Bandolero motorcycle gang to be interesting. But it was when he got to the young woman's description of her rescue that his eyes widened, and he came fully awake. "Holy fucking shit!" His nearby colleagues, perhaps amused that he swaddled his profanities in reverence, raised their heads in curiosity. But Broadscale ignored their unasked questions and hit a number saved on his cellphone.

The Jackson, Mississippi, sun had been up for a few hours, but

Special Agent Thomas Dettwiler hadn't even had time to pour a cup of coffee before his phone rang.

"This is Agent Dettwiler, Jackson FBI. How can I help you?"

"Hey, Tom, this is David Broadscale over in Memphis. I hope you remember me. We worked on the Radley Duvall/Roy McDonald case a few years back."

"Yeah, sure, I remember you. Younger and better looking than me, but I won't hold it against you. How are you doing?"

"I'm doing great. Hope you are, too," he said. "Listen, the reason I called...well, have you read your email today? Seen that report out of El Paso that Washington sent out?"

"No, not yet. I hadn't got done with my regular morning cat-herding yet. What's it say?"

Broadscale chuckled. Playing bureaucrat was one reason he didn't want to be promoted, although the extra pay would be nice. "Instead of having me read it to you, I think you better call it up," he said to the older agent. "I can wait."

Dettwiler turned on his computer and proceeded to the email. "All right. What do you want me to see?"

"Go about two-thirds of the way down. Read over that part where this Muñoz girl talks about being rescued."

The phone went quiet for a moment while Dettwiler read. "Holy crap!" he bellowed.

"Yeah, that's about what I said when I read this. This girl told Cruz that all of the guards at that Idaho camp appeared to be frozen. Are you thinking what I'm thinking? Doesn't that remind you of a certain congressional hearing where everyone in the room was mysteriously frozen in place just before all the guns disappeared?"

"Yeah, it sure does. That doesn't sound much like a coincidence, does it?"

"No, I wouldn't think so. And she said she only saw two people who were part of the rescue team. Two against dozens of well-armed militiamen," Broadscale noted. "Kind of like one lawyer against a room full of politicians."

Dettwiler was silent for a moment as he read further. "OK, did you see that the rescuers gave her their names? Anton and Ellie. If those are the real names. If they are, they are kind of interesting."

"That sounds familiar, but refresh my memory."

"One of the people we questioned about Roy McDonald was a schoolteacher by the name of Ellen Atkinson. She was McDonald's squeeze. She goes by Ellie."

"Now, that's interesting," Broadscale remarked.

"Yes. And you know what's even more interesting? Last year, Ellen Atkinson and some fella she was with stopped by my office to get some information," Dettwiler said. "Wanna know what they were asking about?"

"What was it?"

"Human trafficking. I sent them to a cop buddy of mine in Houston who's kind of an expert on the subject."

"Wow. In the immortal words of Yogi Berra, 'That's too coincidental to be a coincidence,' " Broadscale responded.

"Yes, indeed. Agent Broadscale, do you feel up to a visit to Hernando, Mississippi?"

"Any good restaurants there?"

"I doubt it. But the coffee at Circle K is pretty good."

"You are a master of persuasion," Broadscale. "Let me check my calendar, and I will get back to you in a few."

Dettwiler hung up. *Hernando. Ellen Atkinson. Seems like old times,* he mused.

CHAPTER 7

It wasn't a malfunction by a certain holo-biotrometer "watch." Instead, one might say it simply ran out of time.

No one in the Xylodonian Protectorate knew with certainty the duration of the effects produced by the security service's "Swiss Army Knife." For some reason, that had not been researched by the usually methodical Xylodonians. It was enough that the holos worked as intended. No one knew that once a holo function was initiated, the clock began ticking.

So, it was neither expected nor unexpected that the form of Jonnie Barnes Jr. reappeared.

For more than two years, Jonnie had been living in the form of Roy McDonald, the pseudonym used by Anton-7. Anton, using his holo, had swapped identities with the younger Barnes to fool the Xylodonian "rescue" crew sent to retrieve him. Anton, guised as Jonnie Jr., lived for a short time with Jonnie's father, and Xylodonian authorities received a surprise when the spacecraft stopped to refuel at Neptune Station. Anton used a bogus story about a Vegas trip to elude the father, and Xylodonian authorities sent back the faux "Roy McDonald" to quell further scrutiny by their human counterparts. Anton returned to Ellie; Jonnie/Roy was sent to a black site by the National Security Agency.

Jonnie was being held in a deep underground NSA facility hidden beneath an obscure piece of Virginia countryside. As "Roy McDonald," he was believed to have some connection to Radley Duvall, the person thought to be responsible for the disappearance of America's guns. Some thought "Roy" might even be Duvall in disguise. Those speculators never knew how close to the truth they were.

An armed orderly brought a tray bearing orange juice and toast into "Roy's" chamber. He dropped the tray when he saw Roy was gone and in his place was something that looked like it had just escaped from juvenile detention. Thin. Greasy haired. Red eyed. Acne scarred. But still clad in a hospital gown.

"Who the hell are you?" shouted the orderly.

"I had the same question," replied Jonnie.

"Where's Roy?" The orderly moved his hand to the grip of his sidearm.

"Who's Roy?"

"The guy who has been in here for two years."

"Don't know no Roy. I'm Jonnie. Jonnie Barnes. Jonnie Barnes Jr., to be exact. What am I doing here?"

"Just stay over there," the orderly commanded. He snatched the radio from his belt. "Tell Dr. McClarendon to get to Room X-12 stat. And tell Agent Leinfelder to get here, too."

"Do you care if I sit?" Jonnie asked, not waiting for a reply before sitting on the only bed in the room. He noticed a bit of pink peeking out of his left sleeve. He raised the sleeve and saw a four-inch scar on the underside of his arm. "Did you people do this to me?" he asked accusingly.

The orderly didn't answer the question. "Just sit there and be quiet until Dr. McClarendon gets here."

After about ten minutes, four men entered the room. Three were wearing suits with shoulder holsters visible under their jackets, and one was wearing a white coat—*the good doctor, I presume,* thought Jonnie. All were wearing badges around their necks.

Dr. McClarendon started to approach Jonnie, but one of the "suits" put a hand to his chest. "Let me talk to him first, doc."

"Go right ahead," said the doctor.

The "suit" walked closer and identified himself as federal Agent James Leinfelder. He didn't say what branch of the government he worked for.

"Where am I?" asked Jonnie.

"Let me ask the questions, young fella. Can you tell us what happened to Roy McDonald, the man who was in this room before you showed up?"

"Hey, did you say Roy McDonald? I know a Roy McDonald. That other fella asked me if I knew a Roy, but he didn't say Roy McDonald."

"So, what can you tell us about Roy McDonald?" the agent asked.

"He was that scientist guy who lived in a fancy rig in our RV park in Eudora. Eudora, Mississippi."

"How is it that you're here and he's not?"

"I ain't got no idea. My head feels like it's going in twenty different directions. First, I'm on a spaceship with some strange little dudes. Then I'm at someplace called Buc-ee's Station. Next thing I know I'm in this glass cage getting poked and questioned all the time. Then I woke up, and here I am," said Jonnie. "Where are my clothes? You didn't sex-drug me, did you?" Jonnie reached around with his right arm. "I guess not. Asshole feels alright."

One of the other agents snorted, "A spaceship? Aliens? What a load of bullshit."

Dr. McClarendon interjected, "Agent Leinfelder, make note of the gown he's wearing. It appears to be a size or two too large for his frame."

Leinfelder examined Jonnie for a moment. "Yes, you're right." Then he stared hard at Jonnie. "Where is the man who was in this room?"

"Don't know about any other man. I told you I woke up, and here I was," said Jonnie.

The orderly spoke up. "There's no way out of here. And even if he got out of this room, he wouldn't be able to get past security at the end of the hall. And he doesn't have a badge for the elevators."

Leinfelder raised his hand to signal that the orderly might have said too much.

"I have an idea," said Dr. McClarendon. "When Roy McDonald got here, his fingerprints and DNA were not in our system. Let's take this fellow's...Jonnie's...fingerprints and do a swab and see if we get a match."

"Good idea, doc," said Leinfelder, signaling to one of the other suits. "Go get the print kit and a swab. Please."

The agent returned with the requested items. He took a swab from inside Jonnie's mouth and placed it in a tube that was then sealed. He then inked and printed Jonnie's fingers and thumbs one by one. He then left the room with the materials.

They knew the DNA test would take some time, but the fingerprint results came back relatively quickly.

Leinfelder looked over the results sent to his cellphone. "Jonnie Barnes Jr." He glanced at the pale creature before him. "You've got quite the history of petty crime. Theft. Burglary. Indecency. Nothing too serious, but you're no choir boy, are you?"

"Ain't none of that stuff true. Them courts in DeSoto County is rigged against poor folk like me."

"Yeah, I'm sure they are," Leinfelder said, turning to the doctor. "According to this (holding up his cellphone), this isn't Roy McDonald."

"And, so, the question remains: Where did Roy McDonald go?" said the doctor.

"Why do y'all want Roy? He kill somebody?" asked Jonnie.

The men ignored him. "We are going to have to keep you here a bit longer until we can get this straightened out," said Leinfelder.

"Oh, yeah?" sneered Jonnie. "Well, can I get something to eat? I'm starvin'."

For the next week, Jonnie was interrogated repeatedly, subjected to batteries of lie-detector tests, and injected with a variety of truth drugs. His story never changed, although he did apologize for peeping in a few RV park windows late at night. The agents showed him the metallic object that had been removed from his arm, the source of the scar. Jonnie said he didn't recognize it; the drugs he was given indicated he was telling the truth.

A few days later, a foursome of "suits" came to Room X-12. Jonnie, munching on a bowl of Cap'n Crunch, had been given a gray sweatsuit to replace the hospital gown.

"Get up," barked one of the suits.

"I ain't finished my cereal," Jonnie replied.

The first suited man signaled with a finger for the others to act. Two grabbed Jonnie under the arms and held him up. The third placed zip-tie handcuffs on his wrists. A black hood was put over his head. The four men—one on each side, one in front and one in back—led Jonnie from the room that had been his home for two years.

"Where are you assholes takin' me???" Jonnie yelled.

"Hold up," said the first "suit." He removed the hood and placed duct tape over Jonnie's mouth. The hood went back on.

Jonnie could tell they were going down a hallway. They stopped, and then he could tell they were in an elevator. Eventually, he could tell they were outside. He could smell hay and animal excreta. "Move," said one of the suits. Jonnie felt the sun though the hood. He heard a car door open, and he was guided inside. Someone was seated on either side of him.

He heard the car engine come to life. But before the car moved, Jonnie felt a needle in his right arm. He was soon asleep.

Some time later, a black sedan with darkened windows and no plates pulled into an RV park in Eudora, Mississippi. Jonnie Barnes Jr., still hooded and bound, was dropped like last week's garbage onto the gravel.

The car sped away.

CHAPTER 8

Despite Korphan's admonitions, the story spread like mono in a middle school.

Termas told his partner, Zephyra, who told her mother and two sisters. The sisters told a few of their co-workers. Before long, even with Termas stewing in his domicile, most of Xylos had obtained some knowledge of what two Guardians—make that three Guardians—had done on Earth.

Those who had heard the whispers included a good portion of the newest cadet class at the Protectorate Academy. Julista-5 was taking notes in her Earth languages class when her study partner, Margeen-8, asked if she had heard the rumors.

"No, I've been too busy trying to learn this *sheerok*. What have you heard?" Julista said.

Margeen, keeping her voice low as the instructor lectured, said she had heard about three Centurion Guardians who had broken Protectorate protocols to save more than 1,000 Earth girls from being violated and eaten. Hundreds of human criminals were brought to justice. One of the Guardians had returned to Xylodon and was facing banishment, but the other two had remained behind on Earth and had not yet faced punishment. "I hear they fell in love and underwent the matrimony ritual. So romantic," Margeen said. "Just like that story of 'Juleo and Romulet.' "

Two male cadets sitting in the row below them, Dakkott-4 and Roggbach-12, turned and held fingers to their lips. "We can talk about this after class," Dakkott said.

Margeen replied with a contemptuous gesture, then continued. "I heard that the two who stayed on Earth have been hunted by the Protectorate for some time. One of them is a famous graduate of the Academy. Anton-7," she whispered. "The female Guardian is Juleetha-6."

Julista jolted upright. "Wait. Say that name again. The last one."

"Juleetha-6. Or so I was told. Why, do you know her?"

"Yes, I believe I do. That's my sister."

Margeen gasped. "Oh, *jyxnozz*, that's..."

The two male cadets turned toward them once more, glaring this time.

Julista and Margeen shook their heads in compliance.

After about forty-five minutes, the four grabbed a table at one of the Academy cafeterias; it was the only one that sold the rare but prized Earth coffee. A waiter, who recognized them as regulars, brought over a carafe and four cups and saucers. They were soon joined by two other male cadets, Gorthand-3 and Ungbar-11. The latter were holding hands; they were one of the relatively few same-gender couplings on Xylodon. Julista signaled to the waiter to bring two more settings.

"How is everyone? What's new?" Gorthand asked as he and Ungbar sat down.

Roggbach pointed at Margeen. "Miss I-Never-Met-A-Secret-I-Couldn't-Share has been giving us the latest gossip."

"Oh, do tell. I love gossip," said Ungbar.

Margeen made a face at Roggbach but proceeded to relate what she had told Julista.

"I heard about that," said Ungbar. "Isn't that a darling story? Just confirms why we all joined the Academy."

Roggbach jumped in. "I heard they killed one hundred human criminals and fed them to animals."

"I didn't hear that, but who knows?" Margeen said. "But Julista has something she should add. Go on, Julista."

"I believe the female Guardian is my sister, Juleetha-6," she said.

"Oh, my. This is getting more scrumptious by the second," said Ungbar. "Like that Earth song says, 'Tell me more, tell me more.' "

"There is not much more to tell," Julista said. "I haven't seen Juleetha in about ten years, ever since our parentals died and she went to the Academy. I went to live with an aunt."

"*Jyxnozz!* You haven't seen your sister in ten years? That must be hard," Gorthand said. He then elbowed Dakkott; he knew Dakkott had feelings for Julista, but the taciturn cadet had been too shackled by his shyness to act upon them.

"Ouch. What was that for?" Dakkott asked.

"Didn't you hear what Julista said, you *nimnule*? She hasn't seen her sister in over ten years," Gorthand replied.

"Yes, but what do you want me to do about it?" asked Dakkott.

"Now's your chance to become Julista's hero. Don't you know somebody in the smuggling business? Someone with access to a Dart Lurker?" Gorthand said. A Dart Lurker was a high-speed craft used by Xylodonian civilians. It was smaller than Void Stalkers and other vessels the Protectorate used, but it could accommodate a crew of as many as ten and could be equipped with the latest in anti-detection technology. It was as stealthy as any craft on the planet. Its only disadvantage? Range. But smugglers had answers for that as well.

"What? No, no, no, no, no, no, no. A thousand times no," Dakkott said. By Xylodonian standards, he had grown up on the wrong side of the tracks. His excellent grades in his foundation classes had opened an avenue to the Academy. "I have tried to avoid that part of my family since I was accepted by the Protectorate."

Roggbach continued to press on the same button that Gorthand had touched, while adding a dash of guilt. "You know someone with a Dart Lurker? I bet Julista would like to drop in on her sister. You know, the one she hasn't seen in TEN years."

Julista looked at Dakkott hopefully but held her tongue.

"And guess what?" said Ungbar. "Spring break is not that far away. I wouldn't mind a little trip."

Dakkott tried to bring some calm to the conversation. "It won't work. Dart Lurkers can't hold enough fuel to get to Earth, and if even if they could get there, how would we get back? How would we take off without being detected by the Protectorate? We get caught, our careers are ruined."

"My, my, my. Where others see rainbows, you just see raindrops, don't you?" Ungbar said.

Roggbach chuckled at the jab. "You know, you can secure extra fuel tanks for Dart Lurkers. As for getting back, we can worry about that once we get there. Julista's sister is a full-fledged Guardian. I bet she can get fuel."

Julista slapped the table. "Wait a minute. Who says I want to go? Maybe I don't want to see Juleetha. She hasn't contacted me in forever."

"Oh, don't be a *schlarm fugg,* Julista. Of course you want to go," said Margeen.

"Yes, yes, yes, yes, yes. C'mon, Julista," said Ungbar. "Can you imagine the look on your sister's face when you show up?"

"That presents a bit of problem," Julista said. "We have a general idea where Juleetha is, but where do we go once we enter Earth's atmosphere?"

"I hate it when you're logical," Ungbar said.

That reality cast a pall on the conversation. Margeen smiled. "I have an idea. Guardian Termas likely knows how to find her. Julista, why don't you go to him? If he won't help, throw a fit. Cry if you have to."

Julista remained quiet, then said, "All right. I don't cry for anyone, but I do have some questions for my big sister. I will attempt to get the information. But we have some 'ifs' to deal with. If Dakkott can get a Dart Lurker, and if we can get the fuel. Let's do this. We can meet again in a week. Dakkott, you have until then to get access to a ship. Roggbach, that's your deadline to get the extra fuel."

Dakkott said nothing and tried to remain expressionless amid the hubbub. He nodded his head. *Maybe this is how I get Julista to pay attention to me,* he thought.

"Oh, goody. We have a plan," Ungbar said, clapping his hands. "Let's meet again right here. One week from today."

Julista buzzed her arrival at the entry to Termas' domicile. She identified herself, and the door soon whooshed open. Termas stood at the doorway with a quizzical look.

"Sorry, I don't know...wait a moment. Did you say your name was Julista? Why do I know that name?"

"Yes. Cadet Julista-12, actually. Perhaps you know me through my sister. Juleetha-6."

"Juleetha. Now, there's a name I am not too keen to hear again."

A female voice came from inside the domicile. "Termas, who is at the door?"

"It appears to be the younger sister of Juleetha-6."

"Don't just stand there. Invite her in," said Zephyra.

Julitha entered their abode, and Termas directed her to a chair in the primary living area. She could hear a young one squealing in a nearby room.

"That's our son," Termas said. Zephyra brought drinks for the three of them.

"Thank you," Julista said, taking a long sip to delay—for just a bit longer—making her request.

"What brings you here today, Julista?" Termas asked.

"It's about my sister. I have not seen her since our parentals left us. It's been ten years since I've spoken to her. I know she has been part of our covert forces, but I am hoping to reconnect with her."

"That's terrible," said Zephyra. "Is she your only remaining kindred?"

"Yes. Our lives went in different directions. Guardian Termas, it has become well known that you conducted an operation on Earth with my sister."

"I am aware. Are there no longer any secrets? I wonder how that information got out?" he glared at Zephyra, who calmly ignored him.

"Might I ask how she is doing?"

"Juleetha is one of the bravest, most intelligent, most instinctive Guardians I have ever worked with. She has amazing initiative. She is in good health, I can assure you," Termas said. "She is one of the best of us."

"That is good to hear. What else can you tell me about her life on Earth?"

"One circumstance you may not be aware of—she has taken a life partner."

"She is wedded?"

"Yes. She asked me to perform the bonding ceremony."

"I wish I could have been there," Julista said, looking down. "I know this may be much to ask. Can you tell me where she is now? Tell me how to reach her so that I might congratulate her?"

"I cannot. I have broken enough Protectorate protocols for a lifetime. Two lifetimes."

"But she is my only relative. Please help me. No one will know," Julista said.

The sound of a crying child interrupted them. Zephyra stood. "Excuse me. Let me tend to the little one."

"I am sorry, Julista. I cannot help you."

"What if I offered to watch your son so that you and your wife might have an evening out?"

"This is a kind offer, but I am confined to quarters except for emergencies," he said. "I am sorry, cadet. I cannot aid you."

Julista put her face in her hands; the gesture elicited no change of expression by Termas. She stood. "I understand. Protocol. Thank you for seeing me, Guardian."

"Again, I am sorry I cannot do more." Termas showed her to the door and watched her depart.

Julista felt defeated. Without that information, the cadets' "mission" to Earth would be moot. Tears started forming as she walked away. But she was surprised when someone tapped her shoulder. It was Zephyra, who gave her a hug.

"Now, now, my dear. There's no need for tears," she said, handing the young cadet a tissue.

Julista wiped her eyes.

"You might want to look that over before you throw it away," Zephyra said. "And please do so as soon as you're done with it."

Julista looked more closely at the tissue. There was something written. *"Hernando, Mississippi, USA."* It was followed by a communications frequency code. She put the tissue in a uniform pocket and looked up to express her gratitude.

But Zephyra was gone.

CHAPTER 9

"You're right. This coffee ain't half bad," Agent David Broadscale said as he and Special Agent Thomas Dettwiler left the Circle K in Hernando.

"Yeah, it will give you a jolt," the older agent replied. "Probably something else if you aren't careful."

"Or maybe cure it," Broadscale said.

Broadscale had driven from Memphis to Jackson the day before, staying overnight in a motel before his rendezvous with Dettwiler that morning. It was about a three-hour drive from Jackson to Hernando, which would put their arrival around lunchtime at Hernando Elementary. The two FBI agents hadn't come to northern Mississippi for the coffee; they had come for answers. But first there were more questions.

On the drive over, Broadscale brought up a topic they had not discussed earlier. "You know, I was looking over the reports on the Waffle Barn mass shooting from a couple years ago. You remember much about that incident?"

Dettwiler, who was driving, shook his head affirmatively. "Yeah, we did some of the background investigation on the shooter, that piece of shit Terry Clyde Tolliver. What about it?"

"I had sort of remembered that there was something that never got cleared up. Tolliver pulled into the Waffle Barn parking lot, right? Then he gets out and starts shooting up the restaurant."

"Yep. Killed six people and wounded a bunch more," Dettwiler said.

"Right. And then witnesses said some guy appeared at the edge of the parking lot. Tolliver starts to point his AR at this mystery guy, then decides to point it at himself and pull the trigger. Just like that, no need to hunt down a perp," Broadscale said. "He's at the scene lying in his own blood and brains. So convenient for us."

"I sure didn't complain," Dettwiler replied. "You got a point in there somewhere?"

"Wouldn't you call a well-armed perp with lots of ammo just killing himself kind of a 'miracle?' "

"A miracle, huh? Kind of like Memphis and Washington were miracles?"

"And maybe like Idaho? Course, I don't have much to base it on, but it sure seems like another coincidence," said Broadscale. "And nobody got a look at the mystery man's face."

"They were probably too busy dodging bullets to get a good look. But you're right...kind of interesting."

It was just shy of straight-up noon when the two agents walked into Hernando Elementary; the dervishes squealing on the playground were oblivious to their arrival. As the pair approached the reception desk, a more orderly contingent advanced up the hallway. Dettwiler surmised this group was likely headed to lunch.

A mass of blond hair wrapped in the armor of self-proclaimed authority and carrying a smile as wide as her bust—and every bit as genuine—greeted the two FBI agents. "May I help you, gentlemen?" said the woman, syrup oozing from every syllable. Kendall Guthrie held the title of school receptionist, but she was also the deflector of inanity, giver of judgments, and keeper of all forbidden knowledge. No one cometh to this school but through Kendall. There was a reason she was called "The Great Wall of Kendall."

The G-Men never stood a chance.

In addition to being the preeminent school sentinel, Kendall, as it turned out, was the granddaughter of the aforementioned Ezra

"Gator" Hopkins, for whom Ellie and Michael still maintained an almost reverent devotion.

In what seemed to be a synchronized motion, the two agents reached into their suit jackets and produced badges that carried their photos and the words "Federal Bureau of Investigation" across the top. "Ma'am, my name is Special Agent Thomas Dettwiler, and this is Agent David Broadscale." Broadscale nodded.

"OH MY, OH MY. What could the FBI want at Hernando Elementary? I've already said everything I know," said Kendall with an apple-butter drawl.

The remark caught the agents by surprise. "You've spoken with the FBI?" Dettwiler asked.

"Only by phone," said Kendall. "My niece, Kristi Fleming, was the one who was kidnapped by those awful, awful Patriot whatevers last year. Some nice FBI fellow wanted to know what I knew about the case."

By familial extension, Kristi was the great-granddaughter of Gator Hopkins.

"And did you know something?"

"Why, not a thang," she replied. "I sure hated to waste that fella's time. Had a nice voice, though. So, what can I do for you?"

"We're here to talk with Ellen Atkinson and Michael Gort," Dettwiler said. "Some place with a little privacy would be preferred." Broadscale was content to let him take the lead.

"Why do you want to talk to Ellen? Have you found out something about Roy?"

"I'm afraid its confidential, ma'am," Dettwiler said.

Kendall flipped through some records, possibly schedules. "It appears they both get a break around 12:45. Can you wait till then, or is this urgent?"

"We can wait," said Dettwiler. The two agents found chairs in the reception area, which drew the attention of Principal Helene Appleberry. *The younger one is kind of cute,* she judged. Her heels click-clacked a path to her office's doorway.

"Who are our visitors, Kendall?" she said.

"These two gentlemen are with the EFF ... BEE ... EYE. They are here to talk with Ellie and Mike."

"My goodness," said Helene, making her big hair even bigger. "Well, don't just stand there, Kendall. Go get these fine public servants some tea or coffee."

Kendall raised her eyebrows as her way of posing the question to the agents. "Coffee. Black," said Dettwiler. "Iced tea. Unsweetened," said Broadscale. Before she left to fetch the drinks, Kendall dispatched a student worker with notes for Ms. Atkinson and Mr. Gort to come to Conference Room A to meet with a pair of visitors.

The beverages arrived, and the two agents thumbed through their phones as they waited. A harried teacher walked into the reception area pulling a small boy by his shoulder. "Here's one to see Mrs. Appleberry," she told Kendall Guthrie. The boy looked down at his shoes. Kendall directed him to the last empty chair, the one next to Dettwiler.

"Wait here until Mrs. Appleberry gets off the phone. These two gentlemen are policemen, so you better not bother them," Kendall told the youthful miscreant.

The boy sat with his arms folded and a scowl deep-etched on his face. Dettwiler, who didn't much like being used to scare small children, leaned over. "What's your name, big guy?"

The boy had never been called "big guy" before. The scowl softened. "Tommy. Tommy Shaw."

"That's my name, too," said Dettwiler. "What grade are you in?"

"Second."

"Second grade? That's awful young to be a criminal." Dettwiler winked at the boy. "What brings you to the principal's office?"

"Shelby Addison called me a shitbag."

Dettwiler snorted, and Broadscale, who couldn't help but overhear, spit up some iced tea. Dettwiler continued. "I presume Shelby's a girl. So, what did you do after she said that?"

"I put some glue in her hair. Ms. Harkins saw me and yelled at me. She didn't yell at Shelby."

The two agents looked at one another and did their best to keep from laughing.

Dettwiler turned back to the boy. "Tommy, I got called to the principal's office for much worse than that. It's going to be OK."

Tommy's eyes widened. "What did you do?"

"Oh, me and some guys were spinning out in my car in the school parking lot."

"Did you get in trouble?"

"You bet. Especially when I got home to my old man," he said. "So, what you did wasn't that bad. I bet you're really a good kid, aren't you?"

"I try to be. Except when Shelby calls me names."

Dettwiler took out one of his business cards, wrote something on the back, and gave it to Tommy. "Give this to Mrs. Appleberry and show her the back. This is good for one free pass on any punishment. You tell her the FBI said so."

Tommy became almost gleeful. "Thank you, sir. Thank you."

Just then Kendall signaled that Ellie and Michael were ready. Dettwiler rose, and said, "Good luck, Tommy."

As the three of them headed to the conference room, Broadscale joked, "Handing out pardons today?"

"Kid needed a break. Shelby sounds like a little bitch," Dettwiler replied.

Ellie and Michael stood as the agents entered. "Agent Dettwiler? What brings you back to Hernando?" she asked.

He introduced Agent Broadscale, and they all took seats, with Kendall more or less occupying the referee position. Broadscale indicated that he would be recording the conversation.

"I know we've talked a few times in the past. We had some additional questions that we thought you might be able to help us with," Dettwiler said.

"We will certainly try to help any way we can," Ellie said.

"Some time back, you and Mr. Gort came to my office to obtain information about human trafficking," he said. "Can you tell me why you came to my office?"

At that point, Kendall interrupted. "My niece is Kristi Fleming. She was the girl who was kidnapped. I had asked Ellie and Michael to help me and Kristi's folks get some information because the Albuquerque police had their heads planted firmly up their rectums. I knew Ellie knew somebody in the FBI."

Ellie joined in. "Michael and I went to Houston to see your policeman friend. He gave us a lot of good information."

"Yeah, Nestor (Nestor Ramirez, head of the Houston police human-trafficking unit) is a good guy. What did you do after you met with him?"

"We drove to Albuquerque and met with Kendall's sister and her husband."

"You drove?" asked a surprised Dettwiler.

"Yes. This was during our break, and we wanted to see more of the country."

"Why didn't you just call the Flemings from Houston?"

Michael finally spoke. "The information the Houston officer gave us was on the rough side. We thought the Flemings should hear it face to face."

"I see. Well, imagine my surprise when a few weeks after that, a major human-trafficking ring is broken up in Idaho. Quite a coincidence. You know anything about that?" the agent asked.

Ellie said, "Only what we read and saw on the news. A bunch of those awful militia guys were arrested, right? Not long after we visited with the Flemings, we talked with an Albuquerque law officer. He wasn't very cooperative, but we couldn't believe it when we heard later that he got arrested, too."

Kendall took the conversational baton; Michael was content to let the two women take on the FBI unless he was asked a direct question. "Ellie called and gave me an update. I guess their questions must have lit a fire under somebody because it wasn't too long after that that Kristi was let go."

Dettwiler sensed that Mount Kendall wasn't too far from erupting. "Yes, public pressure can be very useful sometimes," he said. "So, where did you go after that?"

"We went to Santa Fe for a few days. We'd never been there," Ellie said. *It's a good thing I went back and backdated our Santa Fe receipts,* she thought.

Kendall added, "They even brought me some Native American jewelry." She pointed to the silver-and-turquoise pin on her blouse.

"Great food in Santa Fe. You should go if you've never been," said Michael.

"Thanks for the tip. One thing that wasn't on the news was a statement given by one of the girls who was being held at that Idaho camp. She said the girls were rescued by two people. She said they gave their names as Anton and Ellie," Dettwiler said. "Kind of interesting, huh?"

"I guess, but I can't be the only Ellie in the world," she said.

"Suppose not. But you see why we might be curious," the agent said. "Then there is the matter of how the camp guards were incapacitated. It was the same way those folks in Congress were frozen when the guns disappeared."

"Now, that is interesting," said Ellie. "Sometimes I wish I had the power to freeze my students. But as Michael can tell you, I can't even change the tire on my car."

Michael smiled and gave the arms-up, I-don't-know gesture.

"Have you been contacted by Roy McDonald in the past two years?" Dettwiler asked.

"No. I have no idea where Roy is," said Ellie, who knew right where Roy was. She was sitting next to him.

"OK, Ellie, if you weren't in Idaho, then you won't have any qualms with me taking your picture, will you? We could get your photo off our security cameras, but this would be easier," Dettwiler said. "And you, too, Michael."

Uh-oh, thought Ellie. *They are going to show these photos to Isabella. But if we say no…*

"Sure. Go ahead," she said. The agent raised his cellphone and snapped pictures of both teachers.

Broadscale saw the interview was nearing a close but had one more question.

"Were either of you at the Waffle Barn on the day of the shootings?"

Michael replied, "I wasn't in Hernando at that time."

"No. I was at school that day. That terrible day," Ellie said. "Why?"

"Just another unsolved mystery," Broadscale said. "Ms. Atkinson, did you know that Terry Tolliver drove by your school before the

Waffle Barn shootings? We were able to do GPS tracking on his cellphone. And a former Hernando police officer we interviewed recalled seeing Tolliver's truck outside the school that morning."

Ellie turned pale. "No, I was unaware of that. Are you telling me he wanted to shoot the children?"

Broadscale let the question hang. Trying to answer that would have required getting in the head of Terry Clyde Tolliver.

"Tom, do you have anything else?" he asked.

"No, I guess that's all for now. But we may be in contact in the future. You still have my card if you think of anything, Ms. Atkinson?" Dettwiler asked.

"I do. I hope we were able to help."

The two agents strolled back to their vehicle and the three-hour ride back to Jackson.

"Well, we didn't get much that we didn't already know," Broadscale said. "I can get somebody to check out their Santa Fe story."

"Do that," said Dettwiler, sliding into the driver's seat. "I'll get these photos to our El Paso guys and see if it's something."

Kendall left the conference room and went back to her duties. Tommy Shaw, who dodged significant punishment, saw Shelby Addison at lunch and snatched the dessert off her tray. Ellie/Juleetha and Michael/Anton walked slowly back to their classrooms, both wondering, *What the hell was that?*

CHAPTER 10

It was not the first time Xylodon's technology had come to the aid—if not the literal salvation—of its agents in the field.

Ellie and Michael dashed home in her Tesla after the school day was done. Michael grabbed Gator as they hurried to the Hideaway, the secret room in Ellie's garage. The little dog whined, sensing their anxiety.

Ellie sent an encrypted message to Neptune Station, the primary waypoint between Earth and Xylodon. "Urgent: Need cellphone number for human Isabella Muñoz. Believed to be in: City of El Paso. State of Texas. Nation of United States."

They waited. In silence.

The message was forwarded to Protectorate headquarters on the home planet. The message was evaluated and sent immediately to the Protectorate's basement, a virtual coliseum of computers, databanks, and servers. One of the technicians extracted the needed information in little more time than it took to type the human's name. The information was sent to Neptune Station and was relayed to the agents' station in Hernando, Mississippi.

The whole process took perhaps fifteen minutes.

Ellie jotted down the number and pulled a burner cellphone out of a drawer. She sent a hurried text:

"Hello Isabella. Hope you are well. This is a friend from Idaho. Need your help. FBI asking questions. Exposure could be trouble for us. Can we count on you to keep our secret?"

In El Paso, Isabella was scrubbing a motel bathtub when her phone buzzed. She did not recognize the number, but the message was quite clear.

Michael held Gator in his lap; the dog looked up at him with concern in his brown eyes. Ellie's right leg was shaking as she awaited an answer. The burner phone buzzed.

"Yes! Yes! Yes! (three heart emojis)"

CHAPTER 11

After being thrown brusquely onto the gravel road that divided a Mississippi RV park, could Jonnie Barnes Jr. see his luck turn any worse? After all, and not that he had any clear memories of this, he'd been kidnapped by aliens, interrogated on Neptune, returned to Earth in a stupor, arrested and turned over to men in dark suits, and held God knows where for two years. He had been mind-wiped, probed, screamed at, slapped, and drugged at every stop. And just when the fog had begun to lift, he was stuck with another needle.

So, the answer to the question was assuredly...yes.

Jonnie squinted through the morning sun until his vision, adjusting like a camera lens, became entirely focused. He heard a buzz in his ear, then slapped his neck. The bloody corpse of a flying insect was in his palm. *Now I know where I am,* he thought. *Home.*

Not that Eudora, Mississippi, was an unwelcome sight. It was Jonnie's first brush with familiarity in months. But it was also a place he'd struggled most of his life to get away from. He always felt he was just one lottery ticket away from a real life.

Jonnie, still wearing the sweatsuit he'd been given by the black suits and white coats, stretched and dusted himself off. He began trudging up the gravel road amid a gantlet of oversize vehicles toward one he knew quite well. He could hear televisions blaring as he advanced, "The Price Is Right" from over here and "Sesame Street" from over there.

He stopped at the sign bearing his father's name: Jonnie Barnes, Park Manager. *I guess he's still here,* he thought. *That's a good sign.*

He ascended the steps and opened the door. A meaty gray-haired Black woman screamed. "Who the hell are you?" she shouted.

"Who the hell are you?" Jonnie countered. *Wait...didn't I just do this?*

The woman then wielded an iron skillet. "Stay back or I'll brain your ass," she warned.

"You'll only get one swing, so you better make it a good one," he said. As he assumed a defensive posture, he saw some movement from the rear of the RV.

"JONNIE! Oh, my God. It's a miracle!"

Jonnie Barnes Sr., wearing a white T-shirt and boxers, moved past the woman and put his arms around his son. "I can't believe it's you. Welcome home, son."

The woman lowered the skillet. "Jonnie, who is this?" she inquired nervously.

"This is my son, Jonnie Junior. Remember I told you he disappeared a few years back. I haven't seen him since. Until now. Come in, son, come in. Sit down."

Jonnie Jr. took a seat on a Naugahyde couch.

"Who is this, Pop?" he asked.

"Jonnie, this is Shonea. Shonea Johnson. We met awhile back at the bingo hall," Jonnie Sr. said. "We kind of hit it off, and she moved in here."

Jonnie Jr. began to take note of the redecoration inside the RV.

Shonea's attitude suddenly dropped by thirty joules. "Want some eggs? Was scramblin' some for your dad," she said.

"Nah, not right now. What happened to all my stuff, Pop?"

"Well, Jonnie, it's been over two years. I thought you was dead, son. Some of your stuff I sold, some of it we gave away, and some of it's in storage. Had to make room for Shonea's things," Jonnie Sr. said. "We had no idea you'd be comin' back."

"We?"

"Shonea and me. She takes good care of me, don'tcha, honey," he said.

"Got a place for me to bunk up?" Jonnie Jr. asked.

"We can make up one of the bunk beds for ya," his father said. "But first, you gotta tell me what happened to ya. Last I'd heard you'd gone to Vegas with some of your friends. I never heard nothin' after that. Went to the police and the FBI, and they were fuck-all help."

Shonea handed Jonnie Jr. a glass of ice water.

"I don't know nothin' about Vegas." He then did his best to describe what he knew of his whereabouts, but it was like picking tiny pieces of glass out of a giant mosaic. "Last thing I know I was in some strange hospital room. We must have been deep underground because it took a long time for the elevators to get us to the top."

"Was you kidnapped? Didn't get no ransom note," Jonnie Sr. asked.

"I don't think so. It was like they was doing tests on me. Trying to get information from me."

"What kind of information?"

"Believe it or not, they kept asking about one of the guests. Roy McDonald."

"He was that plant expert, right? He disappeared about the same time as you. FBI asked me questions about him. I thought maybe he was with you," Jonnie Sr. said.

The Barnes men continued their reunion as Shonea cleaned up the kitchen. "Not much excitin' around here after you left. Except maybe the explosion."

"Explosion?"

"Yeah, that big government RV that Roy and them others was using just blew up one night. Made a big fire," Jonnie Sr. said. "You can still see the scorch marks. Not much left, though. Them FBI fellas came and took most of it away. Wouldn't tell me what they was looking for."

"That's purdy interestin'. Say, Pop, does that Betsy girl still live here? I remember helping her with her homework." *I remember how she kept her shades open at night,* he recalled.

"Yeah, her and her family is still here. A lot is just the same as when you left," said Jonnie Sr. He seemed to use the word "left" as if it was a choice.

Jonnie Jr. downed the glass of water and stood up. "I think I'll take a walk to see what's what," he said. "Then I'll come back and get cleaned up, if that's OK."

"Sounds good, son. Sure is good to have you back. You hungry? You sure you don't want Shonea to fix something for you?" the elder Barnes asked.

"You gone deaf? He already said no." Shonea scowled but said nothing more. Her world had just been dealt a card she wasn't expecting and didn't want.

"Not right now, Pop. Maybe later."

Jonnie Jr. was beginning to feel he was more outcast than prodigal son. If everything tumbling in his brain was true, then the aliens didn't want him. The black suits and white coats didn't want him. And his own father had replaced him, with a Black woman, no less. Time and again, he was being thrown out like last night's trash.

He retraced his steps on the gravel road. The television programs blasting from the sedentary RVs alongside the path had changed to "Judge Judy" and "Cops." Finally, he came to the large empty space that had once been the site of the strange government RV with its antenna web on top. His father was right; nothing but scorch marks and some melted plastic.

The burn barrel that the government folks used from time to time was still there, so Jonnie went to have a look. He found a piece of metal to stir the ashes with. His eye caught a small bit of paper, burned on the edges, but the writing on it was still legible.

All he could make out was:

Be ...-ere. Casual.

1287 Beauvoir Drive

Ell-...

Jonnie smiled. *Well, now. Who says there's nothing interesting around here?*

CHAPTER 12

It had been weeks since the FBI summary of the Isabella Muñoz interview was sent to Washington. The outgoing FBI director, who announced his resignation to preclude his likely dismissal, had ordered that it be distributed to the various field offices. A copy was set aside for whichever nominee was approved by the Senate, and a copy was sent to the new White House chief of staff. Between the inauguration and bubbling global events, the report became a dust magnet.

Until the first week of the new administration.

The new chief of staff, Georgia Washington, who had long endured dollar-bill and cherry-tree jokes, was busy organizing her office when she saw the FBI document in her in-tray. Intrigued by the title, she thumbed through the transcript. Like the two FBI agents, Dettwiler and Broadscale, she was stopped by the "holy shit" reference contained within: *The guards appeared frozen in place.*

Washington had been at the Capitol but was outside the House hearing room that became ground zero for "the day the guns disappeared." She had spoken with a number of lawmakers and hearing attendees afterward; they all described being "frozen" or "paralyzed." It had not been painful, they said, and the condition ceased soon after "that lawyer guy" left the room. From the scattered details she had gathered, what happened in Idaho sounded eerily similar to what had happened on that fateful day on Capitol Hill.

Washington almost sprinted down the hallway that separated her office from the Oval Office. America's latest president was standing near the middle of the room, overseeing the placement of new curtains.

"Mr. President, I think I have something you should see," she said.

He turned and saw the document in her hand. "You know I hate to read. Reading is for losers and suckers. What is it?"

"It's a summary of an interview done by the FBI."

"FBI? Why do I want to know anything those deep-state assholes have to say? I've done everything I could to keep them off my ass and out of my home," he said. He turned to the curtain workers. "Make sure the gold matches the carpet highlights."

"I understand, but Mr. President this could be vital to national security."

"Well, these curtains are critical, too. I hated what the last guy did with the place. Curtains are important to my image," he said. "All right, sum it up for me."

Washington gave an overview of the interview, emphasizing what happened at the Idaho camp with, "Here's the key part." She then related what Isabella had told the El Paso agent. "The militia members were frozen is what she said."

"Frozen, schmozen. So, what?" barked the president. "Those idiots could have voted for me. Instead, they get arrested."

"Sir, what this young woman is describing parallels what occurred in the House chamber right before most of our guns vanished."

"You don't say? I remember that. Those videos of Big Jim and Little Jim struggling in their chairs were pretty funny. Kind of like Benny Hill."

"Yes, sir. It was a unique and memorable experience for all concerned. Sir, whatever it was that froze those men, that's some advanced technology that the United States doesn't have," she said. "No one has it."

"Russia doesn't have it?"

"No, sir."

"China doesn't have it?"

"No, sir."

"Iran doesn't have it?"

"No, sir."

"North Korea doesn't have it? Never mind, of course they don't. They barely have food."

"No, Mr. President. And we don't either. That's the point," she said. "But this report might be the key on how we can get it."

"A freeze ray. Boy, that would have been handy back when I was dating. Can't date as much now, you know. I could have grabbed 'em without any complaints. Right now, it's my wife who is freezing ME out. And can you imagine my State of the Union if we had this technology? I could freeze the opposition members when they stood at attention. Wouldn't that be great?"

"Yes, Mr. President."

"We need to find this freeze gun or whatever it is. Call my smart generals. Just the smart ones. We can use the military on this if we need to," he said. "Whatever it takes to hunt this down."

"There is a supplemental report that indicates that the FBI might have a lead, sir."

"They do? Why didn't you say so? Who's my guy over at the FBI? Ol' Popeye Face. Get him to light a fire under this," he commanded.

"Yes, sir. Right away, sir."

As Washington turned to the door, the president halted her. "Before you go, what do you think of my curtains…?"

The call from the president's chief of staff left the new FBI director perplexed. *Where does this request fit in with the priorities I was given earlier?* he wondered.

Just that day, the director had appointed a team to investigate a cable television comedian based in Los Angeles who continually ridiculed the president. But the comedian was far from the only person on the "hit list." There was the writer who had revealed the president had not written the books he claimed he had authored. There was the Oklahoma senator who wrote an opinion piece criticizing the president's tax plan. And then there was the New York social media troll who kept referring to the president as "President Schitzenpantz."

Whom was he supposed to go after first?

And not only was the chief of staff applying pressure, but he had also just received a supplemental report that contained a request from two Southern field agents to launch a deeper investigation into this suspected "freeze" weapon.

How could he keep the president happy? The director thought for a moment, twirling his pen, then called in his executive assistant.

"Take this down. Send a message to the chief of staff that confirms the FBI is happy to oblige and that the director will assign the appropriate number of agents to the matter. Now, as to the two agents, tell them that I am studying their report, and it has my utmost attention. Tell them that I will provide them with a more definitive answer as soon as possible."

The executive assistant said, "Got it. In other words, to all of them, fuck off."

"Don't phrase it that way, but yes."

Besides, arresting a Hollywood comedian would get much bigger headlines, he thought.

CHAPTER 13

History has given St. Petersburg an identity crisis of sorts. It didn't help matters that an American congresswoman, Margie Joye Blue of Georgia, had confused the city with the similarly named municipality in the South. "Why would Florida want to attack the United States?" she asked a TV news host who had inquired about election interference.

In its beginnings, the site that became St. Petersburg belonged to the Swedes for several centuries until the fortress-town they had established was taken from them in the Great Northern War. That early-eighteenth-century conflict saw the Swedes matched with forces led by Peter the Great. Tsar Peter, who modestly lived in a three-room log cabin as the settlement was rebuilt and expanded, named the city for Saint Peter and made it the capital of imperial Russia (although his son, Peter II, briefly transferred the flag to Moscow). The port city, a pathway to the Gulf of Finland and Baltic Sea, again became the capital in 1732 and emerged as the cultural center of Mother Russia.

At the outset of World War I, the city was renamed Petrograd to honor the tsar who had tweaked the Swedes. When the country turned red after the 1917 revolution, the Bolsheviks made Moscow the capital. These Soviets-to-be renamed Petrograd as Leningrad in 1924 after the death of the fiery Vladimir Ilyich. Under its new name, the city survived the long, bloody siege by the Nazis during World War II. In 1991, with the creation of the Bolsheviks on the verge of dissolution, the city's citizens, embracing democracy, voted to drop "Leningrad" and restore the appellation of St. Petersburg. The city has prospered under its new-old name; its metropolitan area now boasts a population of more than six million people and ranks as the fourth-most-populous city in Europe. It is home to the Hermitage Museum, one of the largest in the world, and the Lakhta Centre, the tallest skyscraper in Europe. With the gulf at its doorstep and the Neva River cutting through the heart of the city, the river's tributaries and canals give the five boroughs of St. Petersburg a Venice-like feel.

But it wasn't history that was on the mind of Olga Alexandrova; it was the present she was more concerned with as she walked through the ornate doors of the Belmond Grande Hotel Europe. The five-star hotel, located on Nevsky Prospect, one of the city's primary thoroughfares, was one of the grandest in Europe. A uniformed doorman opened the gateway for Olga, who removed her coat as she entered the lobby. She would have liked to pause to admire the wood paneling and shimmering chandeliers, or perhaps investigate the red chairs soldiering in the hotel bar, but she was running a few minutes behind.

Olga avoided looking at the front desk staff; besides, she didn't need a key. She entered the elevator alone and hit the number four on the panel. As it ascended, she removed the pins from her long blond hair and let it fall past her shoulders. After exiting, she moved down the hallway, pausing at a marble-topped table that was the base for a large gold-framed mirror. She adjusted her lipstick, fluffed her coif, and examined her attire for any faults. Satisfied, she strode to Room 424 and knocked quietly.

The door opened, and she was handed a glass of Champagne.

"Hello, my dear," said Nikolai Ivanov. "My anticipation for your arrival was beginning to growl."

Olga and Nikolai clinked glasses and each took a sip of Champagne. "I hope you like the room," Nikolai said. "I could have gotten a suite, but that might have been a bit...ostentatious. If anyone asks later, we were in a critical meeting on national security."

She smiled. "Should I take notes in our meeting?"

"Most assuredly, no. No notes."

Olga, wearing a dark blue satin off-the-shoulder dress that accented her blond mane, looked about the expansive room. Balcony. Plush carpet. Gilded fixtures. Expensive amenities. Four-poster bed. She took off her heels, scrunched the carpet between her toes, and moved to the windows, pulling the curtains aside to observe this part of St. Petersburg that was now at her feet. Heavily bundled people were bustling through the chill, others were queuing up at markets, mothers were pulling stubborn offspring away from puddles. *I am above it all,* she thought, taking another sip of Champagne, which she noted was a good vintage. *Not the grocery store swill Dmitri buys.*

Nikolai spun her gently and took the glass from her hand. His mouth found hers; tongues intertwined. He then kissed her chin, her upper lip, both sides of her nose, and her forehead before moving again to her lips. Their bodies pressed into one another.

He moved behind her and began kissing her left shoulder, his tongue paying particular attention to a bold freckle. Olga tilted her head as Nikolai's lips moved to her neck and earlobe. His hands moved slowly over her body outside her dress. At last, his hands found her breasts, but it was only a tease as he brought them down to her waist. *Dmitri never treated me like this. He never took his time. He got his pleasure, then stopped,* she thought.

Olga felt the zipper of her dress being pulled down, and then the satiny garment was sliding from her shoulders. Nikolai again kissed her shoulders and both sides of her neck. She leaned her head back, and their mouths locked. Olga reached back with her right hand and felt Nikolai's want.

Nikolai unhooked her bra, his hands guiding it to the floor. Then his hands cupped each cool, white breast. Olga moaned.

He guided her to the foot of the bed, gently leaned her forward, then slowly moved her panties downward. He turned Olga around, and she placed herself in the middle of the bed. Her nipples peeked through her blond hair; Nikolai seemed entranced as he removed his clothing. Olga lay back on the pillow pile, legs apart. "Come here," she beckoned with an imperious forefinger..

Nikolai moved onto the bed and took his prize.

After nearly two hours, they were both spent and satisfied. Olga's head was on his arm, her hand on his chest. Nikolai looked at his watch. "Ah. I must get back to the office. I am expecting an important phone call," he said. He leaned over and kissed her warmly. "This was an excellent meeting. I look forward to the next one."

Olga kissed his chest. "I will bring my notepad next time."

"To hell with notepads. Bring that dress."

They showered together, causing Ivanov to wish he had more time. They left the room separately but arrived at the Internet Research Agency together. Olga entered first, carrying a number of folders to fulfill her part of the masquerade. Her hair was pinned up, and she was wearing her work scowl as she marched to her desk. Ivanov pretended to be on his phone and avoided eye contact as he sat at his desk.

Dmitri Alexandrov immediately appeared.

"How was the meeting?" he asked Ivanov.

"You know how such meetings are. Long-winded and boring. Although there were several almost rousing moments," said the director. "Thank you for keeping a watch on things, Dmitri."

The compliment was like patting a dog on the head. "No problem, sir. Here are this morning's reports. Someone representing 'The Benefactor' contacted me and said you should expect his call this afternoon."

"Did this person indicate what time this call would come?"

"No. I get the feeling 'The Benefactor' answers to no schedule but his own."

"You are correct there, my friend. Thank you, Dmitri. That will be all," said Ivanov, hoping Dmitri did not detect Olga's scent.

For the next half hour, Ivanov reviewed the reports. Finally, the encrypted phone buzzed, and Ivanov took the handset. "*Privet* (hello), he said."

"Please hold for Mr. Everson."

After nearly a minute, Everson came on the line. "Nikolai. How are you, my friend?"

Wouldn't you like to know, Ivanov thought. "I am doing well. I'm sure the weather is much warmer where you are."

"Yes, I can imagine that's true. Listen, I wanted to let you know that our little project has been completed, and we are ready to take it on a test drive."

"That is excellent news. What do you need from us?" Ivanov asked.

"Nothing at the moment. We can pick a target and get everything ready from our end, and then we can install the software at your facility. I presume you can mask it? My security is of the utmost importance."

"*Da,* my friend, Maxim."

Everson frowned. Very few people were allowed to use his first name. "So, how do we pick a target?"

"I will give you the honors. After all, it is your software."

Everson thought for a moment, then a smile appeared. "Not many know this, but I was fired from one of my first jobs. My supervisor was an incompetent fool. He once told me he was from some backwater town in Mississippi. Hernando. Hernando, Mississippi," said the billionaire. "Sounds like the perfect place to start to me."

"Very good, very good," Ivanov said. "You bring us your software. We will send this Hernando, Mississippi, back to the Dark Ages."

CHAPTER 14

It had been a trying day at Hernando Elementary, one in which it appeared the students had won. The day's battle was over, but its effects on the casualties remained. Kendall Guthrie, ever alert from her reception-area vantage point, watched as a gaggle of teachers drooped past her office. Among them were Michael, Ellie, Chadwick Cartwright, and The Gurls—Janis Li, Nancy Hernandez, and Wendy Cosgrove. One of the school's teacher-coaches, Jonas "Chalky" Barnett, was acting as rearguard for the exhausted procession.

"Oh, my lord," Kendall said in her booming voice. "Isn't this a sad-looking group. You folks look like someone ran over the Easter Bunny."

Michael wasn't sure what that meant, but he was too tired to respond anyway. Ellie replied, "Not now, Kendall. This day has been a bear."

The reference spurred Michael/Anton to recall the bear encounter they'd had in Colorado last year. *I'm going to remember that every time I go past Ursa Major from now on,* he thought.

"Well, I have the perfect antidote for a day like this," Kendall declared. "It's time to hit The Spot. Hit the spot. Get it?"

Wendy Cosgrove said, "Oh, yeah, we get it. It's not a bad idea, actually. I'm up for it if you guys are."

Ellie said, "I suppose I'm good for a round. Michael?" He shrugged his approval. The others nodded or said, "OK."

"So, get your fannies in your cars, and I'll meet you there in a few after I lock up," Kendall said.

The Spot was the only semblance of a sports bar that Hernando had, and it was tucked into a part of town where teachers might not be identified as paying customers. Some of them called it "Hernando's Hideaway." Its décor hadn't changed in decades, and neither had the smell. One might describe the bar's design style as Taylor Sheridan trapped-in-amber 1950s Fever Dream. Blinking neon beer signs. Broken Formica tabletops. Torn plastic seat cushions. A jukebox that hadn't been updated since Hank Williams died. But the beer was cold, and the prices were amendable to teacher salaries.

Michael and Coach Barnett pulled a couple of tables together to accommodate a group of eight; Kendall was yet to arrive. The seven who were there grabbed chairs; the weight of the day began to dissipate. Chadwick—he preferred Chad—collected drink orders, including Kendall's favorite, and turned them in to the bartender. Michael and Ellie were sticking to their usual, Bud Light.

Chad returned and removed his bow tie. "Uh-oh," said Michael.

"Uh-oh, what?" replied Chad.

"When you take off your bow tie, that generally means you are about to get wild."

"Wild is as wild does, old boy," Chad said in a faux British accent. "Hey, I've got a joke for you."

"Let's hear it," said Janis Li. Chad had asked Janis out a few times, but nothing had kindled. She had since turned her attention to Coach "Chalky" Barnett. ("I'd like to dust his Chalky board," she had told The Gurls.)

"Did you hear about the koala bear that walked into a bar?" Chad began.

Michael whispered to Ellie. "Another bear reference."

"No, let's hear it," Nancy shouted, trying to be heard over the jukebox. The group leaned in as Chad took the "floor."

"A koala bear walks into a bar and grabs a barstool up at the bar. 'What'll you have?' asks the bartender. 'Give me a beer and a bowl of chili. No beans.' The bartender and a customer who is sitting at the bar are both amazed to hear a talking koala bear. But the bartender soon brings over a mug of beer and a bowl of chili.

"The koala bear wolfs down the bowl of chili and then washes it down with the mug of beer. He wipes his face with his paw and says 'aaaahh.' Next thing you know, the bear pulls out a pistol and shoots the customer, leaving him dead on the floor. The koala puts away the pistol and starts to walk out.

" 'Hey, where ya goin'?' shouts the bartender. 'You just killed a man.' The bear turns and says, 'I'm a koala bear. Look it up.' Then he walks out the door.

"The bartender just happens to have a dictionary under the bar. He turns to the entry for 'koala.' The dictionary says, *Koalas. Native to Australia. Members of the marsupial family.*

"Eats shoots and leaves."

Most of the group snorted or chuckled. Wendy Cosgrove said, "I don't get it. Who eats parachutes?"

Nancy looked at her and shook her head. "That's OK, Wendy. I will explain it to you later."

"Good one, Chad," Michael said, patting him on the back.

The drinks and Kendall arrived at the same moment. "Impeccable timing as always, my dear," said Chad.

Kendall's arrival brought the conversation to a crescendo; she was the *e pluribus factum* of all that occurred at Hernando Elementary. "What have I missed?" she asked, with "missed" stretched out over several beats.

"Chad was telling jokes," Janis said.

"You're a naughty boy, Chad. Starting without me. Shame on you," Kendall said.

"Sorry, Kendall. It was an emergency…an emergency case of intense, spontaneous sarcasm," he responded.

Kendall ignored him while the others groaned. As Kendall began to hold court, Chad turned to Michael. "I've got a favor to ask," he said.

"Shoot."

"I have been having a run of bad luck of late in the romance department. There just doesn't appear to be much in the way of proper dating material in Hernando," Chad said.

"What happened with you and Janis, if you don't mind me asking."

Chad nodded his head in her direction. "Chalky happened is what happened."

"Oh. I see that now. Have you tried any of those dating apps?"

"Yes. For what good that did me. I thought I had hit it off with one young lady. Then I took her to dinner. I joked that I had recently defected from the KGB. She says, 'KGB? What's that?' " lamented Chad. "Then there was another woman who I met for coffee. She went into an explanation about how she got her facial scars as a kid from sliding her sled into a barbed wire fence. Now, before you go accusing me of being overly judgmental, I did pay for the coffees."

"That's awful noble of you, Chad."

"Don't be harsh, Michael. A man needs more than personality in a woman. My ex-wife had all the personality I can stand. Personality can clean out your bank account and take your dog with it."

Michael sipped his beer. "So, what is the favor?"

"You caught yourself a winner in Ellie. I was wondering if you or Ellie had any unattached female friends who might be looking for an intelligent, sophisticated man of the South to spend some time with."

"Sophisticated man of the South, eh. Is that the reason you wear bow ties? Is that the new uniform of the sophisticated man?"

"I will have you know that my fashion sense was passed down to me. My father and his father were masters of the chic and suave," Chad replied, holding up his tie. "As you can see, these are not clip-ons. I tie them myself."

"OK, OK. No offense intended. So, what about Nancy?"

"Nancy and Janis are too good of friends. What is said to one is soon known by the other. No, no. And don't ask about Wendy. She didn't even get my last joke."

"So, what are you looking for in a date or partner?" Michael asked.

"She must be astute and have superlative conversational skills. She must be principled but not overly so. No Quakers need apply," Chad said. "Politics don't matter, but I prefer no conspiracy theorists. Height and weight are not major concerns, although I would prefer someone reasonably attractive. A dry and self-deprecating sense of humor would be a plus. So would a huge bank account."

Michael chuckled. "Gee, Chad. You don't ask much. I've been out of the game awhile, but let me talk with Ellie and see if we can come up with any names. You're not a closet serial killer, are you?"

"I never told you my middle name is Dexter?"

"Ha. Your dark passenger just might be a koala bear. OK, let me talk to the Divine Miz E."

"Thank you. An Ellie clone would be just perfect," Chad said.

If you only knew, Michael / Anton thought.

The two men returned to their drinks, but it wasn't long before Chad decided to not fully surrender the conversation to Kendall.

"I've got another joke," he announced.

"Oh, boy. Here we go again," said Janis.

"A cowboy walks into bar and orders a beer. The blond woman bartender brings him his beer, and she and the cowboy get to chatting. After a while, he says, 'I've got a joke for you. Did you hear the one about the blonde who....

"The bartender says, Whoa, whoa, whoa, cowboy. Can't you see I'm blond? Ain't no bottle blond either. And for your information, next to you are four other blondes. One is a Marine drill instructor. Another one has a black belt in karate. The next one down is a SWAT team sniper. And the last one is an MMA fighter. Still want to tell that blonde joke now?

"The cowboy rubs his chin. 'Nah, I guess not,' he says. 'Not if I'm gonna have to explain it five times.'"

Kendall pinched Chad and pointed to her mass of blond hair. "I knew there was a reason I hated you, Chad. Mine didn't come from a bottle either."

After they had finished their beers, Michael and Ellie were ready to depart. "Got to get home to Gator," Ellie said, putting some money on the table. Before they could get out the door, they were headed off by "Chalky" Barnett. It turned out Chad wasn't the only one who was desirous of Michael's assistance.

"I was hoping to catch you earlier, but I didn't want to bring this up in front of everybody," the coach said.

"Need me to leave?" asked Ellie.

"No, no. You can stay. I need a big, big favor, Michael. My grandfather just passed away, and I need to go to the funeral in South Carolina," he said. "I will be out of town for a few days to help clean out his house."

"I'm so sorry to hear that, Jonas." Michael wasn't keen on using "Chalky" to a grown man. "What is it you need me to do?" Michael presumed he would be asked to take on the coach's bus duties. He was in for a surprise.

"I need someone to coach the sixth-grade boys basketball team for me. They have a practice tomorrow and a game on Friday," the coach said.

"Jonas, I don't know anything about basketball."

"That's OK. I don't know much either. All you have to do is tell them to pass the ball when they are on offense and to block out when they're on defense. Get those rebounds," he said. "They pretty much do what they want, anyway."

"Why ask me, Jonas?"

"You, Chad, and I are the only three men in the school. Chad's a nice guy, but look at him. Would you take directions from him if you were on a basketball team?" Barnett said.

Michael hesitated but then got a verbal prod from Ellie. "C'mon, Michael. It will add to your personal growth, and who knows, it might even be fun."

"OK, Jonas. You have a deal."

The coach bear hugged him. "Thank you, thank you. You're a lifesaver," Barnett said, pulling a sheet of paper out of his pocket. "Here's the roster. I've marked the starters and written some notes next to every name."

Michael took the paper. There were eleven names with descriptors jotted on the side. "I will do the best I can. Don't blame me if we lose, though. And payback is going to be…"

"A bitch. I already know," Barnett said. "But really, thanks so much."

CHAPTER 14

Michael and Ellie got into her Tesla. He looked over the roster sheet in his hand. He shook his head. "Basketball? Me? Really?"

Ellie started the car. "Hey, he's Basketball Jonas. We're going to make you Basketball Jones. YouTube, here we come."

CHAPTER 15

Agent David Broadscale read over the response from the D.C. office. "What the hell is this crap?" He immediately called Special Agent Thomas Dettwiler for advice and commiseration. "Have you read what just came down the pipe?" he asked the Jackson agent.

"Yep. Sure did. That is all Washington-speak for stand down," Dettwiler said. "It's just like before 9/11 when the brass sat with their thumbs up their butts despite all the warnings. Remember Zacarias Moussaoui, the guy who wanted to learn how to fly a plane but not land it? That was a big shiny clue. Reports were sent up. What happened? Ignored."

It was certainly not the first time that politics and the FBI had become intertwined, or for politics to become a hurdle to FBI procedures. The father of the bureau, J. Edgar Hoover, was infamous for the files he kept on politicians and others. Those others included antiwar and civil rights activists (including Martin Luther King, Jr.); the bureau's reputation suffered a major blow in the 1970s when its COINTELPRO harassment and bugging operations were exposed. President Richard Nixon—who at one time wanted to join the FBI—told his aides to order the CIA to block the bureau's investigation of the Watergate break-in. Director James Comey placed his finger on the 2016 presidential election with his revelations, or nonrevelations, about Hillary Clinton's purloined emails. More recently, there were attempts to push the FBI to investigate claims, widely proven false, of election rigging in the 2020 presidential race. Not all of the criticism of such so-called "weaponization of the FBI" originated on the left. There were calls to defund the bureau over the FBI's investigation of Russian election meddling; a subsequent special counsel probe found little of substance. During a 2023 congressional hearing, two FBI "whistleblowers" testified that they had been unfairly ostracized and disciplined for the voicing of "alternative theories" regarding the Jan. 6, 2021, insurrection.

Through it all, the bureau's agents have managed to apprehend or silence notorious gangsters, create cracks in crime families and racist groups, and foil Nazi, Soviet, and other intelligence operatives. Its agents have arrested crooked officeholders of all political stripes and stations.

So, the faint odor of politics emanating from this directive was nothing new.

Broadscale said, "I had a little attachment to my version of this memo. They want to investigate the Twitter and TikTok accounts of some Memphis newspaper editors. Supposedly, they endorsed the new guy's opponent."

"Didn't they all? It's kind of comical to see all these media pricks bending the knee and kissing the ring these days," Dettwiler said.

Broadscale replied, "Yeah, he's got 'em running scared. Suing a bunch of them, and some of them are settling instead of fighting. I thought that Stephanopoulos guy had a good case. Hard to prove actual malice on what was basically a fuckup."

"Yeah, not a lot of courage to be found these days," Dettwiler said. "Speaking of, I think I'm going to put in my papers. Looking at the forms right now."

"What? You're going to retire?"

"It's about time, anyway. I've got more than three decades in. Besides, I've got some connections in the private security field that I can tap. Better money and benefits. A lot less bullshit."

"I hear you on that. But listen, two can play this game," Broadscale replied. "I'm going to keep looking into this "freeze weapon" or whatever it is but do it quietly. In the meantime, I will shovel shit to the mushroom suits upstairs."

"Good luck with that, but be careful. Jackson wasn't my choice as a station. Read me?" Dettwiler said.

"Loud and clear. Hey, best of luck as a civilian. And, if I hear anything…"

"…Please let me know," Dettwiler said. "Keep your head down, David, and watch your six."

"Will do. Likewise."

CHAPTER 16

Never had a conspiracy been launched over seven cups of Colombian coffee. Not on Xylodon, anyway.

One of Dakkott's cousins, a tall, dark-clothed native of the planet's sparsely populated west mountains, joined the six cadets. He removed a silver flask from under his cloak and added some amber liquid to his cup.

"I find it cuts through the taste of the city," he said.

Ungbar reached a hand across the table. "Greetings, friend. My name is Ungbar-11, and this is..."

"No names," said the cousin. "You are just passengers one through six to me. I am only here because Dakkott shares our blood."

"All right then," said Julista. "No names. We have been given to understand that you have access to a Dart Lurker."

"This is true," said the cousin.

Julista declared their intentions. "I was able to obtain the necessary coordinates and a way to establish a communications link. We would like to secure passage for a trip to..."

The cousin cut her off with his upraised hand. "I don't need to know that either. It's best that few know."

"Secrets, secrets, secrets. I just love secrets," said Ungbar. "I used to have a secret, but it's not a secret anymore." He playfully poked Gorthand in the ribs; the latter winced.

Dakkott silenced him. "Let him finish."

The cousin continued. "Use of one of our Dart Lurkers is not free. It will cost each one of you five hundred *xyls*. Hard currency. No credit."

Julista asked, "When would we be able to depart?"

"Once payment is received, we will make the preparations. Which of you can fly a Dart Lurker?"

"I can," said Dakkott. "I have flown them two or three times, so I guess I will be the pilot."

His cousin smiled. "Of course. I suggest you train someone to be co-pilot. Just in case. Do it soon."

Dakkott nodded.

"What about extra fuel?" asked Roggbach. "My understanding is we will need additional fuel to get to...our destination."

"We can supply the extra fuel. There are external tanks that can be attached. That will cost one thousand *xyls* more."

"That is a pretty steep price," Julista said.

"*Now* you want to negotiate? The Academy has made you an expert now on fuel costs?" the cousin said tersely.

Roggbach patted Julista's hand. "Don't worry. I can pay his price. I have access to a trust fund. In fact, I can cover any who cannot pay the passage fee."

"That would be me," said Margeen.

Gorthand asked the cousin about the stealth capabilities of the craft.

"You have the best. We are never seen by the humans unless we want to be," said the cousin. "Some of our pilots like to play games with the human aircraft. They turn off the stealth and hit the afterburners. Then they turn it back on."

Roggbach nodded. "Let's do this. I will pay the entire fee now for passage and fuel, and you five can pay me back at some point." Roggbach took out his communicator and scrolled to the desired screen. He passed the communicator to the cousin. "Enter your account information in the designated area." The cousin did so, then passed back the device.

Roggbach said, "I will round this up to five thousand *xyls*. That's to cover any incidentals and secure your silence in this matter."

The cousin looked at his communicator and observed that the transfer was accepted. "Most generous. I did not say this before, but the Dart Lurker will be well provisioned for your needs. This is how we will proceed. All communications will go through Dakkott." The cousin handed Dakkott an encryption device.

"I ask only one favor for myself," said the cousin. "If possible, bring back some Earth coffee for myself and my colleagues."

Dakkott and several of the others nodded.

"Good, good. Any brand will do," said the cousin. "Tomorrow at about this time, Dakkott will receive a set of instructions. You are to follow these instructions to the letter. To...the...letter. Do not deviate. You may receive additional instructions as you proceed. We will be watching to see if you are being followed…" he then looked at Ungbar. "…Or if there is deception."

"Why are you looking at me, old boy?" Ungbar said. "There's not a shred of deceit in my bones."

The cousin did not smile. Standing, he said, "I go now to make ready. Listen to Dakkott." Then he was gone, quickly blending into the night.

"Well, now. Wasn't that just the proper dose of intrigue?" said Ungbar. "All right, children. Earth, here we come."

The six cadets gathered in Dakkott's Academy room after supper the next day. They tried to make small talk, but their collective rising anxiety unraveled attempts at conversation. They had each brought backpacks or light luggage for the change of attire needed on Earth. One dangling issue was soon resolved: Julista volunteered to learn how to pilot the Dart Lurker.

Dakkott's encryptor *dinged* to life. When connected to his personal communicator, he could read this message:

Proceed by hover car to 127 Quartzon Avenue in the Lumina District.

Because of the size of their party, the cadets had to book two hover cars. Within about twenty minutes, they had reached the given address, a pharmacy that had closed for the evening. There was still foot traffic about, but none of the pedestrians appeared out of the ordinary. Night began to settle in, and the other five looked at Dakkott with anticipation. After an interminable half minute, the encryptor sounded.

The next message:

Proceed by foot to 23 Xylor Street.

The address was only six blocks away in total, including a right turn. The six cadets were now above a tube station; the tube on Xylodon was akin to an underground rapid rail system on Earth, if such existed, and if that rapid rail was done with magnets.

Ding.

Take the tube to Nova Station in the Lumina District. Go to the connector lobby. Find a seating area and wait.

The Lumina District was one of Xylodon's most well-known entertainment areas. It provided offerings to suit any taste. The cadets found seats in a tube car; they could barely feel its movement. That didn't stop Julista from gripping her seat tightly. Only the cadets were in the car, but there was no conversation shared among them.

They arrived at the Lumina District station in about ten minutes and trekked into its interior. The cadets found an accommodating seating area and waited. Gorthand procured some cold drinks from a nearby vending machine.

Almost a half hour went by, enough time for Julista and Margeen to refresh themselves. No sooner had they sat down than the encryptor sounded.

CHAPTER 16

> Take the tube to Nebula Station.

Nebula Station was at the end of the north tube line and was some distance outside Xylos. The cadets looked at one another. They knew Nebula Station was the link point to shuttle service to Xylodon's three moons.

This time the trip, taking them into the desolate outer reaches of the capital, took almost forty-five minutes. Once they had arrived, the travel choices were limited. It was either one of three moon shuttles or the tube back to the city. The cadets gathered in a waiting area for what they expected to be the last of their instructions. After a few minutes, it came.

> Take the Khione shuttle. Tickets are already purchased. Identify yourselves as Presidium research group Alpha. Signal once you arrive on Khione.

Khione was the farthest of Xylodon's three moons; it was largely covered by ice. Its distance and climate were the primary reasons Khione was selected as the site of the lone Xylodonian prison. Dakkott approached the ticketing desk and identified the group as instructed. The clerk looked over their identification and then began tapping on a keyboard. In a few moments, six tickets appeared. Dakkott passed them out.

The ticket clerk said, "Proceed down Hallway C. Insert your tickets into the scanner, then follow the arrows to the shuttle craft. A guide will show you to your seats."

After the short walk to the shuttle, the cadets were aboard and seated. There were no other passengers.

A uniformed female guide approached them from the cockpit. "Hello. My name is Xina, and I will be assisting you this evening. Take-offs can sometimes be rough, so make sure you are buckled in. After we leave Xylodon's pull, I will conduct a refreshment service. The expected flight time to Khione will be fifty-five minutes."

Once the shuttle had lifted off, the cadets began to relax. Apparently, their security precautions had succeeded. Several of them lay their heads back and closed their eyes. Dakkott was not among them. Neither was Julista, who was seated next to him. He took her hand.

"Almost there," he said.

As the shuttle craft neared the frosty moon of Khione, the final leg of this portion of their journey, the six cadets became more ebullient; they pointed at this and that, and their chitchattiness increased in frequency and volume. The shuttle slowed during its descent, and its landing was little more than a hard thump.

"Please remain seated," said the guide after the craft shut down. "As you know, Khione is much colder than Xylodon, and the atmosphere is less tolerant for our life forms." She opened a set of lockers. "These enviro-suits are being provided to you for the duration of you stay on Khione." The silver, thermal-lined suits covered the entire body and were secured at the throat. A protective facemask containing a breathing tube and a set of goggles came with the suit. "Please do not lose or damage any of this protective gear. You will be responsible for any damage or loss, and I can tell you, the goggles can be expensive. The suits must be returned to the crew handling your return flight to Xylodon. Any questions?"

"Yes. What are the gravitational differences here? Will that be a problem?" asked Gorthand.

The guide nodded. "Good question. Fortunately, the gravity here is comfortably similar to that on Xylodon. You should have no difficulties. Also, take note of the breathing tubes inside your facemasks. You have nose and mouth tubes as redundant devices. Some Xylodonians have said they did not need to use the tubes, but I would recommend using one or both until you know if you can adjust. Are there any other questions?"

The group met her query with silence.

"Good. You may put on your enviro-suits here. Make sure the suit is secured about your heads and check the fit of your masks and goggles. The station is only a short walk up that lighted path, but our company is not responsible for any freeze burns or other injuries. Check each other's suits; if you secure them properly, you should have no problems. Understood?"

The six cadets took the suits and nodded.

"Excellent. I am now heading into the cockpit area. Once you are all ready, push the button next to the cockpit door. The pilot will then open the exterior doors. As I stated, follow the lighted path to the station. You will not need to use your suit's safeguards inside the station. You may remove them, but you will need to put them back on once you depart from the station. Good luck with your research."

The guide departed, and the six cadets put on their enviro-suits. The suits were one-size-fits-all but could be tightened to accommodate any frame with belts and straps. Dakkott checked everyone's suits afterward; when he was satisfied, he hit the cockpit buzzer. The exterior doors opened, and the group trudged, some more easily than others, toward the station. The exterior and interior were virtual copies of the station they had departed from. Once inside—it was quiet and empty but for a ticketing clerk—several of the cadets refreshed or relieved themselves, and Dakkott sent a simple message on the encryptor.

"Here."

A response quickly came. "Be there soon. Meet outside exit in five minutes."

Dakkott told Julista of the instructions, and they herded their companions outside the station exit. A large yellow-and-black-striped hover craft—*Is that supposed to resemble a zeephar?* Julista wondered, referring to one of Xylodon's wild cat species—soon arrived.

A door on the hovercraft opened, and Dakkott's cousin, clad in his own enviro-suit, appeared in the doorway. He beckoned to the group; he was as terse as before.

"Get in."

Once they were all aboard, the hovercraft, lights off, sped off into the dark, traveling only a few feet above the landscape. Snow and ice blown by the moon's unpredictable wind patterns posed a danger, but Dakkott's cousin, who was piloting the craft, seemed oblivious. A sliver of a crack, barely visible in a far-off glacial mountain, transformed into a canyon entrance as the hovercraft drew closer. The cousin slowed the craft, still with its lights off, and began negotiating the twists and turns of this frozen thoroughfare with instruments—and experience—alone.

The hovercraft cleared the canyon and entered a large, darkened clearing that served as the smugglers' base. It was shielded by ice-topped massifs and peaks, and muted lighting marked the half-dozen or so structures on the base. Dakkott's cousin brought the hovercraft to a stop outside a large white dome. "Come with me," he said.

The cadets followed, and the cousin raised the dome's large pull-down door. He pulled on a large tarp, revealing the dome's occupant.

"Your Dart Lurker," he said.

CHAPTER 17

"TWEEEEEEEEEEEEEEEET!!

The eleven boys in the gym for the after-school practice stopped their dribbling, shooting, and sixth-grade goofing.

Michael Gort/Anton was wearing shorts, basketball sneakers and a T-shirt with the Hernando school logo. He had bought a whistle and put it on a lanyard around his neck. As recommended by Ellie, he had watched a number of YouTube videos to gain an understanding of the fundamentals and tactics of basketball. "Gather round, fellas," he said. "I'm Mr. Gort, and I will be your coach this week."

Jimmy Thompson, otherwise known as No. 12, raised his hand and asked, "Where's Coach Barnett?"

Michael thought he would spare the boys from the complete truth. "He had a family emergency come up, so I'm substituting for him for a few days. That includes your game Friday against Horn Lake." "Chalky" had emailed him an overview of his practice routine, which began with five laps around the gym's interior. "OK, fellas, let's line up here and get our warmup laps in." He blew the whistle, and the boys took off. It didn't take long for them to transform from a group to a gaggle, with the lead pack running almost a court-length ahead of the stragglers. One boy, the shortest player on the team, brought up the rear. The others completed the five laps; the little guy finished last, red-faced and sweating.

Michael pulled him aside. "What's your name, son?"

"Curtis Mouton. Folks call me Little C."

"What position do you play, Curtis?" Michael asked.

One of the other boys, Quintavion Phillips, answered. "Left end of the bench." The rest of the team laughed; Curtis looked at his shoes.

"My daddy says his family is a bunch of Katrina refugees," another boy spurted. "That's what my daddy said. He called them Katrina trash." Curtis continued to look down.

"Well, I don't have many rules," Michael said. "But one of them is, if you show up for practice, then you get to play in the game. Got it? Everybody plays. OK, let's do our dribbling drills, and then we will do some passing drills."

Only Quintavion was particularly adept at dribbling around the cones Michael had set up, which explained why he was the team's point guard. Most of the players couldn't dribble more than a few steps without looking at the basketball. The ball was a good deal bigger than Curtis's hands, and he struggled keeping it under control. The tallest player on the squad, Kenon Jimerson, was pushing six feet and played center. Kenon had some height for his age, but he was trapped in an awkward growth stage, and his arms and legs didn't always go the direction he wished.

When he put the team through some passing drills—chest passes then bounce passes—the boys could do a fair job of passing the ball, but catching it was an adventure. And, again, Curtis struggled; his lack of arm strength made him a liability.

Michael attempted to show the team a basic pick-and-roll play—found by Ellie on YouTube—and attempted to get the boys to move around more on offense and set screens for the better shooters. After Quintavion and Kenon performed three successive pick-and-rolls for baskets, Michael moved on to defense.

"Coach Barnett didn't teach us no defense, Mr. Gort," Kenon said.

"Then I guess you fellas will learn something today," Michael said. "I am going to give you a couple of basic defenses, the two-three zone and the man-to-man. The last one is probably the one you have already been doing, right?"

Jimmy, the team's second-tallest player, said, "Yas, sir...find a man and stick to him. That's what Coach B told us."

"That's right. Very good. The man-to-man is the defense we'll use most of the time, depending on the matchups. But when you fellas see me hold up two fingers (he demonstrated), you switch to the two-three." Michael explained how each player was responsible for protecting a certain area or zone. He placed Kenon in the middle of the back trio and told him he would likely be the primary rebounder and key defender. "You are the last line of defense against opponents driving to the hoop. Make 'em afraid to come at you. If you get in foul trouble, we'll go back to man-to-man," he said.

Michael then had the boys do a five-on-five half-court scrimmage, with Curtis initially on the bench. His lesson on the zone defense was quickly lost. When he subbed Curtis into the mix, the small boy appeared more interested in staying out of the way of the bigger boys. Five-on-five essentially become four-on-five. He was a bit better on defense; being lower to the ground enabled him to slap the ball away from dribblers.

He wanted to show the boys how they could adapt the zone to a double-team trap of opponents in the corners—another Ellie discovery —but he was running short of practice time.

"OK, fellas, let's finish up with some free throws. Don't stop until you hit five in a row," Michael said.

Quintavion hit his first five shots and headed to the showers. The rest of the team was a mixed bag, and Michael feared he might be there most of the night. "Let's change it up. Just hit three in a row."

The new goal was no easier for Curtis. He was more heaving the ball than shooting it; the ball sometimes missed the backboard and rarely touched the rim. His small hands provided little control of the ball. Still, he kept at it as his teammates began to satisfy the three-shot requirement. Soon, only Curtis and Michael were left on the court. *One has to admire his determination*, Michael thought.

The interim coach came over to Curtis and tried to demonstrate a typical set shot—which is what a free throw essentially is. This was something Michael had pulled from "Basketball Fundamentals for Beginners" on YouTube. He had Curtis, who was right-handed, place his left hand on the side of the ball and put his right hand behind the ball. "Then push. Use your left hand to steady and guide the ball and use your right hand as your launcher. Line up your right hand with the basket, then push. Give it a try."

Curtis tried to model what Michael had shown him, but his small hands worked against him. He could barely reach the rim. "OK, let's try this. Have you ever shot underhanded? There was an NBA player named Rick Barry who made a career doing that." Michael went to the foul line and demonstrated the technique. He finally made a basket on his third try. "I didn't say I was any good, but that's how you do it. Give it a shot."

Curtis took his position on the line, placed his hands on both sides of the ball, and flipped it upward. The ball hit the backboard, then caromed through the net. Michael awarded him with a high five.

"Do I have to hit two more, Mr. Gort?" Curtis asked.

"Nope, since that was a new technique, then you're good for today."

"YAY!" the boy shouted, then he joyfully dashed to the locker room.

When he got home a half hour later, a weary Michael/Anton sank into the living room sofa. Gator pawed at his legs, and Ellie gave him a pitiful look.

"How was practice?" she asked.

He looked at Ellie with half-closed eyes. "We have no prayer. You mix a Chinese fire drill with the Ringling circus, that's what I got," he said. "But you'd better show up tomorrow. If I'm going down, you'd better be there to catch me."

There was one somewhat important detail that "Chalky" Barnett had not given Michael. Horn Lake was Hernando's biggest rival, one that had claimed eight straight victories against their neighbors to the south. Even among sixth-graders there was no love lost. The stands in

Hernando's gym were filled with parents and fans for both teams: Hernando's blue and gold on one side, Horn Lake's white and red on the other. Some fans even had signs with various messages of encouragement or invective.

The Gurls were there in full force—Wendy Cosgrove and Janet Li were selling tickets, and Kendall Guthrie and Nancy Hernandez held down the concession stand with its offerings of popcorn, candy, and water bottles. Ellie Atkinson sat in the stands a few rows up from the Hernando bench.

The Horn Lake players were smaller on average than the Hernando players—they had no one as tall as Kenon. But they generally handled the ball better, and their passing was superior—when they passed it. Both Horn Lake guards liked to dribble and drive, missing plentiful opportunities to pass to open players on the wing. That allowed Kenon to block and alter a number of shots. He also started drawing fouls, which caused his backcourt teammates to abandon their assignments and collapse on the drivers, who then passed to cutters for easy layups time and again.

Quintavion made three baskets for Hernando and orchestrated one pick-and-roll play for Kenon. At the end of the first eight-minute quarter, Horn Lake led 18-8.

The second quarter was even worse. Hernando committed turnover after turnover, mishandling the dribble and sending passes into enemy hands. When Quintavion wasn't managing the offense, Horn Lake would send two or even three players at the Hernando ballhandler, who would then panic and give up the ball. Kenon continued to use his height to his advantage, scoring eight more points, mostly on offensive rebounds and putbacks. But at halftime, the scoreboard had Horn Lake in the lead 37-20.

As he headed to the locker room, Michael looked at Ellie and shrugged. She gave him the thumbs-up sign for encouragement.

That encouragement was what he doled out to his downcast team. "You guys are playing hard, and we all appreciate the effort. Those guys aren't better than you are, but they are taking advantage of our mistakes," he said. "Let's remember to keep our hands up on defense. They have been passing the ball over you guys. When they try to dribble in, cut 'em off and take the charge. Quintavion, how are you feeling?"

"I feel just fine, Mr. Gort."

"When Quintavion is in the game, let him bring the ball up court. You other guards, as soon as Horn Lake tries to double-team you, pass the ball to Kenon or Jimmy. Even if it's a lob. They can outreach and outjump those guys," he said. "And try to set some screens. Quintavion can out-dribble any of 'em, but he needs some help. C'mon, we can do this."

Michael's halftime suggestions apparently sank in; now it was Hernando that was taking the ball away, deflecting Horn Lake passes and taking charges. The tide began to turn; Horn Lake had no one who could keep up with Quintavion, and the tactic of beating double teams by passing to either Kenon or Jimmy worked more often than not. Hernando even hit every one of its third-quarter free throws—all three of them—but Horn Lake still led the game 44-36 going into the fourth quarter. Hernando was playing a steadier game, but Quintavion had picked up two more fouls, giving him four.

Horn Lake's quick guards turned a pair of Hernando blunders into baskets, but then Hernando's defense turned stingy. Or got lucky. Hernando held Horn Lake scoreless for more than three minutes, and the Quintavion-Kenon duet continued to sing, allowing the blue-and-gold to draw within two points, 48-46, with less than two minutes to play.

Horn Lake extended the lead to four points when one of their guards connected on a floater over Kenon, but Quintavion closed the gap with a layup that had the benefit of an unintentional double screen by Jimmy and Kenon; Jimmy had been knocked out of position but into the right place at the right time. Horn Lake's center was called for a foul on the play, and Quintavion watched his free throw make three revolutions around the rim before it fell in. Hernando trailed 50-49 with thirty-eight seconds left.

Quintavion then gambled and tried to steal Horn Lake's inbounds pass, but he tripped and crashed into one of the opposing players. It was foul number five; it was a non-shooting foul, but Quintavion, Hernando's top scorer, was out of the contest.

Michael looked at his bench. Suddenly, he had a hunch.

"Curtis, you're in." Quintavion and the rest of the bench looked at Michael with stunned expressions.

"M-m-me, coach? Are you sure?" quaked Curtis.

Quintavion whispered to one of his teammates, "You know what Little C stands for? Little Choker."

Michael told the small boy, "Yes, Curtis. You're in for Quintavion. I believe in you. Guard your man close. Tell Jimmy that when we get the ball back, he's going to shift to point guard, and he's to bring the ball up court for us. Got it?"

"Yes, coach."

"Go on, now. Get out there and have some fun."

Horn Lake crossed midcourt, and their two guards tried to squeeze the clock as much as they could, dribbling around and passing the ball to themselves. Michael yelled, "Jimmy!" He signaled for Jimmy to rush the Horn Lake ballhandler. When he saw the taller boy running at him, the Horn Lake player made a weak pass to his fellow guard.

Curtis was able to snatch the low pass before the Horn Lake player could secure it. Hernando had the ball trailing by a point with eleven seconds left. Michael screamed, "Timeout!"

The Hernando boys huddled around Michael. "All right, fellas, get in here. They are probably going to pressure the inbounds pass, so, Kenon, you toss the ball in. You can pass over them, so get the ball to Jimmy. We have another timeout left, so use it if you get in trouble. Jimmy, once Kenon gets set up down low, try to get him the ball. Kenon, take the shot if you have one or try to get fouled," Michael said, then turning. "You other three, move out to the wings to clear out for Jimmy and Kenon. But listen up. Jimmy, Kenon, if you feel like you are about to be trapped, pass the ball to an open man. The clock isn't our friend. Got it?"

"YES, SIR!"

Michael looked up into the stands at Ellie. She held up crossed fingers.

The ref blew his whistle, and Kenon flipped the ball high to Jimmy, who dribbled toward the top of the key while Kenon headed toward the basket. Two Horn Lake players cut Jimmy off from driving, so he made a pass to Kenon, throwing the ball up high where only he could catch it. Kenon had to jump to make the catch, giving Horn Lake, whose coach had anticipated the move, enough time to surround him with three players. Kenon tried to turn, but Horn Lake hands were grabbing at the ball. Out of the corner of his eye he spotted an open blue jersey and passed the ball in that direction in desperation.

Curtis Mouton found himself with the ball in his hands with three seconds left. And...simply...froze.

"Shoot, Curtis!" yelled Michael.

Little Curtis, Mr. End of The Bench, the Hurricane Katrina refugee, threw the ball underhanded toward the basket. The ball seemed to reach the gym rafters before it began its descent. Those in the gym uttered a collective gasp.

The ball came down and hit the back of the iron, bouncing almost straight up above the backboard. The ball hit the top of the backboard squarely, bouncing upward. Then it came down once more.

Swish.

The Hernando side of the gym erupted; the Horn Lake partisans were in shock. His teammates mobbed Curtis; Kenon then grabbed Little C and hoisted him onto his shoulders. Even Quintavion said, "Nice shot." Michael stood, clapped, and patted him on the shoulder. "See, I told you you could do it," he told Curtis. The boy was grinning too widely to respond.

Michael walked over to Ellie, who took his face in her hands and kissed him with a loud smack. She followed with a hug. Then he leaned back.

"Did you have anything to do with that?" he asked.

"You might say I 'watched' that last shot until it went in," she said, glancing at the holo on her wrist.

"You 'watched' it, huh? Well, good for you. You just made one little boy extremely happy."

She smiled. "I love good deeds. Hey, you've done your share. And if we go home right now, I might be able to make a big boy happy."

"Why, Ms. Atkinson. The things you do say."

CHAPTER 17

The next morning, Michael received a text from "Chalky" Barnett. "How did it go?"

"Great. We won the game," was the reply.

"You beat Horn Lake?"

"51-50."

"We haven't beat Horn Lake in forever. How did that happen?"

"Curtis made the last shot."

"CURTIS!?!?!"

"Yep. Made it underhanded. Seemed like it took an hour to get to the basket, but it won the game. You should have seen it."

"Wow. I wish I had. That's amazing. You are the man. Once again, thanks for filling in for me."

"Sure thing. But no more. I'm retiring with a career coaching record of 1-0."

"(Laugh emoji) Good deal. See you soon. Thanks again, Big Mike! (Fireworks emoji)"

Ellie came into the room carrying a coffee and a leash. Michael said, "So what's it like being married to the only undefeated coach in Hernando history?"

"Gator needs a walk, Dr. Naismith."

CHAPTER 18

As he walked down the sidewalk, with Gator ahead of him and Ellie on his arm, Anton-7/Michael Gort was filled with appreciation for the turn his life had taken. The sun seemed brighter, the air sweeter. He no longer felt like a fugitive. Yes, he still had his secrets and a mission to conduct. But the caution and doubt he had felt in recent years had been replaced by...security and confidence.

Ellie/Juleetha was much more unsettled. She paid more attention to current events than Michael, and while she might deny it, she had one foot more firmly planted on Earth than on Xylodon. At least in Hernando, Mississippi.

Anton could sense when his *sh'ana,* his life partner, was disconcerted. She was quiet, but in a certain way.

They passed houses of various shapes and colors, although the basic floor plan seemed the same. The homes might have been constructed to house plant workers in a past generation; now they were filled with retirees and beginning buyers. Gator investigated new scents and left his mark where he felt needed. The sidewalk offered a small degree of treachery; it was cracked and uneven in some places. Thorned rose vines climbed across fences while trying to escape their confinements. An outright evil pyracantha bush terrorized the faint of heart at the end of the first block.

Ellie's quiet made Gator's occasional yip seem louder. Anton knew her inner fires were burning; the longer he waited to inquire, the more incendiary she would become. "What's got that beautiful face of yours in a frown this morning?" he asked.

"Have you ever been in one of those situations where you see a problem, know what the solution is, but have absolutely no ability to match the problem with the solution because there are others who are more interested in some shiny bauble than they are in the actual solution?"

"That's both extremely deep and extremely unspecific at the same time. What are you referring to?"

"America's new president wants to abolish the Department of Education. Or maybe dismantle it from within. His education secretary is a former professional wrestling puppeteer who doesn't even have a college degree," she said.

Anton sighed. "America has long been an educational system and a health-care system shy of being a civilized nation. It's a matter of values. On Xylodon, we have codified a value system that places our citizens above profits. As you know, we have a more equitable pay-scale system that reduces the desire for profit. It is much less of an issue there. That hierarchy of needs put into pyramid form by the human psychologist Maslow is barely a bump on our planet."

"Yes, yes, yes. I know. There's a reason Maslow made gut-level wants much larger on that pyramid than those emerging from the heart and mind. It's just so frustrating," she said. "Funny that you mentioned value systems. Didn't many of the Europeans who came to America do so to escape religious strictures? But now some states are putting the Ten Commandments in classrooms. Which is funny in and of itself because the content of the Ten Commandments varies between the Jewish, Protestant, and Catholic holy books. I can't wait to hear how some of these Puritans explain 'adultery' or 'idols' or 'covet' to my third-graders. And do they care about the Muslim or Buddhist kids in a class? Or the agnostics? And you must have asked a key question to yourself: What value system gives greater rights to guns than to books? Surely, that crossed your mind before you made the guns vanish."

Anton tugged on Gator's leash to refocus the nosy dog on the walk. "You are nothing but right, of course. But you certainly have an amazing propensity for bringing up subjects that we can do absolutely nothing about. We can't even vote here, much less change the Constitution," he said. "Speaking of, isn't the Constitution more or less at the root of the Education Department question?"

"Look who's up on their reading."

"I try," he replied. "But I just know the contours of the subject. I presume you have some thoughts on the issue?"

"There are those who think the Constitution should be strictly interpreted. They say that what's not in there should be left to the states. The Constitution doesn't prescribe a federal role in education, so *pppffffftttt*, leave it to the states," Ellie said. "Others see that as a short-sighted view, because, for example, the writers of the Constitution had no foreknowledge of spaceflight, social media, artificial intelligence, and other innovations. Additionally, there's no equal playing field for the states in America. On the one hand you have California, which has one of the world's largest economies, and on the other you have states like Mississippi. Our friend Janis teaches special needs kids how to read. Kids with dyslexia. Do you think Mississippi would fund programs for those kids if it didn't have to? What about vouchers, some humans will argue. Going to a more privatized system, especially in the Mississippis of the world, will just create more haves and have-nots."

Anton nodded. "Mississippi. Where innovation goes to die. Sadly, it's not alone in that regard. So, here's a related question for you. You and I have both talked with human parents who love their offspring and appear to want the best for them. Including an education. Why do you think so many of them voted for a candidate who might endanger their children's educational opportunities?"

"Don't you mean: Why do so many people vote against their own interests?" Ellie said. "Good question, and I've struggled to come up with an all-encompassing answer. You remember my friend Bobby Gene Holloway?"

Anton rolled his eyes.

"Yes, I know what you think of him. But he was a policeman, and he told me he voted for the man who has thirty-four felony convictions. Can you imagine? A cop voting for a crook? Anyway, I'm no expert, but from what I have observed, human knowledge can be subdivided into shared facts and shared beliefs. Often, the beliefs are held more strongly than any multitude of facts—especially when you have a counterforce undermining the institutions that are responsible for producing facts. That brings us to the question of, 'Why do some humans choose beliefs over facts?' I think humans make an active choice; they want to believe rumors and misinformation because it supports a narrative they fancy. In a fast-changing society, they see beliefs as a foundation they can cling to."

"Interesting. Choosing beliefs—unsupported beliefs—over facts. Quite the opposite on our planet," Anton said. "Wouldn't an example of what you are referring to be that case in Ohio of the supposedly illegal Haitian migrants who were accused of eating cats and dogs? None of that was true—and the migrants weren't illegal—but many humans believed it to be true despite being given information that refuted those beliefs."

"Yes, and I can give you dozens of other examples," Ellie said. "There is a common denominator in these stories. Fear. When there are gaps in what is known, fear often fills those gaps. As in your example, a fear of 'the other' served to close many ears to the truth. The fear of 'the other' is very much related to the fear of the unknown. A good example of the latter would be those drones that were spotted along the East Coast in 2024. People didn't know where they came from, so they contrived stories to fill in that information gap."

Anton looked at Ellie in mock wonder. "Why, Ms. Atkinson. Who made you so wise? You must be a teacher or something."

Ellie chuckled. "Sometimes it's difficult to teach here without violating our protocols."

"Yes, our protocols. Do you ever miss Xylodon?"

"Sometimes. I don't miss living in Xylos. I couldn't breathe there. I can breathe here," she said. "I miss traveling across the plains. I miss eating a plate of fried *zurgot*. I often miss the sunsets. You?"

"Sometimes. But less and less while I'm by your side."

"You have told me little about your childhood," Ellie said. "What was little Anton like?"

"I always liked to read. Books were often my best friends. Histories. Mysteries. My father, like his father before him, was in the Protectorate, so he was gone much of the time," Anton said. "My mother was an artist. A painter and sculptor. She sold a few of her works."

"It sounds like you were alone a lot," she said, taking his hand.

"Oh, it wasn't bad. I never lost a game of *jeeparna*. Still undefeated," he said. "I participated in athletics teams. I could run. Had endurance. And what about you?"

"What about me? My sister and I fought a lot. Made our maternal crazy most days. I used to beat up the boys. That made my paternal crazy," she said.

"I bet you broke a few hearts as well."

"Only my own, as it turned out."

"Sore subject?"

"You might say that. But it's why I went to the Academy."

They walked in quiet reflection for the next half-block. Anton broke the silence.

"Here's another question for you. Now that we are partnered in marriage, are you still 'Ms. Atkinson'? And are we really married if there is no document that makes that declaration?" he asked.

"That's two questions. As to the first question, to keep the Kendalls of the world happy, yes, I'm Ms. Atkinson," she replied. "I have never thought about the second question. Don't you suppose Termas told the Protectorate that he conducted the *sh'ana'ala* (union) ceremony for us? If so, the scribes would feel a bureaucratic compulsion to record it."

Anton and Ellie reached the end of their six-block route and began to turn back. She wrapped her right arm in his left and squeezed.

"I love these walks with you," she said. "I love you. I love our dog. I love our life. I should try to focus more on what is good in this world. I look at my students, and I can't help but have big dreams for them. They deserve so much."

"There is no question about your fondness and empathy for these children. That is probably why you were willing to risk it all to bring those child traffickers to justice."

"Those men were terrible. Khione would be too good for them."

"Uhhh...speaking of children. That is something we have not discussed," Anton said. "Would you wish to become a maternal someday?"

Ellie paused and looked Anton in the face. "There are few things that I wish for more. I yearn to raise a *dziecko*—a seedling—with you. But I think we would agree that Earth is not the right environment."

"You are probably right. I just wanted to see if you were open to the idea. And I was trying to switch to a more pleasant subject; one we do have the power to do something about."

"Aren't you the clever one. And what about you?" Ellie asked. "What are your thoughts on having a little Anton-8 running around?"

"Of course, I would love that. But as you indicated…timing and all that," he said. "In the meantime, practice is quite enjoyable. Teacher."

Xylodonians weren't supposed to be able to blush, but in her human form, Ellie did.

"I think it's time for some ice cream, hotshot," she said.

CHAPTER 19

Pegasus, the white winged stallion of Greek mythology, became an inspiration to poets, sculptors, and painters, perhaps a product of his favoring brooks and streams frequented by the Greek Muses. Surely, that fascination must have had less to do with his origin. Pegasus, and his twin brother Chrysaor, were sired by Poseidon, the sea god. Their mother? The hideous Gorgon Medusa. The creature with a snakelike coif was pregnant with the twins when she was beheaded by Perseus; the two foals sprang from her spilled blood and literally took flight.

Pegasus became the better known of the brothers; Chrysaor appears famed mostly for producing a three-headed progeny that was slain by Heracles. In addition to flight, Pegasus had the ability to move between the mortal and immortal realms. The white stallion was also tasked with carrying Zeus's lightning bolts, and his wings could produce thunderclaps. He also had the ability to create tranquil, entrancing springs with his hoof strikes. Pegasus was transformed into a flying warhorse by Bellerphon, who used an enchanted golden bridle fashioned by Athena to bend the horse to his will. Bellerphon then used Pegasus to conquer the chimera.

The modern version of Pegasus is no victim of subterfuge; instead, it thrives upon it. One might even say it is the ultimate Trojan horse.

This Pegasus, one of the most advanced spyware programs thus far developed, was created by the NSO Group (the acronym represents the first names of the Israeli company founders), and it has abilities every bit as broad and frightening as its flying namesake. It is perhaps the most daunting challenge facing corporate and governmental chief information officers / chief information security officers.

The Pegasus invader requires zero clicks; it is installed via receipt of a text message. The spyware allows complete access to a user's smartphone, whether iOS or Android. Its tentacles—remember Medusa? —can reach into the user's photos / videos and every email and text message sent and received. It can access the phone's microphone—even when the user is not using the device—and listen in and record what is being said around it. It can access the phone's screen. It gives access to the phone's GPS. It opens a door to the applications uploaded on the device; the text sender can then delete their original message to remove traces of an incursion. Additionally, the Pegasus software can monitor keystrokes, allowing passwords to be stolen. Meanwhile, the device user is completely unaware they have a very real monster in their palm. What of that encryption in the WhatsApp application? No match for Pegasus.

The information Pegasus gleans can be used in any number of ways. One popular option? Extortion of a phone owner using the "private" information found on the device or their overheard conversations. Those pictures of young girls on Congressman X's phone could yield spectacular leverage.

The NSO Group created Pegasus with the intention of turning its cyber intelligence skills into shekels and dollars, but only to government clients. The Israeli government classifies Pegasus spyware as a weapon, and it must approve any sales. The company claims that the spyware provides a weapon to its government buyers to combat crime and terrorism. However, according to an investigation by the British newspaper The Guardian, the spyware has been used against dissidents, activists, and journalists—including Jamal Khashoggi. Israeli law enforcement has been accused of using Pegasus for warrantless domestic surveillance. Pakistan was a victim of Pegasus espionage. Trojan horse, indeed.

WhatsApp and Facebook's parent, Meta Platforms, sued the NSO Group in 2019 under U.S. computer fraud statutes. Apple filed a lawsuit against NSO in 2021, and the United States has forbidden American companies from supplying and assisting the Israeli firm.

Pegasus spyware takes advantage of—*exploits* in cyber nomenclature—zero-day bugs in software. These flaws are unknown to the vendor, who then has "zero days" to manufacture a fix or patch; the bug has already been accessed and exploited. Or not. Some members of the hacking world treat zero-day bugs as a commodity, selling them to the highest bidder. Government intelligence services will often warehouse known zero-day bugs for use at an opportune time.

Using the chosen language of the hacker, a zero-day vulnerability is considered "alive" if there is no public knowledge of its existence. If the flaw has been found, but not patched, it is deemed to be "dead." Vulnerabilities that have been patched in updated software versions, but still exist in older versions, allowing further exploitation, are called "zombies." When software manufacturers are negligent in maintaining their products, allowing "alive" vulnerabilities to continue, those bugs achieve "immortal" status.

Zero-day bugs became a growth industry in 2024; a variety of corporate network-control mechanisms, including Ivanti Connect Secure, Cisco Adaptive Security, and Check Point Quantum Security Gateways, reported being subjected to zero-day exploits. Zero-day vulnerabilities are often targeted in ransomware attacks and software supply-chain compromises. In 2023, Apple iOS and Google Chrome were among the more notable victims of zero-day bugs.

The NSO Group is far from being the only player in the zero-days game. Amnesty International discovered that the Serbian government had exploited zero-day flaws in Qualcomm software to plant a Pegasus variant called "NoviSpy" on Android phones. The primary targets? Those pesky activists, protesters, and journalists once again.

For Maxim Everson, one of the richest men in the world, the temptation to dip a toe into the spyware pool to monitor competitors and colleagues was simply too great. Besides, there was money to be made.

He had managed to purchase a version of Pegasus, and with a tweak here and a tweak there, had developed his own version—SuperMax. He had come up with the name himself, chuckling at the allusion to the U.S. federal prisons that boast the strictest security.

Everson had used his private jet to come to St. Petersburg and was quietly sipping tea in the office of Nikolai Ivanov when the IRA director returned from lunch. Ivanov appeared flushed. Everson watched as Ivanov's assistant, Olga Alexandrova, who had entered the building with Ivanov, hurried away with some files under her arm.

Ivanov removed his coat and sat down. "I am so sorry to keep you waiting, Mr. Everson. I had, how do you say, one of those fires that needed putting out."

I bet you did, Everson thought. "It's quite all right, Nikolai. Your staff took care of me quite nicely. And speaking of being taken care of, you must have been comforted to learn that the American Pentagon has decided to cease offensive cyber operations against your country."

"Yes, yes, yes. Our Operation Krasnov has been most successful in putting Washington on a chain, as it were," Ivanov said.

"Good for you. But enough small talk. You must know that I would rarely wait (looking at his watch) forty-five minutes if the matter were not so important."

"Yes. Indeed. Please forgive me, my friend. You have come a long way. Is there anything else we can get for you?" Ivanov asked.

"No, but there is something I can give to you." Everson reached into a jacket pocket and then held up a silver metallic thumb drive. "Let me introduce you to SuperMax."

SuperMax did not come cheap. Everson was to receive $500 million in two installments sent to a secret offshore account. The payments were on hold pending a successful result in today's test run. The target for the demonstration was Bogdan Leonov, a midlevel executive with Gazprombank. One of Ivanov's IRA technicians had easily secured Leonov's smartphone number and had prepared a perfectly innocuous text message for him, should he even look at it.

Everson and Ivanov watched as the thumb drive carrying SuperMax was inserted and soon began its cyber coupling with an IRA server. Once the mating was complete, a text message was sent to the phone of Bogdan Leonov. The message offered last night's hockey scores and complete analysis. There were no scores and no analysis.

Within seconds, Everson and the IRA had complete access to Leonov's smartphone. A search of the device found an application for Gazprombank. An IRA technician was assigned to keep watch on Leonov's phone screen until he accessed the app. It was only a matter of time. Everson and Ivanov went back to the director's office for more tea. They had barely stirred in their sugar and milk when the technician signaled that Leonov had opened the application. The IRA technician recorded the username and password. Leonov had then checked a few client accounts, then closed the app. But the application was not closed to everyone.

With Everson and Ivanov watching, the technician went into the application, accessed one large client account and then transferred one million rubles to an account number Ivanov had given him. They waited until their tea had been consumed, then Ivanov told the technician to transfer the rubles back to Leonov's client. There would be a record of the transactions somewhere, but Leonov would not likely see it.

Everson and Ivanov clinked their empty tea cups. "See? It works perfectly. As I said it would," Everson said. "You can tell your masters in Moscow to send me my money now."

Ivanov made a call; Everson nursed his phone until he confirmed that he was $250 million richer. *Not bad for one day's work,* he thought.

"Thank you, Nikolai. Now, what's for dinner?" Everson asked. "For tomorrow we are eating Hernando, Mississippi."

CHAPTER 20

MMMM-WAAAAAAHHHHH!!

For all intents and purposes, the Brangus heifer should not have been there. The cow and its calf, along with a few dozen other Brangus steers and heifers, had recently been placed in this vast field outside Hernando. A gas pipeline ran under the field; having the cows there to consume the dewy grass above the pipeline provided an agricultural tax break to the property owner.

The heifer and its tag-along calf had sauntered over to a less traveled area of the field when the mother went headlong into something solid. But unseen.

She bellowed at the obstacle. *MMMM-WAAAAAHHHH. Mmmm-waaahh. MMM-WAAAAHHH!*

The calf watched its mother curiously as she attempted to move forward once again, only to be met by a *clunk-thud* sound of rejection. A third attempt achieved the same result. The confused heifer then turned around and went back the way it had come, with the calf close at its heels.

"I believe those are called cows," Dakkott told the five other cadets who had lined up at the pilot's window to view the creatures.

"They are so peaceful," Margeen said. "Oh, look at that little one drink from its mother. I wish we could take them back with us."

"That would only violate about a dozen of our laws," Julista said. "In addition to the dozen or so we are breaking already."

Margeen shrugged. "I hate it when you're right. And besides, there's no room anyway."

The Dart Lurker had landed in the field during the pre-dawn dark. Dakkott had kept the craft in its stealth (invisible) mode since nearing Earth's atmosphere. To human—and nonhuman—eyes the vessel wasn't there, although the impression left in the grass and soil would have been evidence that *something* was there.

The trip from Khione took nearly a week and had gone without incident. In fact, it was almost boring. Dakkott and his smuggler cousin had charted a course well clear of Xylodon's resupply station on Neptune, one that avoided the most widely used Xylodonian flight paths. Once past Neptune's ears and eyes, Dakkott taught Julista how to pilot the vessel. Days later, as the craft neared Earth, Dakkott and Roggbach had initiated the Dart Lurker's stealth capabilities to avoid detection by the surveillance equipment that Xylodonian agents had placed on the planet's moon in the 1960s. The cadets had been unaware of the well-camouflaged devices—as were Earth explorers—and their unapproved adventure would likely have been detected if not for a warning from Dakkott's cousin.

The cadets had come up with a plan of sorts—Julista and Ungbar would travel to Juleetha's domicile in Hernando while the others remained on the Dart Lurker. Dakkott wanted to accompany Julista but was needed to pilot the Dart Lurker should an emergency arise. Margeen was entrusted with the vessel's various countersurveillance equipment, looking for incoming signals and sorting any nearby heat signatures. So far, the latter had all been of the four-legged variety. Gorthand, who had downloaded several global positioning applications and had managed to gain access to an Indian spy satellite, was scouting the area. The closest human structure was nearly three miles away along a two-lane road. After refocusing the satellite camera lens, Gorthand was able to get an enlarged view of the facility. It appeared to be some sort of combination food and fuel supply establishment, Gorthand told them. Human vehicles and their drivers would stop at one section of the facility and use the refueling machines; other humans would enter the other section and reappear with white paper bags of consumables.

"I can't say for certain what they are obtaining," he said. "All I know is that the humans walk in, then they walk out eating something that is circular and drinking something in cups. Who knows? Maybe it's coffee."

Just hearing the word "coffee" made them all smile.

Roggbach assisted Julista and Ungbar with the selection of the human cover personas to be created by their holo-biotrometers; Ungbar quickly settled on the guise of a young Caucasian female. He had wanted to use a Black male persona but was voted down given the cadets' collective knowledge of Mississippi history. Julista took longer to select her persona—the hair and other features had to be just right—but was also using the form of a Caucasian female. She and Ungbar would be college-age pals exploring the Mississippi countryside as part of a class assignment. Although no expert, Roggbach did what he could to coach the two "girls" on their voices, dialects, and vocabulary.

"Ooo. Ooo. Ooo. Don't you just love an adventure?" Ungbar said, clapping his hands. Then he added loudly enough for Gorthand to hear, "I wonder what these Earth boys are like?"

The landing site the cadets had selected had its advantages and disadvantages. It was far removed from roadways, making human detection unlikely, but its remoteness created hurdles for satisfying the primary purpose of this mission—reuniting the two sisters. The craft was resting nearly a dozen miles outside Hernando; accomplishing that distance on foot was not impossible but would be difficult. The progress of Julista and Ungbar could be monitored from the Dart Lurker via signals from their holos. For at least part of their journey, the Dart Lurker could come to their aid should they encounter difficulty. But once they were in the city proper, they would be on their own.

Thanks to Dakkott's cousin, Julista and Ungbar had access to a limited supply of human clothing, footwear, and currency—another reason the other four needed to remain behind. Margeen had rummaged around the Dart Lurker and had found some gear resembling backpacks that would add to the pair's hitchhiker/explorer cover story. The pair lacked human identification and other credentials; they would just be "Julie" and "Amber" should anyone ask. Any questions would have to be settled with the use of their holos.

The six cadets went over their plan, such as it was, one last time before Dakkott opened the Dart Lurker's outer door. Julista and Ungbar descended and began walking through the field. While the two Xylodonians and the Brangus residents of the pasture were mutually curious, they did not approach one another. Earth's atmosphere and the milder temperature posed no problems for the pair, but the planet's heavier gravity, which they had not trained for, caused them greater exertion. The pair negotiated a barbed wire fence and then reached the roadway. They trudged in the direction of the human facility that Gorthand had input into their holos, remarking how green and moist Earth was compared to Xylodon. Every plant, every insect, every piece of human debris became a new wonder to reflect upon.

"Now I know why Juleetha likes it here. Even the air tastes wet," Julista/Julie said.

They had dressed similarly: jeans, long-sleeved shirts over T-shirts, and sneakers. Ungbar/Amber wore a baseball cap. They paused frequently to adjust to Earth's gravity. The road was sparsely used; they didn't encounter any humans until more than thirty minutes into their journey. A large truck roared past them in the direction they were headed. A few minutes later, another vehicle (later determined to be an open-top Jeep with a roll bar) appeared, this one headed in the opposite direction and carrying four human males. One of the humans whistled as they passed, and then the vehicle screeched to a loud halt. There was a "Muck Ole Fiss" sticker on a rear bumper. The driver then began backing up until the vehicle had drawn even with the two cadets.

"Hey, do you ladies need a ride?" shouted one of the human males. All were grinning and each was holding a can or bottle in one hand. "We have plenty of room."

"It doesn't appear you are headed in the same direction we are," Julista said.

"Baby, we are headed any direction you want to go in," said the driver.

"Thanks for the offer," said Ungbar. "But we are on a class field trip. Finding items along this thoroughfare is part of our humanities assignment."

"Thoroughfare? Awful fancy word for this piece-of-shit road," said one of the males in the back of the vehicle. "And, hey, you found us. Don't we count? We ought to be double class credit." The four laughed and high-fived.

"I think it's the other way around; you found us. Anyway, we have a time limit for this exercise. We have to be on our way," Julista said. She noticed a message from Dakkott on her holo: "You are stopped. Everything OK?" She ignored it for the moment.

"C'mon. How about a couple beers? You can tell your prof you just found 'em," said the driver.

"Really, we're fine. Thanks for the offer, fellows," Ungbar said, eyeing the Jeep occupants warily.

"Fellows? Man, these chicks are weird. They talk like Ole Miss sorority bitches," said the backseat passenger. He tossed his empty bottle near Julista and Ungbar. The vehicle sped off.

Julista holo-replied to Dakkott: "We are fine. First encounter with humans. Interesting."

The rest of the journey to the human facility—it turned out to be a Shell service station hosting a Dunkin' Donuts franchise—was uneventful. They arrived almost exhausted, and the pair went into a restroom to freshen up. "This is a first. I've never been in a female relief chamber before," Ungbar said.

"And just think. You had to come to Earth to accomplish that," Julista countered.

The service station was part convenience store, and the two cadets had hoped to purchase burner cellphones, but here the plan went awry. The cadets had been told that ground transportation could be purchased through human for-profit entities called Uber, Lyft, or taxi services. Uber and Lyft require phone applications tied to a credit card; the cadets had been given one by Dakkott's cousin. The store did not carry cellphones, but there was a pay phone outside. With cellphones no longer an option, Julista messaged Gorthand for a tutorial on how to use the pay phone. While they waited for his response, the pair walked into the Dunkin' Donuts side of the facility, finding a welcome surprise.

"Coffee!" they both said at once.

They both ordered coffees and, not wanting to be impolite, were talked into plain cake doughnuts by the clerk. "Nectar of the gods," Ungbar said after the first sip. "And these round things are pretty good as well. Too bad we can't bring some back to the ship."

The word "ship" startled Julista. "Shhhhh, you *nimnule.*"

"Sorry, sorry. This is me shutting up now," Ungbar said.

Gorthand messaged them both with instructions regarding the pay phone and had even found a phone number for a local taxi service. They finished their coffees and went outside.

As Julista picked up the phone receiver, the same vehicle they had encountered before pulled into the station with a cloud of dust in its wake.

"Well, now, look who it is. We meet again, ladies," said the driver.

"It looks like we're your destiny," said one of the backseat riders. The four cackled.

Ungbar turned to Julista and whispered, "I've got an idea. Just follow my lead."

"Amber" walked over to the Jeep. "You fellows seem awfully nice. Can any of you tell me what time it is?"

The driver said, "There she goes with that 'fellows' crap ag---…" Before he could finish the sentence, there was a barely discernible flash of light. The four young men stiffened in place inside the vehicle. Ungbar said something to the two riders in the rear, and both got out and went into the Dunkin' Donuts. Ungbar jumped into the back of the vehicle and then signaled for Julista to join. As she did so, she whispered some information to the driver, who began his lesson in Xylodonian compliance by pulling away from the station with his new passengers.

They reached Hernando in about ten minutes.

CHAPTER 20

Anton was in the kitchen fretting over a recipe, with Gator at his feet hoping for some spillage. He was trying to surprise Ellie with some homemade bread, his first-ever attempt. Flour just seemed to go everywhere, and he couldn't find a rolling pin.

"What are you doing, tiger?" Ellie said, peering over his shoulder. "Whatever it is, it looks like the other side is winning."

He gave her a quick kiss. "I would tell you, but it's on a knead-the-dough basis, Ms. Atkinson."

She pinched his behind. "Lord. You are terrible."

Gator's ears perked up. The chiweenie dashed into the den and jumped up on his favorite sofa perch, one that allowed him to spy out the window. He began barking.

"What is it, boy?" Ellie said, walking over just in time to see a Jeep drive away hurriedly from the front of the house. A moment later, there was a knock at the door, which caused Gator to bark more furiously.

Ellie opened the door and saw two young women on her doorstep. *Oh, no...what are they selling?* she wondered. "Can I help you?" Ellie asked.

The visitor who was nearest the door gave a galaxy-wide smile. "Hello, big sister."

CHAPTER 21

How loud does a bell have to ring to be heard on two planets? As it turns out, a silent alarm can be deafening.

Maxim Everson had a self-satisfied smirk on his face; his SuperMax was about to demonstrate his superiority and put these Russian slugs in their place. His smug confidence was demonstrated in his attire choice—under his suit jacket he was wearing a T-shirt that bore the phrase CAN HACK IT.

Several of the IRA agents working for Nikolai Ivanov had already accomplished the first task by obtaining cellphone numbers for multiple officials at six banks in Hernando. The duplication was merely for backup. It was now early evening in St. Petersburg; there was a nine-hour time difference between the old capital and Mississippi. The agents wanted to be ready when the banks opened for business. At precisely 9 a.m. in Hernando, a similarly worded text message was sent to the selected bank officials. It really didn't matter if the message was read, but it was intended to be innocent and intriguing at the same time.

It read: "Will Nick Saban be the first commissioner of college football?" There was a hot link that took the curious to the Southeast

Conference athletics website, but there was no further elucidation concerning Saban, the former Alabama coach.

One by one, the Russians gained access to eighteen cellphones. Two were of little use; their owners were not at work that day. SuperMax's keystroke recording function provided a variety of passwords, which were the primary targets, but the Russians were amused by some of the images in the photo albums of these upright citizens of Hernando. Some of the images, along with text messages and emails, were archived for later use.

Everson wasn't concerned with petty extortion; it was the accounts data he was after. The Russians soon had it.

Julius "Ju Ju" Williamson, executive vice president of inaptly named First Security Bank, was at his desk contemplating his Little League team lineup and had no idea his phone was allowing cyber thieves from across the globe into his bank's vault. The IRA agents began infiltrating the bank's client accounts, taking the first twenty found in alphabetical sequence. The First Security accounts included some that were private, some that were commercial. The Russians emptied the accounts, transferring the funds to a recently created account controlled by Everson and Moscow. Their efforts netted almost $315,000 in just seconds.

Under normal circumstances, a transfer this large would be flagged for possible fraud review and then placed on hold if deemed questionable. However, since executive accounts were being used, this and the other transfers bypassed the internal security protocols.

Chester ("call me Chet") Cunningham, the manager of Trustmark, was equally oblivious to the invaders. The agents employed a similar strategy in each case, emptying the funds in the first twenty accounts found in alphabetical order. They knew the zero-day bugs on the "infected" devices would allow return access if desired. From Trustmark, the Russians transferred about $455,000 into their cyber money bag.

They completed the same operations on phones belonging to executives at Bankcorpsouth and SecurTrust Federal Credit Union—the latter's name drawing chuckles from the Russians—collecting their first $1 million-plus haul from the former and about $387,000 from the latter. Everson and Ivanov smiled at how easily SuperMax, hiding in the cyber shadows, made the thievery. The next target was a smaller institution, Community Bank DeSoto, but the Russian keyboard crooks still managed to pull $288,000 from the twenty infiltrated accounts.

Everson and the Russians had agreed to infiltrate only six banks on this first run, and the final bank was supposedly the smallest institution on the list. The agents had penetrated the cellphone of Susan Lovelace, manager of Sycamore Bank, just as easily as they had the others. After rummaging through the device, they opened the account of AAA Plumbing and were shocked to find $152 million sitting on a nest of vulnerability. Several of the Russians whooped loudly as if they'd found the Golden Goose.

"Holy shit," said Everson. "Nikolai, I think we just found one of the places our cartel friends from south of the border have been stashing their cash. Either that, or this is the most profitable plumbing company in the world."

The $152 million, like the rest, was quickly dumped in the cyber money bin and would soon be transformed into cryptocurrency. In about twenty minutes' time, the Russians had purloined more than $154 million from the six banks. Everson and SuperMax took a bow. "Just wait until we hit LA or New York," he told Ivanov.

The effects of the cyber chicanery were felt almost immediately. Imani Allen was attempting to pay for her groceries at a FoodMart when the clerk handed back her bank debit card. "I'm sorry, ma'am, there are insufficient funds in this account," the clerk said.

"That can't be right. I just checked it this morning," Imani said. She tapped on her phone to get to her account at Trustmark. The total in her account came up zeroes.

"Oh, my lord. OH, MY LORD. I've been cleaned out," she said, beginning to weep. "My babies, my babies."

The clerk asked if she had another card. "Don't got no other card. What the hell just happened?" she asked between tears.

A similar scenario played out at the QuikBiskit Café, where Jeremy Billings was trying to pay for his breakfast of scrambled eggs, toast, and bacon. After an "I'm sorry, sir…" from the waitress, Billings found that he, too, had been pilfered. He managed to find enough cash in his wallet to pay for the meal, then he called his Bankcorpsouth branch. His stomach almost emptied when he was told there was not even a Lincoln penny left in his account. Most of his retirement nest egg had vanished.

Imani Allen and Jeremy Billings weren't alone. Soon, dozens of Hernando residents and businesses were calling their respective banks. Bank officials began contacting the Federal Deposit Insurance Corporation; officials with that agency, once they had examined the collective evidence, labeled the theft as a cyberattack. The FBI was then contacted.

But those managing the account of AAA Plumbing could not contact Sycamore Bank, the FDIC, or the FBI. This account belonged to a unit within Xylodon's Protectorate and was responsible for funding surveillance and intelligence operations across Earth. Hundreds of Xylodonian operatives were now financially stranded. A lone Guardian assigned with monitoring account activity had detected the attack and had informed his superiors.

"Girgach, girgach, girgach!" screamed Sub-Protector Korphan when told of the incident on Earth. He picked up his communicator and reluctantly informed the Presidium what had occurred. An immediate council meeting was ordered; most of the Presidium's fifty delegates were in attendance.

"Do you have any explanation for what happened, sub-protector? We were told our financial accounts on Earth were protected from such incursions," said Praetor Norvet-Bar-3, the elected head of the Presidium. Praetors were rarely addressed by their names; the title had become historically preferred.

"That is true, Praetor. We have established cybersecurity mechanisms and procedures that would thwart an infiltration of this kind," Korphan said. "But…"

"Then what happened?" the Praetor demanded.

"As I was about to say, the culprits caught us at the wrong time. We were in the process of transferring funds from our original account in Barbados to one we had established in a small American town. Our security measures were to be completed later this week."

"Are you saying the Protectorate is a victim of bad timing? I would say misfortune, but there is no fortune. Not anymore. What necessitated this change in accounts?" the Praetor asked.

"We felt it was an obscure location. Additionally, two of our best operatives are based there," replied Korphan. "On paper, it was an optimal site."

Many of the Presidium delegates chuckled or snorted. The Praetor quieted them. "All right. All right. That sort of reaction is not helpful," he said, then he turned back to Korphan. "Have you formed any plan for proceeding? Our entire Earth operation could be in jeopardy now."

"First, we must re-create a secure account with broad access for our off-world operatives. We have enough funds to satisfy our operational needs until the end of the year," Korphan said. "We will base this account in a new location with Protectorate-level security."

"And after that?" countered the Praetor.

"I envision that full funding will soon be restored," said the sub-protector.

"You envision. What do you mean?" asked the Praetor.

"What do I mean, Praetor? I intend to get the money back. All of it."

CHAPTER 22

Maxim Everson gestured toward an aide, and the man produced four bottles of top-shelf vodka. Glasses were found. "Here's to SuperMax," he said to Ivanov and the IRA team. "Here's to the Benefactor," responded Ivanov. Glasses clinked, and the "sorrow water" poured for the next hour. Ivanov's top assistant, Dmitri Alexandrov, joined the group for a short time, as did Alexandrov's wife, Olga. Everson couldn't help but notice that after Dmitri returned to his duties, Olga moved closer to Ivanov. At one point it appeared her hand brushed across his crotch.

As their victory celebration wound down, Everson pulled Ivanov aside in the director's office. "We've had a good day, my friend. I know I have. Moscow has just paid me the remainder of my fee, and twenty percent of today's take has gone into a separate account," he said. "But I would suggest waiting a bit before letting SuperMax off the chain again. Perhaps pick a new country. Let Washington stew in its own juices for a bit."

The funds stolen from the six U.S. banks had been turned into cryptocurrency and then funneled to the "crypto wallets" of Everson, the Russian leader, and a handful of his cronies. The complexity of the passwords—often as long as sixty-four letters and numbers—that are the keys to these "wallets" necessitates that they be written down. There is no "save password" function, and without the password, there is no access to the money. Thus, the passwords are often kept in safes.

Ivanov voiced agreement with Everson's suggestion. "*Da.* Good idea. Our joint venture today brought back fifteen times what was taken in 1994. That is about to stir up quite a few of the alphabet agencies in the United States. I will pass along your suggestions to Moscow. I am hoping for a little bonus from today as well."

Everson reached for his coat, hat, and gloves. "Well, then, our business appears to be concluded. I don't believe I will be needed to chaperone your next venture. But if questions arise, you know how to reach me. I think I need to go visit a warmer clime for a bit."

"*Spasibo, spasibo* (thank you). Yes, go enjoy the sun, my friend," Ivanov said.

Before he exited, Everson turned to Ivanov. "Oh, and Nikolai?"

"Yes, my friend?"

He winked. "Give my regards to Olga."

The retirement papers of FBI Special Agent Thomas Dettwiler had not yet been fully processed, so he was dispatched from Jackson to Hernando along with a dozen other agents from various locations. As far as the FBI was concerned, only a bit more than $2 million had been pulled from the six banks; not even Sycamore Bank was aware of the massive AAA Plumbing account. That account had been a secret to all prying eyes until SuperMax knocked its electronic door down.

Still, the agents found a city in shock and disarray. The local police felt helpless; they had no idea how to help the citizens they were supposed to protect. There were families who couldn't eat or pay rent. There were businesses that were forced to close temporarily. Churches and support groups came to the aid of some of those afflicted, but it was a weak balm. There was no salve for some; once he learned his phone had been the source of his bank's cyber intrusion, Chet

Cunningham tendered his resignation. His wife found him dead inside their closed garage a few days later.

The FBI's computer experts and contractors did what they could to seal the zero-day backdoors, but there was no guarantee all were found. Dettwiler wrote a lengthy report, hoping it would be his last, on his weeklong investigation of the cyberattack and forwarded it to Washington. The key and perhaps most volatile section of the report was at the end—the investigators pointed an accusatory finger at Russia. Dettwiler's superiors in D.C. reviewed the document and decided their best option was to hand-carry it to the White House.

The FBI director and assistant director entered the Oval Office, where the president's chief of staff invited them to sit down. The new president, meanwhile, was futzing with the end of his long red tie, trying to remove a cola stain. The FBI officials remained silent until the president's attention was secured.

"Mr. President, I am sure you are aware of the infiltration last week of six banks in a Mississippi town. Our agents have investigated the attack, and these are their findings." The director gave a folder to the chief of staff, who then placed it on the president's desk. The president flipped through it.

"I'm hearing all kinds of things about it. You know, this wouldn't have happened at one of my banks. I'm too smart for that," he said.

"Yes, sir. I'm sure that's true, sir. Would you like for us to give you time to review the report?"

"No, just give me the bullet points. That should be all I need. I'm a genius, you know," he said. "No other president has been as smart."

"Yes, sir. As you can see in section two, our agents outline what was taken from each bank. Only twenty accounts at each of the banks were affected," said the director. "Why the attack was limited to six banks and only twenty accounts at each one is unknown, sir. This certainly could have been a broader assault."

"You keep using words like 'attack' and 'assault'. Was this an invasion?" asked the president, sipping on a new cola. "We have two big, beautiful oceans. How can we be invaded?"

The director looked at his assistant, then continued. "It's an invasion of the cyber variety, sir. Cyberattacks don't pay heed to oceans or any other geographic barriers, for that matter."

"Yeah, yeah. OK. So how did the crooks pull this off?"

The assistant director then explained in broad, simple terms how the scheme was likely perpetrated. He emphasized how the thefts originated with the surreptitious seizure of the executives' cellphones.

"My phone has always been secure. They can't get to mine," said the president. "So, what's next? We need to hurry. I have a golf game."

"Yes, sir. The next sections include anecdotal accounts from the Hernando residents and businesses who suffered from this hit and the initial actions taken by the NSA and FDIC in response," said the FBI director. "The last section details who our experts believe is responsible and outlines possible retaliatory options."

The national security adviser entered the Oval Office and took a seat.

"Well, don't make me guess. Who did it?" asked the president. "Some fat slob living in his mother's basement? Russia? Don't say Russia. It can't be Russia, Russia."

"Yes, we believe it was a foreign actor, sir, and all signs point to Russia. This penetration has all the earmarks of an operation of the Internet Research Agency," replied the director.

"Russia, Russia, Russia. Are we going through that again?" barked the president. During and after the recent campaign, a good number of the president's aides and supporters found themselves in a boiling legal broth over their back-channel contacts with Russian officials and intelligence operatives. It didn't calm those who held suspicions of the president's consistent placating of Russia that he had once wanted to build a hotel in Moscow. "Couldn't it have been some Iranian kid at a Radio Shack?"

"It could, sir, but it's not likely. This attack was too broad, too sophisticated."

"There you go with that 'attack' word again. Well, have we tried to contact any of the folks in Moscow? What do they say?"

"They have issued the usual denials, sir. They think we should look at the Chinese," said the assistant director.

The president looked at his chief of staff. "What is it you think I should do? Order an airstrike? Where would we bomb?"

The chief of staff simply shrugged and looked at the national security adviser, who then said, "Well, sir, we could…"

The president cut him off, then addressed the two FBI officials. "I know what we can do. You fellas go find that freeze ray that was used by that left-wing nut against Congress a few years back. I think we need to get that thing and go freeze some people. Especially those fake-news people. Yeah, that's what I want. Get it done."

"Yes, sir, we will boost our efforts in that area, sir."

"All right, then. I've got a tee time. See ya, fellas."

CHAPTER 23

Korphan had never been one to issue empty vows. After his debriefing with the Presidium, he immediately went to the cyber intelligence unit within the Protectorate. The unit took up three entire floors; such space was needed for servers housing the collective knowledge of the known universe.

Aside from the two Guardians killed in accidents on Earth, the Sycamore Bank theft was the greatest blow ever suffered by Xylodonian surveillance operatives. *Yes, one can say the loss was an accident wrapped in bad timing, but this is not supposed to happen to us,* Korphan thought. *We have been at this too long. We got clumsy...or lazy...or both.*

Cybersecurity and counter-cyber operations were not within Korphan's area of expertise; he had scores of younger Guardians who were more adept with Xylodon's advanced computer systems to assist in those regards. He had placed a veteran Guardian, Lurkon-4, in command of the cyber unit, and it was his office that Korphan now entered. Lurkon stood at attention.

"Greetings, Lurkon," said Korphan, gesturing for the officer to sit. "I don't suppose you have found the antiseptic for our infection while I was coddling the Presidium, have you?"

"Not yet, sub-protector, but I have our best Guardians working on the problem," Lurkon said. "I was just about to check their progress. If you have the time to accompany me, we can do so together."

"Yes, let's do so."

Their destination was a floor below, accessible by stairs or hover-vator. As they approached the latter, Lurkon gave the sub-protector a brief tutorial on human cyber criminality.

"One of their primary tools is what is termed clickbait or phishing. This is a type of trap that requires some action, usually a click or tap, by the intended target," Lurkon said. "That click or tap can send the victim to a bogus website that may then seize your device, or it might install ransomware, which could prove very costly. One of my favorite human schemes that we have observed is called 'obit pirating.' "

"Obit pirating?"

"Say a colleague or relative dies. Using a browser search, you come across a tribute page or something similar dedicated to that deceased individual," Lurkon said as they both stepped upon the hover-vator and began their descent. "There might be remembrances or other comments that you must click on in order to read them. The tributes are generally vague plaudits and are recirculated for repeat use. Each time you click on one of these comments, it generates advertising revenue for the creator of the page. So, while you are attempting to pay homage to a friend, you are also paying a cyber crook."

"That's insidious. So, these humans are profiting from death," Korphan said. They whooshed to the desired floor and began heading toward a cluster of Guardians cloistered among computer screens.

"Insidious, yes. Perhaps more insidious are the human criminals who use artificial intelligence to deceive elderly humans into believing loved ones have been kidnapped or are in need of bail money after being arrested. The criminals use AI trickery to mimic the appearances and voices of the supposed kidnap victims."

Lurkon continued. "Many of these human cybercriminals choose to launder their ill-gotten gains as something called cryptocurrency. It is an extremely fast method, and it offers anonymity and the benefit of crossing national borders on Earth," Lurkon said. "Although difficult, we have been able to track a good number of these cryptocurrency transactions. If my memory is correct, we monitored some $24 billion in such transactions last year."

"*Girgach!* That is unbelievable. Whoever it was from long ago who decided that we must monitor the humans was more correct than he or she will ever know," the sub-protector said.

The Protectorate investigators had determined that the human thieves had converted the stolen funds into cryptocurrency. But, as clever as they were, the crypto crooks relied on security algorithms that use Earth's current level of computing technology. Quantum computers, still in a relatively infantile stage, would be able to surpass that technology but were not yet widely available. In any case, the Xylodonian supercomputer—the Galaxium Matrix—was several steps above human conception and was quickly bloodhounding the culprits. Galaxium was a well-guarded Protectorate secret.

The gaggle of Centurion Guardians began to rise, but both Korphan and Lurkon signaled for them to continue. A second-brevet Guardian, Jenklor-9, was overseeing the team; it was she whom Lurkon asked for a progress report.

"We actually have had a good bit of luck, commander. Sub-protector, some of this terminology can be quite technical, so please feel free to ask for clarification whenever necessary. As we suspected, the cybercriminals who struck us almost immediately attempted to launder the account funds as cryptocurrency," Jenklor said. "There are countless crypto exchanges available, but there appear to be a handful that are used with the most frequency. Perhaps these exchanges are more trustworthy, or perhaps the criminals are just lazy. Or simply arrogant. Hard to say. In any case, we began our investigation with these most-frequently used exchanges, and we ran across an old friend. Cheezwiz."

"Cheezwiz?" asked Korphan.

"Yes, sir. The criminals like to give names to the exchanges they use. A sort of shorthand, I suppose," said Jenklor. "My team examined recent activity on the Cheezwiz exchange, and we found transactions that match the funds stolen from the six human banks."

"Bravo," Korphan said. "I must say I'm impressed. But how does identifying the...what, crypto exchange...help us find the perpetrators?"

"After the funds are laundered through a crypto exchange, in this case Cheezwiz, the crypto coins are transferred to the respective 'crypto wallets' of our thieves. The criminals leave traceable patterns. We have been able to determine the internet address for those responsible for the exchange transfers related to the bank thefts. It's a site of origin that is well known to us. We have also secured the identities of some of the 'wallet' owners who were rewarded by Cheezwiz."

"And whom do we have to thank for this pilferage?" asked Korphan.

"The exchange transfer was performed from within the Internet Research Agency, a human construct based in St. Petersburg, Russia. It has long been known for such nettlesome activities."

"And the 'wallet' owners?" asked Lurkon.

"Familiarity again aided us here. A good portion went to a 'wallet' belonging to the Russian leader. Other funds went to wallets controlled by the leader's inner circle," Jenklor said. "There is another wallet that received a sizable transfer from the exchange, but we have not been able to identify the owner as yet. We are getting closer, and I will advise you once we do."

"That's excellent, Jenklor. Keep at it," Lurkon said. "And, yes, let us know when you have the final puzzle piece."

Korphan bade good luck to the team, and then he and Lurkon began walking back to the latter's office.

"I must say your team zeroed in on the criminals much faster than I would have imagined," the sub-protector said. "You have chosen your people well."

Lurkon nodded in appreciation of the remark. "What do you intend to do once we have pinpointed all of those responsible?"

"I plan to squash some bugs," Korphan said. "Permanently."

CHAPTER 24

Ellie was stunned into silence. Words, which had long been her forte, would not emanate.

Ungbar/Amber gave Julista/Julie a slight push. "Go on, then. Go hug the sister you haven't seen in ten years."

Julista threw her arms around Ellie's neck and buried her head into her shoulder. "Juleetha. It has been so long. So long. I've missed you." Tears began to flow.

Ellie began sobbing. She still couldn't speak.

Ungbar, still on the porch, said, "Well, this is awkward."

A flour-covered, apron-wearing Anton emerged from the kitchen but was halted by an invisible barrier of confusion. Gator's ears were perked, but he was equally perplexed.

"Uh, hello?" he said quizzically.

The two women continued to hug and weep, their sobs intermittently louder. There would be no immediate explanation coming from them.

Ungbar stuck out his hand to Anton. "Hello, I'm Ungbar-11. If you allow me to enter your domicile, I think I can clear things up."

"Yes, please, by all means, come in. I'm Michael. Uh, Anton. No, Michael Gort," he said.

"I already know who you are, Anton-7. You are a hero to our cadet class at the Protectorate Academy," said Ungbar, who then tapped his holo to reveal his Xylodonian form.

"*Grudukh!*" exclaimed Anton, who rushed to close any open curtains. A surprised Gator began to bark until Anton picked him up. Ungbar returned to his Amber persona.

The two sisters were still not speaking, at least not in sounds Anton understood. They were now stroking each other's faces and hair. A flummoxed Anton told Ungbar, "Come with me. I have to check my bread."

Ungbar was uncertain what "bread" was, but he complied nonetheless.

"So, you are a cadet," said Anton, finally getting his concoction into the oven.

"Yes. All six of us are," he replied.

"Six?!?! You mean there are four more of you?" said an astonished Anton. *This day is just getting better and better*, he thought. "You'd better sit. Do you want something to drink?"

Ungbar settled into a chair, crossing his legs. "Do you have any coffee?"

As Anton prepared a pot, Ungbar launched into the backstory. A sad, orphaned sister. Supportive friends who were like family. A secretive journey to Khione. Travel to Earth on a smuggler's spaceship. Landing on Earth and being greeted by cows. The strange sequence with the human males in the roofless vehicle.

"Where are the other four of you?" asked Anton, somewhat disoriented by the male voice coming from Ungbar's female persona.

"Back on the ship. But I'm sure they would just love to come meet you and Juleetha," he said. "You two are adorable. And that ship is filthy, filthy, filthy. Smugglers have no sense of décor."

Anton handed Ungbar a cup of coffee, then poured cups for Ellie and her sister. They had stopped hugging long enough to accept the beverages. Gator was sniffing to determine his acceptance of Julista's presence, soon signified by a wagging tail.

"Is this what humans call a dog?" Julista asked, stroking the pup's head.

"Yes. He's a chiweenie. A chihuahua-dachshund mix. But hold on, there's someone I want you to meet. Michael, I want to introduce you to my sister Julista," Ellie said, tear streaks still visible on her cheeks. "Julista, this is Michael. My *sha'no*, Anton-7. My husband, as they say on Earth."

Anton gave her a hug. "I guess that makes you my sister-in-law."

Julista gave Ellie a surprised look. "You went through the coupling ceremony without inviting me? Your only relative?"

"It was sort of sudden. And it was done on one of our vessels," Ellie said, before giving a shortened version of their Earth adventures.

"Still, it is yet another part of your life I was unable to share in," Julista said.

"I'm so sorry, sister...I wanted so much to leave my life on Xylodon behind. I forgot that there were parts of that life that I should have held on to. Please forgive me."

Anton attempted to change the subject as they found places to sit in the den. Gator sat next to Ellie but kept his eyes on Julista. "OK, we can reminisce and express our recriminations later," Anton said. "We have two Xylodonian cadets in our home, and four more hiding in a smuggling ship out in a field. What are we going to do about that?"

Ellie asked, "You six conspired with smugglers to come to Earth? Do you realize how crazy that is and what the consequences might be if you got caught? Is the Protectorate looking for you?"

"I thought you would be glad to see me. We are all we have now," Julista said. "We were on break, and a member of our study group is related to a smuggler. I don't think anyone in the Protectorate knows we are gone yet."

"Well, you are just going to have to head back before you are missed," Ellie said in her teacher's voice.

Ungar entered the room. "This is some really good coffee," he said, taking a sip. "There's just one hiccup with our return. There's a bit of a fuel problem."

"No. Don't tell me you don't have enough fuel to get back," Ellie said.

"Well, we might be a t-e-e-e-e-nsy bit short," Ungbar said. "We convinced ourselves that you and Anton could help with that. Being heroes and all."

Anton let Ellie lead the inquisition but thought: *The only thing that could top all of this would be for the FBI to show up.* "That's not our only problem," he said. "How are we going to get the other four, and where are they going to sleep?"

"I can shuttle two at a time in the Tesla. We can get some sleeping bags on the way back," Ellie said. "I guess we can put a couple in the guest room and give the couch to another one. Maybe one can use the den floor, but the rest will have to use the Hideaway. That's our 'spare' room hidden in the garage. At least the garage is heated, so you will be comfortable."

Ungbar said, "We can give the guest room to the girls. Just put me and Gorthand together some place."

"Gorthand?" asked Anton.

"He's my boyfriend. At least for now. These human boys are kind of cute," Ungbar replied.

Ellie took charge. "OK, then. Julista, you contact your companions and tell them to decide who will be the first two passengers. Tell them to get their human personas ready and to come to the road. It will take us twenty or twenty-five minutes to get there, and I don't want to have to go looking for anyone. We can go to the store, then drop off the first two, and then go back for the others. Anton, show Ungbar the garage and the spare room. Since he's here, he gets first choice on where to sleep."

Anton gave a mock salute. "*Oui, mon capitaine.* Do you want me to order some pizzas while you're out?"

"Pizzas?" Julista asked.

"It's Earth food. Trust me, you'll like it," Ellie replied. "Yes, that would be a great idea."

"Juleetha, do you want me to come with you?" her sister asked.

"Call me Ellie. And you're Julie, remember? Get used to using those names. Yes, you can come. You have the directions to the ship so you can guide me." Ellie quickly inspected Julista's attire. "I guess what you're wearing will work for now, but we might have to go visit the Goodwill later."

"Goodwill?"

"Don't ask," said Anton.

Julista sent a message to the four cadets on the ship, and then the sisters got into the Tesla for the first part of their retrieval mission.

Anton went to check on his bread, then gestured for Ungbar/Amber to come into the garage. There were palettes and other art supplies about, but those could be moved aside to accommodate the unexpected guests. He then revealed the contents of the "spare room": a cot, chair, and an array of computer and communications equipment.

"Welcome to our sanctum sanctorum," he told Ungbar.

"Amazing. This is quite an impressive setup."

Anton then noticed a blinking red light on the communications system. "Give me a second," he told Ungbar, then he sat down to decrypt the message. It was marked "URGENT" followed by "TOP SECRET." Anton skimmed through the first few sentences. His reaction was most un-Xylodonian.

"Holy fucking shit."

About an hour and a half later, Ellie and Julista returned with Margeen and Gorthand in their newly created human personas. After the introductions were completed and Gator quieted, Anton pulled Ellie aside.

"You need to read this."

Ellie's eyes widened as she read the missive. The cadets' chattering continued in the den. "Oh, my God. All of the Earth accounts are gone?"

"That appears to be the case," Anton said. "And Korphan wants us to help get them back."

"And how do we do that?" she asked.

"Look at the end. He says he will send further instructions when the Protectorate has fully identified the perpetrators."

Ellie gave a weak smile. "I guess this means we are back in the Protectorate's good graces."

"Yes, looking on the bright side, there is that. And I suppose it was wise of us to put our teacher earnings in a different account," he said. "At least I will be able to pay for the pizzas."

"Right. The pizzas. You take care of that while Julista and I bring back the other two cadets. It's going to be crowded in here tonight. Just curious. Why weren't the operatives the Protectorate already has in Russia picked for this mission?"

"It's not entirely clear. There's a reference to recent events in Ukraine and North Korea that need continual monitoring. Those are a long way from St. Petersburg."

"Is that the destination?"

"Apparently so. We can talk more about this later tonight," he said, waving the message. "Go get our guests, and I will take care of dinner."

The pizzas were waiting when Ellie, Julista, Dakkott, and Roggbach arrived, sending the exuberance level inside the home to a new level. Anton smiled to himself; it was all so remindful of his cadet days.

"Hey, this pizza compound is very good," said Gorthand. "I especially like the one with the little red circles on it."

"Anton called them pepperonis. Can't you remember anything, you *nimnule*?" Ungbar retorted.

"I think we should bring the recipe back to Xylodon and start a restaurant. We can become rich," said Gorthand.

Dakkott chuckled. "Are you forgetting about the Academy? And how are you getting back to Xylodon? We are almost out of fuel."

Gorthand looked downward, and Roggbach placed a hand on his shoulder. "Don't you hate it when he's right all the time?"

As the pizza disappeared and the evening drew to a close, Ellie directed Julista and Margeen to the guest room, gave Ungbar his choice of the sofa (Gorthand took the nearby floor), and got Dakkott and Roggbach situated in the garage. A few minutes later, she was in bed with Anton looking over the message from the Protectorate.

Anton sighed. "Who said Hernando is dull?"

CHAPTER 25

As Nikolai Ivanov and his Kremlin cohorts conferred to select SuperMax's next target on the geopolitical cyber board, Jonnie Barnes Jr. was determining his next target as well. In Jonnie's case, the victim was not a bank—it was the sixteen-year-old daughter of the Salvadoran-American family that had just moved to Eudora and taken up residence in his father's RV park.

Jonnie didn't know the girl's name, but that was of small importance. What was important, to him, was the fact that she had not placed aluminum foil up on her window as the rest of the family had. He had become enamored with her variety of thongs and the nightshirts that clung to her jiggly bosom, and so she became an integral performer in his nightly routine. Jonnie had found a tree not far away from the girl's window, providing him with some degree of concealment for his visual encroachment...and for the activities that went hand in hand with his peeping.

The morning in Eudora was sunny, but a slight chill had declined to surrender to the day. Jonnie, wearing a light jacket, was smoking a cigarette outside his father's RV, the one bearing the manager's sign. He smiled as he watched the Salvadoran girl emerge from her vehicle and carry her schoolbooks to the bus stop. He was enjoying the memory of the previous night.

Jonnie's old running buddies were all at work or in prison, so the day loomed as yet another tedious experience of watching TV reruns with his father until some of the no-longer-incarcerated got home. Even after nearly two years, his former friends were just as trapped in Mississippi as he was.

He flicked his spent cigarette toward the gravel road that divided the RV park, then he remembered something. He reached into his jeans pocket and pulled out a charred slip of paper, the same scrap he had found in the burn barrel. It bore a Hernando address and the name Ellie.

Ellie. I wonder if that is the same woman I saw hanging around with that federal guy Roy McDonald. She was hot, Jonnie recalled. He lit another cigarette and then entered the address into a search window on his cellphone, obtaining directions to the address.

Shit. I ain't got nothin' better to do. Why don't I just go pay this Ellie a visit? he asked himself.

He went inside the RV, grabbed his father's truck keys without explanation, cranked up the vehicle, then headed up State Highway 304 toward Hernando.

Anton yawned widely as he entered the den from the bedroom he shared with Ellie. There were two sleeping bags folded neatly and placed under the coffee table. He heard sounds from the kitchen and found Ungbar and Gorthand busy making breakfast.

"Good morning, you sleepy nonhuman," Ungbar declared. "Dakkott brought some supplies from the ship, and we thought you might like a home-cooked Xylodonian meal for a change."

Anton rubbed his eyes. "Coffee?"

"Right here," said Ungbar, pointing to a carafe. "Gorthand made it, so I can't vouch for it. I hope you don't mind us rummaging through your cabinets."

"No, make yourself at home. For now," Anton replied with a slight smile.

Ellie soon joined them in the kitchen, an action that somehow sent a telepathic signal to Julista and Margeen to emerge from the guest room. They were wearing the same attire as the previous day.

"Ugh. This won't do. I am going to have to take you girls shopping," Ellie said.

Dakkott and Roggbach then made their entry, both looking slightly disheveled.

"I hope you both slept well," said Ellie.

Dakkott replied for them both. "Yes, we were quite comfortable. Thank you, Guardian Juleetha."

"Ellie. Please. Just Ellie," she replied. Julista rolled her eyes and sighed.

It didn't take long for two or three or four separate conversations to erupt in the den and kitchen, which was confusing—amusing?—to a certain chiweenie unaccustomed to such racket. They all sampled the breakfast created by Ungbar and Gorthand, which earned them compliments from the other cadets and an expression of "thanks for the welcome change" from Anton and Ellie.

Anton sought a brief escape from the noise and went to the Hideaway in the garage. He didn't mind that he was suddenly on Ellie's back burner; Julista was her only relative, and she hadn't seen her in a decade, after all. Still, he felt a small bruise on his ego.

He sat down before the communications array and sent an encrypted message acknowledging receipt of the Protectorate's communiqué. Without giving many details, he also mentioned that six Academy cadets had found their way to his Mississippi domicile. He included their names in case any worried relatives required soothing. He also mentioned that they would need fuel to return to Xylodon. At the end of his reply, Anton indicated he was awaiting further orders.

Six cadets made it to Earth without the Protectorate's knowledge. There might be some heads rolling over this, he thought.

He went back into the house for a coffee refill. Julista and Margeen, holding Gator, were on the sofa with Ellie. The male cadets were all in the kitchen. *Of course they are. That's where the food is,* Anton thought.

"What is it like to teach human children?" Margeen asked Ellie.

"They are lovable for the most part, and they give me hope. Many of them come from less than ideal circumstances. This is not a rich county. But they show up every day wanting to better themselves," Ellie said. "Now, I did say 'for the most part.' I did have one boy who I had to take to the principal's office because he was selling marijuana during lunch. He told the principal that it was the family business and that if he didn't do his part his father would punish him."

"Marijuana?" Julista asked.

"It's a mild hallucinogen," Anton answered. "Similar to our *xenphoria* herb."

"And the boy was selling it on campus? *Gradakh*," said Margeen.

Dakkott had apparently gone unseen to the garage. After returning, he approached Anton. "Guardian Anton, there is a red light blinking on your communications system. I thought you should know."

"Thank you, Dakkott." Anton had not expected such a quick reply. He decrypted the message, which apparently had come from Sub-Protector Korphan himself. The first part of the message addressed the theft of the operation funds. Xylodonian cyber sleuths had tracked the attack to Russian sources, namely the Internet Research Agency, the Russian leader, and various oligarchs. There was another player whom they were still trying to identify. As the IRA was at the heart of the cybertheft, Korphan suggested they begin their investigation there. The communiqué listed a Nikolai Ivanov and a Dmitri Alexandrov as the director and sub-director of the Russian agency and suggested either one or both of these men could be possible targets for extracting key information.

Anton was a bit surprised by the next operational suggestion. To expedite the probe—creating new personas and identification credentials would take some time—Korphan said Anton and Juleetha should travel to a secluded area on the Mississippi River and rendezvous with one of Xylodon's Deep Watch vessels for the journey to Russia. These ships could travel by air or underwater; the Deep Watch teams had constructed several undersea bases at the bottoms of the Atlantic and Pacific oceans for observation and operation. The message gave coordinates and a set time for the rendezvous. It was three days hence.

The message ended with a brief discussion of the six missing cadets. In short, Korphan indicated that the missing funds were the immediate priority but that he planned to deal with the cadets at a later time. Anton was unable to determine Korphan's level of rage or discontent.

As Anton acknowledged receipt of the Protectorate message, Jonnie Barnes Jr. drove slowly past the home of Ellen Atkinson. He paused across the street, lit a cigarette, and rolled down the driver's side window to allow a better look into the home's den window. He saw an attractive brunette who was sitting facing the window and talking with two younger women. At least that was his guess. *So, that's who ol' Roy was banging,* he thought, smiling to himself. *Found you.*

Jonnie continued smoking and staring at the house until one of the younger women stood and happened to look his way through the window. Jonnie pressed the accelerator and drove off.

"Sister, were you expecting a visitor today?" Julista asked Ellie.

"No, why do you ask?"

"There was a male human parked across the street. And when I looked at him, he appeared to get nervous," Julista said. "Then he just drove away."

Ellie was puzzled. "What did he look like? Anything remarkable?"

"No, he was just...just…"

"Just what?"

"What is the human word? Creepy. He was just creepy."

CHAPTER 26

Maxim Everson sat back in his poolside lounge chair in St. Croix; his right hand held a hurricane glass filled with a combo margarita mixture. There was a strawberry margarita on the bottom, and a mango-colored concoction on the top, along with the traditional umbrella and straw. The sun felt replenishing after his stay in bleak St. Petersburg. Bleak but profitable, he would likely say to anyone who asked.

His companion for the day, a blonde about half his age, was tanning face down in the chair next to his. She had loosened her bikini top before entering a drowsy state. Everson put some of the frozen drink on his forefinger and ran it down her back. Her surprised jump gave him a Cracker Jack surprise—a quick glance of an as yet unbronzed breast and nipple. He smiled at his successful ploy. *That will be my prize in a few hours,* he thought. There were some expenses at this all-expenses-paid hotel, and she was one of them.

For those who knew him, the drink could have been a metaphor for Everson's life. At the top, the mango level, was what everyone could see. Everson had accumulated vast wealth. He employed thousands of people. He had contributed numerous technological innovations to society. His opinion was respected and sought far and wide. He contributed to charitable causes. He had written a few books.

But below the surface, the strawberry level, there was something darker, something far less selfless. Despite all his achievements, much of Everson's life slate was barren.

There were no libraries named for him.

There were no museums named for him

There were no parks bearing his name.

There were no college wings or buildings carrying his name.

There were no foundations in his name.

His companies were under continual federal scrutiny.

His seed had fathered children, but he had not wed any of the mothers, creating a tattered legacy at best. But when that legacy plays to an audience of one, what does any of that matter?

But all of that was far removed from Everson's present thoughts. He knew his Russian friends were planning to use SuperMax in a second attack, but he was not privy to their discussions of the intended target and timing. *What if they hit one of my accounts?* he thought. *That loss could far exceed my return percentage. I probably should have a word.*

Everson called his assistant. "Javier, please bring me my 'special' phone. It's in the room safe," he said. By "room" he meant presidential suite. "Thank you, Javier. I'm at the main pool."

A few minutes later Javier arrived with a hand-size black device. He thought for a moment; his message had to be stated in an appropriate manner. The Russians would not react well if they thought they were being told what to do by an outsider. He prepared his encrypted message and hit send.

"Nikolai, my friend, I hope you and your superiors are finding SuperMax to be a useful tool. If you would be so kind, please give me some warning as to your next target so that I might take precautions if necessary. I would like to avoid any unnecessary pain if possible. Thank you, my friend."

Everson passed the device back to Javier, then gave his blond companion's derriere a mild spank.

"Time to wake up, my dear. You have work to do."

Ivanov was in a Kremlin conference room when Everson's message arrived. He read it and smiled; he actually had only the smallest of concern for the American billionaire's anxiety—Benefactor or not. *But perhaps it is better to avoid a rift in our relationship*, he thought. *A short forewarning cannot hurt*. He replied to Everson that he would pass along that information once it was agreed upon.

In addition to Ivanov and the Russian president, there were a half dozen other participants in the meeting, half in uniform, half not. The discussion had gone round the table for nearly half an hour. How much did they want to stir up the Americans? The Hernando heist had apparently created barely a ripple in Washington, largely thanks to the new president's desire to avoid another Russia controversy. So where to strike next? American cities from the West Coast to East were being mentioned as options. The positives and negatives of each were tossed onto the table like dog bones.

Finally, the Russian leader waved his hands. "Enough. We are not getting anywhere. Why not take a bite of the Big Apple? Would not targeting New York cause the greatest disruption in the American financial system?" he asked.

"Indeed, it would, Mr. President," Ivanov said. "But perhaps you would enjoy some beans with your apple."

"Explain, Nikolai."

"Boston, Mr. President. Boston is known as Beantown. We could hit banks in both cities," Ivanov said.

"This sounds like a massive undertaking, Ivanov. Is this even possible?" asked the president. "How would you do it?"

"It will take some time, but it can be done. There are hundreds of banks in New York and Boston. Not all of them have the same level of security. Security protocols even vary among employees," Ivanov explained. "The first step will be gaining phone numbers of as many bank employees as possible. Then we will employ SuperMax by using various text messages sent to those phone numbers. After the doors are opened, we will see where they take us. We will then infiltrate as many accounts as possible."

The president smiled. "Excellent. I am impressed, Ivanov. We will soon enjoy a feast of beans and apples. We need to keep pace with our Chinese friends. Their leader has been boasting to me about their recent penetration of the system used by the U.S. Treasury, including the computer of the Treasury secretary. Do you have enough people to perform this operation, and do you have an idea of how long your first phase will take?"

"Your second question is a bit of an unknown, Mr. President, but perhaps a few weeks. I think our staffing is adequate, and I can get the agency started immediately."

"*Da*. Please do so. Get the ball rolling, as the Americans say. Keep me apprised on your progress."

Ivanov nodded, then made a call to the IRA.

CHAPTER 27

A half world away, another conference had just concluded in the back room of a garage in Hernando, Mississippi. Anton and Ellie had reviewed Korphan's order to rendezvous with a Deep Watch ship. On the one hand, they were excited—neither had been on a Deep Watch ship, one of the most advanced vessels in the Xylodonian fleet—but on the other hand, they were more than perplexed.

What to do with the six cadets while they were on the St. Petersburg mission?

The two veteran Centurion Guardians came to a joint conclusion—take the cadets with them. At least some of them. "We don't dare leave them here. That Ungbar will want to go to a club and get them all caught thirty minutes after we're gone," Ellie said. "They can stay on the ship while we are in Russia. Besides, the trip over will give me more time to reconnect with my sister."

"Those are all good points. I hate playing the parent, but I think that's what we have to do," Anton replied. "And I have to agree with your observation about Ungbar. Ezra would say, 'That boy's a hoot.' "

"Ezra. He had such a way with words, didn't he? I still miss him," she said.

"As do I, dear. As do I. Let's get Korphan's thoughts on this."

The two Guardians posed their idea to the Protectorate commander. At first Korphan demurred. *Take cadets on a mission this important? Ridiculous,* he thought. But after reviewing the position of Xylodonian operatives in Russia—they were all monitoring the Ukraine conflict—the idea became more appealing. He gave his assent. "Keep them safe, Anton-7," he stated in his reply.

They pulled the cadets into the den and explained what had happened to the operational funds and outlined the Protectorate's plan to retrieve them.

Julista looked puzzled. "This seems highly classified. Why tell us?"

"Because, sister, you are coming along," Ellie said.

Anton repeated the order. "You are coming with us on a Deep Watch vessel, but you might be remaining on the ship, depending upon operational needs." The cadets exchanged the Xylodonian version of high-fives.

"Ellie and I are both third-brevet Guardians, and as such are your superiors. Now, I know following orders has been a low priority for you in the past, but it is imperative that you do so now," Anton said. "Understood?"

He didn't mention that they had only recently received notice of Ellie's promotion to the third-brevet rank; Anton held the same rank but held seniority.

The cadets nodded their acknowledgement.

"Good. Ellie and I must return to our teaching duties tomorrow. We need you to stay inside the house and do not answer the door," he said. "To keep yourselves busy, we need some research done on the city of St. Petersburg, Russia, and on a secretive entity called the Internet Research Agency. The latter is at the heart of this mission, and any details you can find could be useful. Feel free to use Ellie's laptop or the computer in the spare room. I know memories can fail, but be careful with anything you write down or print out."

Dakkott and Roggbach volunteered to obtain details on the IRA from the garage computer since they were ensconced there anyway. Julista said she would look for information about St. Petersburg on the laptop. Ungbar warned her not to "hog the machine" because he might want to "shop for outfits."

The next morning found the cadets going about their duties or trying to stay out of the way. Ellie and Anton headed to Hernando Elementary with figurative fingers crossed.

As it turned out, it was Michael Gort, Anton's human persona, who ran into trouble—trouble in the bow-tied form of Chadwick Cartwright. If anyone could catch a Xylodonian "off-Guardian," it would be Chad.

Michael was furiously grading some class papers when Cartwright sat down in a chair across from him. Chad said nothing for nearly a half minute. "Hello, Michael."

"Hey there, Chad, what's new?"

"Michael, I wonder if you can confirm some information I just got from Kendall."

"What's that, Chad?"

"I hear that one of Ellie's cousins is in town."

Oh, no. How did that get out? he wondered. "Yes, she's visiting from out of town. I don't know how long she's staying."

"Well, Michael, not to be a scold or a hector, but I do believe you owe me an introduction. If she resembles Ellie in even the slightest, it certainly would be worth my time."

"I am well aware that I owe you a favor, Chad. I have no idea if Ellie and Julie—that's her name, by the way—have any plans tonight, but I can check. Maybe we can make it a foursome if they are free."

"A dinner for four would be just delightful, Michael. Give me a call once you know something. Still have my number?"

"It's right in here, Chad," said Michael, holding up his cellphone.

Cartwright stood, rubbing his hands. "I look forward to hearing from you. I'll let you get back to your busy bee-ness."

Michael then texted Ellie. *How did Chad find out we had visitors at the house?*

Ellie sent a sad-face emoji. It was followed by: *Kendall saw one of the female cadets through the window as she was driving to school this morning. Damn curtains!*

Great. Now he wants to go out to dinner. Do you think one of them can pull it off and get Chad off my back?

I can ask.

While driving home after school, Ellie gave him the answer. "Julista said she'd do it. Just as long as we come along."

"That's the plan. Fratello's steakhouse work for you? We liked it before," Michael said. Ellie nodded, and then he called Cartwright. "Be at the house around seven."

"That gives us about two hours to get her prepped," Ellie said, suddenly appearing to enjoy the idea.

"Not us. You. I tell you what. You make her into a pretty human, and I will come up with her back story. How's that?" he said.

"That works."

When they got to the house, the cadets were excited that one of them was going to be able to interact with a human. All except Dakkott. He said nothing, which fairly summed up his impression of the idea of Julista dining with another male, of any species.

Ellie helped make some adjustments to Julista's human persona. They couldn't be twins, but there needed to be enough close features that they appeared related. Then she found a dress and some shoes that could work—although Ungbar found it too frumpish. "Show them cosmic orbs, girl. Flaunt what you got," he said.

Ellie hushed him. "Ungbar, if you say one word about cleavage, I'm going to holo you and set you in the yard like a scarecrow." He put his hand over his mouth and walked away.

She then helped her sister with her hair and the application of a little makeup in the bedroom's adjoining bathroom. As she started to add some lip gloss, a flash of memory gave her pause. This is what their maternal did for her when she reached adolescence; now, she was repeating the ritual with her baby sister. Ellie felt tears forming.

"What's wrong, my sister? Are the applications not working? Am I too ugly?" Julista wondered.

"Nothing's wrong," Ellie relied, wiping her eyes. "And you look beautiful."

Anton watched the process while he worked on "Julie's" back story; he could sense the emotions stirring within Ellie. *It's like two little girls playing with dolls,* he thought. *But they are not so little anymore. And there are shared memories to navigate.*

He jotted down some notes for her to use. Age 26. Was born and raised in Winter Park, Colorado. Is a graduate student at Colorado State in Fort Collins. Majoring in civil engineering or something similar. Likes all kinds of music, particularly Bob Dylan ("Just say 'Tambourine Man' if he asks what your favorite Dylan song is."). Favorite food? Pizza. He tossed in a few other details but didn't want to overwhelm her.

Ellie and Michael went into the den, making way for Julie's entrance. "Ta-daaaahhhhh," said Julie, doing a twirl. All of the cadets, save one, cheered and clapped.

When it neared seven, the cadets fled to the garage. The ever punctual Chadwick Cartwright pulled up at the curb seconds later and was at the door seconds after that.

Ellie made the introduction; Julie smiled and shook Cartwright's hand. Michael could already tell that Chad, assuming the role of Southern gentleman, was pleased with his "date." Cartwright offered to drive and play tour guide for Julie on the way to the restaurant.

Fratello's Italian Steakhouse was the best of its kind in Hernando, not that there was much competition. The four were seated at a round table with a red-and-white-checked tablecloth with a candle centerpiece. Breadsticks and olive oil were brought to their table, and Michael allowed Chad to select the wine. He chose a 1994 California pinot. Julie sipped it cautiously, then raised an eyebrow in approval. She was bewildered by the menu, so she asked her sister-cousin, "What's good here?" Ellie suggested the pasta bolognese with Italian sausage, and she made that her dinner choice. The others joined her in ordering pasta dishes.

Julie fielded Cartwright's inquiries marvelously, occasionally filling in some details from her own life. For instance, Chad wondered if she was a skier, and she went on for several minutes about various ski resorts she had visited in Colorado. She managed to elude his query about her civil engineering major by asking, "I'd rather hear how you became a teacher and how you deal with these children." Anton was impressed. *She will make a good operative.*

Ellie was also impressed with her sister; Julie knew just how to giggle when Chad would lean toward her and touch her arm. Her verbal fencing was every bit as good as Cartwright's—although she did slip up once by saying "Creek Beaver" instead of "Beaver Creek." Cartwright didn't seem to notice. He seemed to be captivated by the young "Colorado" woman.

"It's so nice to go out with someone who can offer some intelligent conversation for a change," Cartwright said.

"What are we, turnips?" sniped Ellie.

"No offense meant. As opposed to third-graders was the intent of my remark," Chad said. "Of course, there was the time that I went out with a young lady, an LSU grad as I recall, and, as gentlemen do, I was detailing my work history bona fides. I then joked that my second job was right after I defected from the KGB. She asked me, 'KGB, what's that?' I do believe she thought it was some sort of fraternity. Not the brightest bulb on the tree, as they say."

Julie didn't let on that she had no idea what the KGB was as well. "Oh, my. How disappointing to see your joke spoiled." *That was a masterful response*, thought Michael.

The night went on, with Cartwright holding court for the most part. He later ordered glasses of a lightly sweet wine to accompany their desserts. "I hope I can still teach tomorrow," Michael said.

"Maybe I should order a bottle," Chad said. "It might be more fun that way."

It was almost ten by the time they left the restaurant and arrived back at Ellie's house. None of them noticed the pickup parked along the street a few houses down. Ellie and Michael led the foursome to the front door, where they paused. Chad took Julie's right hand in both of his and told her, "It was such a pleasure meeting you. I had a wonderful time, and I hope you did as well."

His eyes widened in surprise when she kissed him on the cheek. "Yes, it was delightful. I loved your stories. Too bad I didn't get to hear more of those jokes I was told you are famous for."

"Well, maybe next time..."

"We'll have to see about that, Chad," said Ellie. "Have a good night. Thanks for driving."

CHAPTER 27

The other cadets had waited until Cartwright was well down the street before they besieged Julista with questions, Margeen in particular. Anton was pleased that he had fulfilled his promise to Chad. *That should keep him happy until the end of the school term.*

Dakkott had remained in the backyard with Gator, not relishing the idea of listening to Julista recount her experience. As he walked in the shadows between the house and garage, Gator uttered a low growl. Dakkott then spotted a shadowy figure behind Ellie's Tesla. The figure would raise its head above the Tesla's rooftop for a moment and then bob down again.

Dakkott set Gator down. The chiweenie immediately bolted toward the figure, then assumed a defensive stance while yap-yap-yapping in canine bravado. As Dakkott approached he heard a slap, then a sharp yelp from Gator. "Damn dog. I hate little fucking dogs," the figure said, standing and drawing back a leg to kick the canine. But the figure was now face to face with Dakkott.

There was a flash of light.

Dakkott, carrying a shaking Gator, entered the house through the front door. "I think we have another visitor," he told Ellie and Anton.

The cadets quieted as the figure walked mechanically into the den. His eyes stared straight ahead, and he made no sound. Ungbar held a hand to his nose to diffuse the odor emanating from the shabbily dressed intruder.

"Does anyone know who this is?" asked Ellie.

Anton grimaced. "I'm afraid I do."

"Well…?" she inquired.

"Everyone, let me introduce you to Jonnie Barnes Jr."

CHAPTER 28

If ever a Xylodonian Guardian commander could have a bounce in their step, then certainly Lurkon had a veritable spring and a skip as he entered the office of Sub-Protector Korphan. He carried a small video-projection device with him to assist in his presentation.

"Come in, Lurkon. Come in. I take it you have some good news for me," Korphan said.

"Yes, sub-protector, indeed I do. If you will permit me, I can show you what my team has uncovered thus far. Can we darken the room?" Without waiting for Korphan to respond, Lurkon dimmed the office lights, placed the projection device on the sub-protector's desk, and activated it. The air molecules became a screen for the image, which depicted an outline of the Earth nation of Russia.

"As you know, by using Galaxium we were able to trace the cyberthefts to this human nation. We were further able to pinpoint the intrusion to this facility." Lurkon advanced to a new image within the city of St. Petersburg. "This building is the location of an entity called the Internet Research Agency and is well-known for a variety of nefarious activities."

A new image, this one of a mustachioed human, was projected. "This is Nikolai Ivanov, the director of this Internet Research Agency. If he did not participate in this theft, then he certainly approved it or oversaw it." The next image depicted the Russian leader and six members of the Kremlin inner circle. "These are some of the men who profited from the theft of our funds. Ivanov did as well. As you are aware, there was one person outside the Russian sphere who we have been trying to find. We believe this human is the creator of the software that facilitated the thefts."

"Have you found this human?" Korphan asked.

"Yes. Through the efforts of the Galaxium Matrix, along with our own foresight and this human's ego, we have been able to identify him and determine the location of his primary residence. I say 'primary' because he has almost as many residences as the entire Presidium. But before I continue, let me give you some history."

Lurkon advanced the presentation to an image of a somewhat rectangular object. "This is one of the 7,000 or so satellites placed into Earth orbit over the past five years as part of a network called Skyweaver. This Skyweaver is a for-profit communications system that utilizes the satellites and their links to transceivers on the ground. Subscribers pay to use the Skyweaver system. There is a sister satellite network called Skywall used by various human defense entities, also on a subscriber basis."

Lurkon continued. "The satellite you are looking at was one we captured and examined aboard one of our operatives' vessels about two years ago. We added some enhancements, you might say, to this satellite and placed it back in orbit. Among other things, those enhancements allow us to monitor all communications within a designated area. We recently activated the satellite and focused it upon this Internet Research Agency. We were able to intercept all communications to and from the facility, even encrypted communications. Galaxium was quickly able to decrypt those messages for us."

A new image was projected: Maxim Everson's face appeared.

"This is the creator of the Skyweaver and Skywall systems. As it turns out, the decryption of his messages to the Internet Research Agency establishes him as not only one of the culprits but as the designer of the software used in the thefts."

Another image was put forth, this one depicting a grotesque

example of one of the human mega-mansions often jeered by Xylodonians. The obscene extravagance used to house a single human was illustrative of the vibrant income inequality prevalent on Earth, something that was beyond the scope of Xylodonian understanding.

"This is the home of Maxim Everson. Or one of the homes, I should say," Lurkon stated. "As I indicated, it appears to be his primary domicile. It is located outside the city of Austin, Texas, in the United States. This Everson is a technology entrepreneur, and his wealth approaches that of the Protectorate's budget."

"So, the natural question would be: Why does he need more wealth?" Korphan proffered, in what was more judgment than question.

"Remember earlier I mentioned that we were aided by human ego? It was this human's conceit and vanity that I was referring to. Not only did the satellite bear the logo of his company, but he also repeatedly referred to a program called SuperMax in his discussions over payment with the Russians. One must presume he named the program."

"Bravo, Lurkon. You and your team have done some excellent work. We need to forward this information to our operatives on Earth."

Lurkon turned off the projection device. "I should add, sub-protector, that we have secured the blueprint details on both the Internet Research Agency and Everson's home in Texas."

"Even better. Make sure that information is sent along as well. How do you think we should proceed from here?" Korphan asked.

"As I understand it, our operatives will be transported by a Deep Watch ship to St. Petersburg. The operatives should conduct surveillance of the Internet Research Agency, targeting this Nikolai Ivanov in particular, as perhaps a way to gain entry. This agency is the beating heart of this criminal activity; it stops when the heart stops. Perhaps we can even reverse the blood flow through the heart. Everson we can deal with separately at a later time," Lurkon said.

"We are leaving much in the hands of our two operatives, Anton and Juleetha. Is there anything more you can do to assist them?"

"Perhaps, given the right circumstances. The Russians are quite the mischievous folk. They have had their commercial vessels dragging their anchor chains in waterways like the Baltic Sea in order to cut the undersea cables of foreign adversaries. However, Russia recently experienced a massive internet blackout; perhaps one of their vessels cut the wrong cable? Who knows? But members of my team thought this might be something we could exploit," Lurkon replied.

"Certainly. Let's keep that in mind," Korphan said. "Anything else?"

"No, sub-protector. We will be monitoring the mission, and we will step in to help if and when needed. One question. What of the six cadets who went to Earth?"

"Anton has indicated that they will not be a problem. He may even use them in some way. I have no choice but to trust his judgment."

"Understood, sub-protector. Thank you."

"Thank you, Lurkon," said Korphan.

The sub-protector paused at his desk as Lurkon departed. It had been years since he had been a Centurion Guardian, many more since he was an Academy cadet. He reflected upon his first mission, a reconnaissance of one of the moons of Elysium, Xylodon's nearest planetary neighbor. It had been simple and nonthreatening. He had spent nearly seven decades in the Protectorate, the past twelve years as sub-protector, head of the Protectorate and answerable only to the Praetor. The responsibility was often a torment. *How many times have I ordered young people into danger's path? How many times have I asked them to do what I dare not attempt? How many lives have been cut short at my behest?*

Korphan turned to rationalization for comfort. *Monitoring Earth is a necessity for Xylodon's growth and perhaps its very existence. That effort requires funding. The thieves must be dealt with. This mission must succeed.*

Now it's in Anton's hands, he thought.

CHAPTER 29

It was Roggbach who drew the short straw.

Anton and Ellie had decided that leaving all six cadets behind was too big of a risk, and leaving even a holo-sedated Jonnie Barnes in their home alone was an unpleasant thought as well. Besides, who would take care of Gator?

So, the cadets drew broom straws; Roggbach would not be coming on the mission.

It wasn't easy, but Ellie and Michael had secured a week off from Hernando Elementary so Ellie could entertain her visiting "cousin," deflecting Kendall Guthrie's aroused curiosity in the process. The school managed to find substitutes to cover their classes.

As for Barnes, he was kept "frozen" in the garage. His truck was moved to a grocery store parking lot to steer the inquisitive to a different location. Providing an explanation as to who this Jonnie Barnes was forced Anton to travel over some old ground.

"You might say we are one and the same person. Of a fashion," Anton said as the questions flew after Jonnie was discovered.

"Enough with the double talk. Just spit it out. This human was outside our home," Ellie said.

"Most of the story you already know, Ellie. I was using the persona of Roy McDonald then. For the benefit of the rest of you, let me take you back to the night of Roy's (Anton made air quotes) disappearance. Ellie and I missed our pizza date because I had been ordered to rendezvous with one of retrieval ships. Only I didn't want to go back to Xylodon." Anton looked and nodded at Ellie. "I found a reason to stay on Earth."

Julista asked, "So, where does this Jonnie Barnes fit in?"

"Well, *someone* had to go back to Xylodon. Jonnie Barnes took my place. I shape-formed him into Roy McDonald, and he was transported away. Sadly, I became Jonnie Barnes for two weeks until I found a way out. His is not an existence you would wish to have."

"And the retrieval crew had no idea they were carrying a human? They didn't force a change back to your...his...whatever... Xylodonian form?" Dakkott asked.

"Apparently, I benefited from having two of Xylodon's laziest or most incompetent retrieval crew members. No, according to what I was told later by Sub-Protector Korphan, the crew placed him in a holding room and didn't learn of the deception until after reaching Neptune Station. Barnes was mindwashed and returned to Earth. I have no idea what happened to him after that."

"I must say, that was very clever of you, Roy-Michael-Anton," Ungbar said. "How do you keep them all straight? I mean separate. You know what I mean."

"Which brings us to tonight. What do you think he was doing here?" Ellie wondered.

"As to that, I have no answer. Maybe he had followed Roy once from Eudora," Anton said. "Now, he did have a bit of a reputation. To learn he was peeping through a lady's curtains is no surprise. Julista, was he the same human you saw across the street a few days ago? What was the word you used to describe him?"

"Creepy."

"And there, my friends, you have a one-word summary of the life of Jonnie Barnes Jr."

In the days after the Barnes encounter, Anton and Ellie prepared for the journey to St. Peterburg. The almost forty-degree difference in temperature between Hernando and St. Petersburg would require clothing purchases for the two Guardians and five cadets. They also had to arrange for a rental vehicle that could accommodate seven passengers with room for luggage and equipment.

Anton and Ellie had another stop to make—a visit to the Eudora cemetery to visit the grave of Ezra "Gator" Hopkins. It was something Anton had done before going to Washington, and the visit was repeated before he and Ellie traveled west to confront the Aryans. It was through Ezra that Anton and Ellie had found one another, and it was because of Ezra that they felt a special warmth for humankind. Xylodonians believed the spirit—or essence—of a living being never went away. That essence was also energy. Earth's Albert Einstein discovered what Xylodonian scientists had determined centuries before—that energy can never be destroyed, "it can only be changed from one form to another." Anton and Ellie were hoping, once again, to tap into the energy of their friend.

"Gator, I hope you aren't tired of us yet. We are coming to you hat in hand once again," Anton began. "We are about to embark on an endeavor that will require an old seaman such as yourself to watch over us and our young friends. It could be dangerous, and we know you were always a steady hand at the wheel. You've helped to steer a straight path for us before, at least we like to think so, so we're asking you to do it again."

"That's right. There was no one like you, Ezra. You were definitely one of a kind," Ellie said. "I miss your Waffle Barn rants and the sea stories you told over and over. Wherever you are, I hope Lillian is making you change those awful flannel shirts."

"And I hope the coffeepot is hot and you have a flat-bottom mug in your hand," said Anton.

"Take care, Ezra. Watch over Lillian," Ellie said softly. Then they both stood silently for several minutes, remembering the past, before returning to the car.

The preparations were more extensive than for the New Mexico-Idaho trip. Ellie had suggested the cadets could be used as lookouts, as assistants to the crew, or in other roles—Gorthand had demonstrated his expertise with computers and surveillance equipment. Even the slightest possibility of having a small role in this drama excited the cadets.

It was also during this time that another Protectorate communiqué was received; this one identified Maxim Everson as being one of the key players in the bank thefts. Everson's name, often found in news stories and heard on broadcasts, came as a surprise to the two Guardians. Everson's SuperMax software was considered a threat to Xylodonian interests, and the Guardians were ordered to destroy it or compromise it in some way.

The coordinates for the rendezvous with the Deep Watch ship were for a secluded area southwest of Natchez. Anton had created a new persona and credentials for the van he had rented; should the vehicle be damaged or stolen while the Xylodonians were away, it would not be traced back to them. Returning to Hernando without the van would be a hurdle to consider should it arise.

The drive would take nearly four hours. They all went to dinner around 6 p.m. on Monday, dropped Roggbach off at the house, and began heading west-southwest.

Just before midnight, Anton pulled the van into a truck stop outside Natchez, allowing his "team" to purchase drinks and snacks. At exactly midnight, a beacon was activated by the Deep Watch ship, which was submerged near a stretch of Mississippi River shoreline accessed by a rutted dirt road. Perhaps it was a fisherman's route to the river. Anton had to drive slowly in the coal-black night, without streetlights or the moon providing illumination, to avoid bypassing the correct dirt road, adding almost forty-five minutes to the trip. When at last it was found, the final route to their rendezvous point turned out to be more trail than road. The closer the van got to its destination, the quieter the cadets became.

They reached the shoreline, and Anton sent a signal from his holo. As Anton attempted to hide the van as best he could, the cadets stood in awe of the mighty Mississippi racing toward the Gulf of Mexico. The river was making a low, steady rumble, much like a distant thunderstorm, as it carried tons of water downstream. Closer to the shore, they heard gurgling and sloshing near the bank. Adding to this nocturnal concerto were the croaks, hoots, and chirps of wary night creatures.

"So much water. Just look at the power. We have nothing like this on Xylodon," Margeen said.

"It reminds of the *heerquus*, running wild in the plains," Julista observed. "I could stay here and watch this river all day."

Ellie smiled. "And this is not even the longest river in this country. One called the Missouri holds that honor. C'mon, our ride is here."

A dark-colored craft began to emerge from the river's depths and move toward the shore. The Deep Watch craft was large and could only get so close to the bank. A smaller vessel appeared, and its pilot ferried them three at a time to its mother ship; Anton, who had placed a "Road Closed" sign up the dirt trail, was the last to board.

"Welcome aboard. I am Ganplor-6," said the Deep Watch captain, extending a hand to Anton. Ganplor, like his crew, was still using his Xylodonian form. "You and your team must be weary from your travels, so feel free to make use of our ship's mess for replenishment. If you need sleep, we have empty bunks available in our crew quarters."

"Thank you, Ganplor. Have you been briefed on the mission?"

"Yes. But first, be advised that we have already made Xylodonian history. This is the first Deep Watch vessel to go upriver. As to the mission, my understanding is that I am to get you to St. Petersburg, Russia, as quickly and quietly as possible and to lend you any support that you might need. I and my crew are here to provide whatever assistance that we can."

"Thank you. How long will it take you to get us there?"

"If our route is unencumbered—American submarines can be quite the pests—we should arrive in a little over twenty-four hours. We will need to make a brief refueling stop at our undersea base along the way."

"Understood. Excellent. If you're ready, let's get underway," Anton said. "Just curious. How did you find this rendezvous point?"

"In addition to the drone boats that you used to board, we are equipped with aerial drones that can be used for scouting. We dispatched several as we came upriver. The aerial drones are not very stealthy, so we use them after nightfall. By the way, the drone boats are also submersibles."

"Good to know. That may be handy later."

The Deep Watch crew secured the tear-shaped vessel and set a course for the Gulf of Mexico. The ship's hydrodrives were extremely quiet; sensors below the craft kept its position at a consistent five feet off the river bottom. Other sensors, akin to radar and sonar, sent directional beams out a half mile or more in front of the craft to detect underwater objects such as trees or sunken boats.

While the cadets scoured the mess for "real Xylodonian" food, Ellie and Anton went to the bridge to watch the vessel's progress. There was not much to see; the river was murky, and it was still nighttime. Still, the occasional bump with a catfish or other river dweller provided an amusing distraction.

"My understanding is that there is a significant alligator population along this river, but we have yet to encounter one. That would be an interesting sight," Ganplor said. "I believe they reside primarily in the river's tributaries."

As the vessel neared and passed Baton Rouge, Louisiana, the crew slowed to accommodate barge and tugboat traffic. Deep Watch was undetectable by human technology, but that fact didn't preclude chance accidental encounters. A few years ago, a Deep Watch vessel assigned to monitor Chinese naval exercises in the South China Sea narrowly avoided a collision with a Chinese submarine.

The Xylodonian Protectorate had initiated Operation Deep Watch some five decades ago with the construction of a base at the bottom of the Pacific Ocean's Mariana Trench. That base, which now was home to more than 300 operatives and scientists, had dual purposes: research Earth's largest ocean to see what benefits could be gleaned for the water-deprived planet and monitor Earth's militaries and space programs. For many years, human spacecraft had often splashed down in the Pacific; not so much after America began its shuttle program and privatized programs began to spring up. Some Xylodonian pilots grew bored with the inactivity and occasionally played cat-and-mouse games with U.S. Navy aircraft, confounding officials in Washington and wracking more than a few nerves in Xylos.

Eventually, the Protectorate established another base—code-named Atlantyss Complex—in the deepest portion of the Atlantic Ocean for similar purposes and as a transit hub for Xylodon's land-based operatives. Although smaller than its Pacific cousin, the Atlantic base had been the busier of the two bastions of late, largely because of the Earth conflicts in eastern Europe and the Middle East.

The craft picked up speed once past Baton Rouge, then slowed again near New Orleans for the same reason as before. Water visibility improved as daylight arrived, and the craft entered a new body of water.

Ganplor turned to his passengers to mark the occasion. "Here we are. The Gulf of Mexico."

Ellie snorted. "Don't you mean the Gulf of America?"

"What? I don't understand. My maps say Gulf of Mexico," Ganplor replied.

"You need to keep up with current events, my friend," Anton said.

Ganplor, a bit confused, pleaded for understanding. "You know, we don't get many news channels at the bottom of the Atlantic Ocean."

"Touché," conceded Anton. "Just use what's on your maps. Ignore the xenophobic recasting."

"Thank you, That eases my mind," Ganplor said.

A progress report was transmitted to the Protectorate. The cadets, who had not yet earned their holo-biometrometers, were then supplied with a basic form of the device. This version could perform communications, medical treatment, and emit the "freeze" light beam.

"Juleetha...I mean, Ellie...I still haven't got used to that. Ellie, do you think we will have to use these?" Julista asked.

"I hope not," Ellie said. "But there is a saying on Earth: Better to be safe than sorry."

Julista nodded, and Ellie gathered the cadets in the galley to lead them through some holo drills.

The ship was a few hours away from the Atlantic base, so Ellie and Anton eventually left the bridge to get some sleep. Being senior Guardians, they were given their own cabin.

The cabin was spacious and had an attached bathroom. Ellie looked at Anton with a mischievous eye and then gave him a long kiss. "Have you ever *priasomared* below an ocean?" she whispered in his ear.

"Loin joining? No, never," he said, taking her in his arms and reacting quickly to her aroused pheromones. "Have you?"

"No. Let's make our own history." She moved into him, forcing his back against the cabin door as their lips and hands found one another. She began untucking his shirt and unbuckling his belt; he began unfastening her buttons.

Then, without turning, Anton reached back and locked the door.

CHAPTER 30

Ellie and Anton were still asleep when the Deep Watch craft—which had been named The Chthonic by Ganplor and his crew—passed between Florida and Cuba then skirted around Nassau in the Bahamas. The Chthonic's helmsman plotted a course through the Northeast Providence Channel and into the open waters of the Atlantic. The Xylodonian base was located on the ocean floor southwest of the Azores. They would send their next progress report from there.

The five cadets had been invited to the bridge to witness the vastness of Earth's undersea world. They didn't know the names of the species, but they watched in stunned fascination as the ship passed through the deep blue beneath huge schools of bonito, menhaden, tarpon, Spanish mackerel, and yellowfin tuna. Ganplor spotted something of interest on one of the vessel's screens and sent up a drone to investigate. The drone's camera soon gave an enlarged view of a pod of blue whales with at least two calves that were visible.

Julista gasped then dashed to the Guardians' cabin, knocking softly on the door. "Juleetha. Sister. You need to come see this," she said.

"What is it?" she asked from behind the door.

"Hurry! You'll miss it."

"I'm coming. I'm coming."

Ellie followed her sister to the bridge but quickly came to a halt. Some members of the whale pod were slowly sounding. "Oh, my. They are so beautiful," Ellie said, putting an arm around her sister. The drone's microphone captured the haunting sound of the blue whales' language.

Anton joined the group and was equally fascinated. "How can the humans hunt such creatures?" he murmured.

Ganplor recalled the drone, and The Chthonic began its descent to Atlantyss Complex, which sat nearly three miles below the surface. After clearing security protocols, the vessel pulled into a bay inside one of a dozen massive pressurized chambers. The vessel's stores would be replenished and the hull and sensitive equipment checked for damage during the brief stop.

"Welcome to our home away from home," Ganplor said.

Ellie and the cadets were given a brief tour of the base while Anton and Ganplor went to the communications center. Anton's encrypted message read: "Reached Atlantyss Complex. Everything on schedule for approach to St. Petersburg. Any updates?"

The reply from the Protectorate came moments later: "Excellent. Have detected indications that IRA has entered early phase of new operation. Critical you intervene but leave no trace. Safe travels."

"Acknowledged," Anton replied. "Atlantyss out."

Anton and Ganplor returned to The Chthonic and awaited the others. Ellie led the chattering cadets onto the vessel and asked Anton about the instructions from Xylodon.

"It seems that the Russians have begun some new activity," Anton replied. "The Protectorate didn't say it in so many words, but I got the impression that expedience is desired."

"Have you put together a plan for when we reach St. Petersburg? I don't think we will require accommodations," Ellie said. "We can use the ship if necessary."

"You are so cute when you're right," Anton said. "Here's what I have come up with. Tell me what you think." He outlined his current strategy and tactics.

"So, flexibility is the key," she said.

"Indeed. Like a rubber band."

The Chthonic eased out of the supply bay and back into the depths of the Atlantic, following a north-northeasterly heading. In an hour or so, the vessel was on the doorstep of the Norwegian Sea, splitting the difference between the United Kingdom and Iceland. As the water turned colder and denser, the Chthonic automatically compensated to keep its passengers comfortable and its sensitive equipment running.

Ganplor, Ellie, and Anton were on the bridge monitoring the course. "You know, the island of Greenland is just north of here. It is vastly underpopulated but is rich in resources," Anton said. "I wonder if the Protectorate has ever considered putting an outpost there. It is strategically located as well, what with the growing interest in the Arctic region and all."

"Greenland as a base? You raise a good point, Guardian. We should establish one before someone else does. Perhaps you should make that recommendation," Ganplor said. "You might include that it seems every navy on Earth operates in this region. Speaking of that, look on our central screen."

The ship's sensors were picking up a large underwater entity several miles ahead.

"Do you have any idea what it is?" Ellie asked.

"What you have before you is an American-made Virginia-class cruise missile attack submarine. It is one of the quietest submarines ever built by the humans. It and its sisters form one part of the Americans' triad nuclear defense strategy, although these types of submarines, with their torpedoes and Tomahawk missiles, are usually on the prowl for other nations' ballistic missile submarines. It's a hunter-killer, this one is," Ganplor said. "Luckily for us, we are quieter, stealthier, and when so equipped, more dangerous. To the crewmen anchored to their screens on that submarine, we might as well be a stray barracuda."

The Chthonic passed within 300 yards of the American submarine, which gave no indication that another undersea craft was nearby. Although it was still daylight above, the vessels moved past one another as "ships in the night."

"By its signature, this one is called the USS Virginia," Ganplor said.

"We have met this one before. We played our version of 'follow the leader' almost to its base."

"Was that wise?" Anton asked, quickly realizing he was likely one of the last who should be questioning a fellow operative's wisdom.

"No, but it was more exciting than doing climate change studies," Ganplor replied.

The Chthonic was not quite as invisible as Ganplor thought, but it wasn't recognizable either. In fact, it was quite the mystery to sonar technician (ST) Ric Bowen. His brow furrowed as he squinted his eyes; the readings he was seeing couldn't possibly be right.

"Sir, could you come look at this," Bowen said to the Virginia's executive officer, "Black" Jack Vanore. The XO, in his eighteenth year in the Navy, had some expertise with sonar. But this signature had him just as baffled as the enlisted man.

"I know this can't be right, but is that...a whale? Aren't we too deep for whales?" asked Vanore.

"Yes, sir. That's what I thought, too, on both scores," replied Bowen. "That's why I wanted a second opinion."

Vanore waved at the sub's captain, Derrick Suehs. "Skip, come take a look at this."

Suehs peered over Bowen's shoulder. "OK, what am I supposedly looking at? You fellas are the experts on sonar."

Vanore said, "Bowen and I think this looks like a whale. But I've never heard of a whale going this deep before."

Suehs shrugged. "Maybe it's a dead whale? On his way to the bottom?"

Vanore and Bowen looked at one another with the nonverbal "maybe" expressions.

Suehs had no wish for the Virginia to make any new headlines. In November 2024, the submarine got trapped in the nets of a Norwegian fishing vessel. That was embarrassing enough, but the vessel drew more attention when it became a political pawn in March 2025 after Norway declined to resupply the Virginia during a spat with the American president. Suehs didn't need a repeat of those incidents.

"Well, keep an eye—or ear—on it, and let me know if something changes," Suehs said.

"Aye aye, skipper," said Bowen.

In this case, a false image was as good as "no" image. No suspicions were aroused on the American submarine.

The Deep Watch vessel left the Americans behind in the Norwegian Sea and then entered the North Sea, moving toward the Skagerrak Strait and its meandering path among the Scandinavian countries. The Xylodonians weren't aware, but they were passing under the site of one of humankind's most famous battles of World War I, the Battle of Jutland. That battle, which saw Britain's Jellicoe defeat Germany's Scheer, was the last sea encounter fought primarily by battleships. The airplane would dominate the next world conflict.

After passing through the Skagerrak Strait, bounded by Norway, Sweden, and Denmark, the Chthonic cruised into Kattegat Bay, with its shallower depths and treacherous reefs. Ganplor had not navigated this seaway before—no Xylodonian had—but he had extensively researched it once the mission was placed on his plate.

"We will have to reduce speed and let our sensors guide us. Our tiny friends with the artificial intelligence will do all of the piloting, all the work. At least for a bit," he told his passengers.

Anton could feel the tension rise among those on the bridge as the craft moved through the bay, but those tensions calmed when a human-dredged path was found. The deeper the better, the Xylodonians thought.

"Now comes are next challenge. The bridge over the Øresund strait," said Ganplor. "This is a tricky one. It's actually a bridge and a tunnel. But we can't go over the tunnel without becoming partially visible."

The Øresund bridge was a combination automobile-rail route linking Sweden and Denmark, thus providing rail access to Central

Europe via Germany. The structure was completed in 2000, delayed slightly by the discovery of some detritus from World War II—sixteen unexploded bombs. The bridge, with four lanes for vehicle traffic and two lanes for rail, stretches above ground for five miles from Sweden to the artificially created island of Peberholm, or Pepper Islet. That island, so named to complement its northern neighbor, Saltholm Island, features one end of the Drogden Tunnel. The tunnel portion is less than three miles long and connects the artificial construct to Denmark's natural island of Amager.

The top of the tunnel is only 10 meters below the surface, thus Ganplor's eschewing of that route.

"There is an opening in the bridge for ship traffic. Once again, we will have to use sensors and avoid any human vessels," he said.

After another tenuous thirty minutes, the Chthonic picked up speed as it entered the Baltic Sea. In about the same amount of time it took for the vessel to clear the bridge area, it cruised swiftly and uneventfully past Poland, Lithuania, Latvia, and Estonia. Soon, with Finland on its port side and Estonia to starboard, the vessel entered the Gulf of Finland.

Ganplor turned to the Guardians and cadets. "In about fifteen minutes, my friends…St. Petersburg."

CHAPTER 31

A FEW DAYS BEFORE THE ARRIVAL OF THE CHTHONIC...

Nikolai Ivanov lay stretched out on the king-size bed in his usual room within the Belmond Grande Hotel, swaddled in the pleasures of the flesh. He twirled his mustache as watched a nude Olga walk imperiously toward the bathroom, her blond hair falling almost to the twin ivory mounds of her buttocks. She left the bathroom door open, allowing him to admire the long, slender legs that only moments before had been wrapped around him, as she reapplied her makeup.

He reached toward the floor for his trousers and pulled a small leather box from a pants pocket. After ensuring Olga could not see his activity, he removed the contents of the box and slid it under the bedcovers. He propped himself up on some pillows and folded his hands behind his head. In a few moments, Olga returned; she had repinned her hair and freshened her lipstick. She reached down for her bra.

"Not so fast. I have something for you," he said.

"Oh? I thought you had given it already," Olga said, smiling. "What is it you have for me?"

"Pull back the covers."

Olga did as she was asked, discovering a diamond-encrusted

emerald necklace stretched across Ivanov's midsection.

"Nikolai! It is so beautiful. Thank you...thank you." She reached for the necklace, but Ivanov caught her wrist.

"Just a token of my appreciation. But before it is yours, there is one more service you must do."

Olga smiled then bent her head to his hips. In a few moments, Ivanov had his release and Olga had the necklace.

"You are a bad boy," she said. "Now I must redo my lipstick."

"Now, now. No scolding. You know how I greatly enjoy our Tuesday conference meetings." They both chuckled.

A short time later, they were forced to trade the opulence of the Belmond for the drab morosity of the IRA building. Once again, they assumed the charade of bored, tired bureaucrats as they went their separate ways on their assigned floor. Without going to his office or removing his overcoat, Ivanov strolled over to check on the progress of the "SuperMax Squad," as he called it. Dmitri Alexandrov, standing nearby, thought he detected a familiar fragrance as Ivanov paused. *It's nothing,* he thought. *He and Olga were in the same elevator.*

"How goes it, Dmitri? Any updates?" Ivanov asked.

"SuperMax is working perfectly yet again, comrade director. We have gained access to nearly twenty accounts in New York and nine in Boston," Alexandrov said. "We are infiltrating more and more accounts each day. We have done some preliminary tests, withdrawing a few dollars from a New York firefighter and from a Boston hair-stylist. Everything appears ready to go as before. We await your orders."

Ivanov twirled both ends of his mustache. "Let's give Moscow and Washington a taste of what we can do. But I like round numbers," he said. "Once you gain access to a tenth Boston account, then strike. Clean them out. Then I will check with Moscow on how to proceed."

"*Da*. Acknowledged, comrade director," he said. "C'mon, fellows, you heard the boss."

Across the globe, the chief of staff and national security director for the new administration walked into the Oval Office as the president was checking the stock market updates on his phone.

"Yes, what is it this time?" the president asked. "It's never good news when you two are together."

"Sir, we are receiving reports of additional cyber incursions. This time the hackers are attacking banks in New York and in Boston," said the national security director, who, until nominated, had been running a FedEx office in Idaho.

"Yeah, yeah. And I suppose you are going to tell me the Russians are behind it, right?" said the president.

"Yes, sir. We believe that to be the case," said the national security director.

"Sir, this time one of the victims is a U.S. House member who contributed to you and whom you endorsed," added the chief of staff.

The president threw a plate of french fries at the wall. "Well, ain't that eighteen shades of hell. Too bad for him, and too bad for me," said the president. "No more contributions, I guess."

The national security director and the chief of staff looked at one another. The former spoke first. "Sir, what kind of retaliatory action would you like for us to undertake? The same suite of options that I presented to you after the first such attack is still available to us."

The president sat silently, looking at his phone.

"Have we found that freeze ray yet?" he asked.

The national security director closed his eyes briefly and shook his head.

"I told you before to get on it. So, get on it. Why isn't anyone listening to me," shouted the president. "I want that freeze gun."

"Yes, sir."

"Yes, sir."

The pair left the Oval Office disconsolately. "I pray for America," said the chief of staff.

"As do I," said the man entrusted with the nation's security. "As do I."

CHAPTER 31

The initial forays into the banks of the Northeastern U.S. saw almost $10 million purloined from the account holders, including the Boston congressman. There were scores of other cellphone numbers that Ivanov's employees collected; it was a target rich environment. But the IRA pulled its punch for now, awaiting acknowledgement from the Kremlin on whether to continue. Tweaking America no longer required the delicacy that it once did, but still…

"Excellent work, comrades," he told the SuperMax team. "I envision more riches to come for all of us."

CHAPTER 32

Ganplor placed the Chthonic on the Gulf of Finland sea bottom about a half mile from the Russian shore. Commercial traffic would not be an issue at this depth, he said. As the crew waited for nightfall to arrive to launch an aerial scout drone, Anton, Ellie, and four of the cadets—all but Gorthand—labored to create their Russian personas and learn a bit of Russian, one of the many Earth languages in which Anton was fluent. As for Gorthand, the computer virtuoso, Anton ordered him to stay aboard the vessel. To appease his disappointment, Anton told him, "Don't worry. I will have a special job for you later."

The six members of the "shore team" would guise themselves as older Russians—the elderly tended to draw less suspicion. They would need to dress warmly—hats, overcoats, scarves—to accommodate for the weather and to reduce eye contact with humans. Their holos had a video function that could send a feed back to Gorthand and Ganplor for recording and diagnosis.

Getting to St. Petersburg, as arduous as the journey had been, was but step one in their mission. They next had to get ashore undetected and find a base of operations; the Xylodonians hoped the drone would find a solution to the latter problem first. The next would be to locate the building housing the Internet Research Agency and set up surveillance in two-person teams—Anton and Margeen, Ellie and Ungbar, Dakkott and Julista—to find a way inside. If necessary, they could make four teams with the two Guardians and the two cadet duos. For this stage, Anton's plan would require flexibility and ingenuity. They had very little information about what was inside the building or even which of the four floors was most critical. As they were not likely to receive two opportunities to penetrate the facility, sending in an initial scout was shelved as an option.

Anton, Ellie, and the cadets gathered on the bridge for the drone launch and flight. Anton, Ellie, and Ganplor agreed that using the submersibles to travel along the Neva River would be the best route into the city. "Follow the Neva and look for any closed or abandoned buildings," Anton told the drone operator. "Something we can use and not be disturbed."

Cruising slowly at an altitude of several hundred feet, the drone activated its camera once it reached the mouth of the Neva River. Scouring the shorelines of the Neva took much longer than expected; there were shops, restaurants, active warehouses, and historical sites all along the waterway. The city's ancient fortress was too well lit and lured too many tourists. Joggers and cyclists seemed to enjoy the river route at all times of the day, further compounding the search.

The drone passed over a bridge just east of the fortress and maneuvered into a decaying, tumbledown section of the waterfront nursing a cluster of businesses barely sewn together by this ragged and rough stretch of Shpalernaya Street. As the drone flew between the street and river, Ellie exclaimed, "Stop!" Back up a bit."

The operator did as Ellie requested, pausing the drone over a building with faded lettering on one side. "Looks to be some sort of seafood restaurant, according to the sign out front," Anton said.

"Not anymore. Look at it. It doesn't have any windows, and there don't appear to be any electrical lines connected to it," said Julista.

Anton smiled. "My sister-in-law has a keen eye. Can the drone do a once-around the building?"

The drone was so maneuvered; the inspection left little or no doubt that the weary structure was abandoned.

"That looks like home. Drop a homing beacon so it can guide us to the building," Anton said. The drone descended, hovered over the building, and dropped a small disc onto the roof.

"We can take the submersibles to under the bridge, but the river is lined with levees and river walls. We'll need scaling equipment to get from the river to street level," Ellie said. "Then we can walk over to our new headquarters."

"Will rope ladders suffice?" asked Ganplor. "We sometimes have to make use of them on shorelines."

"Perfect," Anton replied. "We will soon no longer have darkness on our side, so I suggest we get some rest and make ready for tomorrow night."

As evening approached the next day, Dakkott and Julista placed spare clothing, some rations, and other equipment into their submersible. There was no telling how many days of surveillance would be required.

"Are you nervous about tonight?" Julista asked.

"Just a bit. But I have confidence that Anton and Juleetha...er, Ellie...know what they are doing," Dakkott said. "Besides, they have the hard job. We only have to keep watch and pretend to be old humans."

Julista laughed. "Too bad we don't have any experience with elderly humans to model after. Not even Chad was that old."

Dakkott grimaced at the mention of Cartwright's name. "I wish Anton had picked Margeen for that excursion. I did not like the thought of that human touching you."

The comment took Julista by surprise. "I had no idea you felt that way, Dakkott. You have not even asked to spend alone time with me," she said.

"I...I...I have always been too nervous around you. You are so...confident," he said. "You always seem to know what you want, where you are going. I am not that way."

She took his hand. "If it were not for you, we would not be here. You arranged for the Dart Lurker. You piloted it across a galaxy. You helped me find my sister."

He didn't respond for a time. Then he said, "I'm glad we are paired. You can rely on me to keep you safe."

"Thank you." She leaned over and kissed his cheek.

He blushed. "Anton is signaling that it's time to go. Let's get into the submersible."

The Chthonic rose just enough to allow the three submersibles to drop and clear the mother ship. The small craft would be guided by the Chthonic until they reached the drop-off point. With Anton and Ellie in the lead, they headed toward the harbor area at the mouth of the Neva, then up the somewhat winding channel. The submersibles had canopies that opened for entry and exit, and these would have provided a view of the river bottom had it not been so dark. Ganplor had launched an aerial drone to monitor the progress of the three vessels and act as a backup should the homing beacon fail. He messaged Anton once the trio had passed the city fortress to the port side. "You should be nearing the drop-off point in thirty seconds," he said.

Anton ascended and opened the canopy. He was able to propel the craft manually to a dark section near the river wall. The cold wind and river current made it difficult to stand, but he managed it and tossed a rope upward. The attached hook bit around a railing, and Anton ascended. Ellie tied the rope to the rope ladder, and Anton pulled it up and secured it. Ellie sent up the supplies, including a small bit of special equipment, closed the canopy, then ascended herself. Anton signaled to the Chthonic, "Submersible one ready for return." The small craft descended.

Ellie kept watch on both directions of the street, but the thoroughfare remained deserted, as if deliberately removed from the city's ascendance. Anton and Ellie repeated the process with the cadets on the other two submersibles. Once the last submersible had been emptied and descended into the river, they loaded their meager supplies and the ropes into their backpacks and headed to the beacon location.

Anton whispered to Ellie, "Are you ready to enter Mordor?"

"What? Oh, Mordor. What are we, the Fellowship now?" she said.

"You are wearing a ring, aren't you? So 'Fellowship' works for me."

Ellie looked at her ring finger. "Of course, I am wearing it. Would never leave it. So, which member of the Fellowship am I? You better not say Gimli."

"Why, the beautiful elf, of course," he said. "Me, I'm just hoping we won't need Gandalf's magic to get this done."

They traveled in pairs as they approached the abandoned restaurant, keeping some distance between them, huddling together against the chill. Lights could be seen across the river, where nightlife was still being enjoyed. There was only one working streetlight in this area. Anton followed the homing signal and soon reached the derelict structure. A wooden back door, cracked and with peeling paint, was secured only with a rusted padlock, but Anton made short work of that hindrance. Within a few minutes, all six Xylodonians were inside.

A kitchen, storeroom, and office provided seclusion from the eyes of passers-by. There was no heat, however, so the Xylodonians had to make an adjustment to the life-support functions of their holos to account for the lower temperatures.

Anton sent another message to the Chthonic. "Made it the gathering point. All accounted for."

Ganplor replied, "All submersibles have returned. Will dispatch when requested."

"Affirmative."

Turning to the others, Anton said, "Day one of surveillance begins in a few hours. We know the general location of the offending entity, and we have all been provided with photos of its director, Nikolai Ivanov. He doesn't stay in his facility day and night, so let's concentrate on locating him and tracking his movements. Any questions?"

"And if we spot this Ivanov…?" Ungbar asked.

"Message me or Ellie. Don't do anything on your own unless absolutely necessary. Does anyone have any other questions?"

No one did or they were too cold to ask.

"OK, let's try to get some rest."

CHAPTER 33

If the exterior of 55 Savushkina Street was dreary, the working conditions inside the building rested somewhere between miserable and bleak. The heavy security supplemented the grimness with a heavy dose of paranoia.

The building shared a parking lot with a nearby apartment complex, and its employees entered through guarded turnstiles by using special security passes. Their salaries differed according to their duties and assignments—those working in the esteemed "American Department" could earn between $1,300 and $2,000 a month. Lower "trolls" earned about $1,000 a month along with bonuses. Being a minute late for clocking in could earn fines; those who were as much as an hour late might be penalized a day's pay.

The daily tasks of the various trolls depended upon the floor to which they were assigned. Those on the first floor wrote "news" articles that referred to blog posts created on the third floor. The nonbloggers on the third floor would write comments on social media posts under false identities, sometimes pretending to be Ukrainian (Ukrainian girls drew the most attention). The marketing teams assigned to the second floor would spin this web of misinformation and disseminate it to the world's social media.

The fourth floor—Ivanov's domain—was where the real rogues got to play.

The tentacles of paranoia were not confined to the building's exterior; they stretched across all four floors as well. Each desk and computer screen was angled in such a way so that anything being written might be visible to that station's neighbors. Contact with fellow employees—even by those commenting or elaborating upon each other's work—was kept limited. "Consultations" came during smoke breaks or in the cafeteria.

The décor—call it "Kremlin foreboding"—contributed to the drab atmosphere. The walls were bare, the furnishings were cut-rate, and the windows were heavily draped. Little outside light entered these halls.

Such was the cyber citadel that the Xylodonians were hoping to storm. But they did have one factor in their favor, one they were unaware of.

It was Tuesday.

Anton, Ellie, and the four cadets had prepared their human personas and placed what equipment they felt might be needed in their coats or backpacks. Ungbar and Dakkott would be college students—there was a medical university not far from their destination —while Anton, Ellie, Margeen, and Julista would be guised as the boy's parents or aunts. Ellie had obtained Russian rubles during their Atlantic station stop, but none of them had proper credentials. They would have to talk—or holo—their way out of any difficult encounters. There was a park near Savushkina Street—named in honor of the 300th anniversary of the city—that was convenient for giving the illusion of family gatherings...and for watching.

Their target was nearly six miles from their makeshift base, but that inconvenience was of little concern. They left in pairs—Anton and Margeen were first—at ten-minute intervals and walked to a bus stop on Shpalernaya Street. They took the bus across the Neva River and disembarked at the second stop, near the entrance to St. Petersburg's Metro rapid transit subway system. The Metro was as clean, cheery, and elegant as the IRA building was not. The former World War II bomb shelters had been transformed into a rail conveyance with few equals in Europe. The tunnels were lit by opulent chandeliers, and the stations featured ornate columns placed evenly on beautifully tiled floors. The underground system lacked air-conditioning, but that didn't matter to Anton and his cadet companion. The Metro got them quickly and efficiently to where they wanted to go.

They were the first team to enter the park. The morning sun had not transcended the night's chill. They bought some hot tea and pastries for themselves and some seeds for the birds. Then they sat on a bench and waited.

The other "teams" appeared shortly afterward, and Anton messaged Ganplor: "In place." The three pairs then strolled leisurely to different areas of Savushkina Street. Sometimes they drank coffee or tea, sometimes they pretended to look at street maps, sometimes they just walked by with the "college student" assisting his "aunt." The guards outside the IRA appeared bored and paid little heed to the *babulyas* (grannies) swaddled in scarves and oversize coats ambling along the sidewalk across the way.

Ellie and Ungbar had stationed themselves southeast of the IRA building, occasionally going into shops or "resting." They had a clear view of the building's primary entrance, and they both went on alert when an Aurus Senat pulled up and stopped.

"That doesn't look like it belongs here," Ellie said to her cadet.

"Indeed. A bit fancy for this area," he replied.

The car's driver got out and opened the back door nearest the building. Two people soon emerged from the glass entrance—a prim, blond woman carrying a purse and briefcase, and then a mustachioed man wearing a fedora and overcoat—and got in the vehicle.

It was Ivanov.

"That's our man," said Ellie.

The driver resumed his position, and the car began to pull away but had to pause to allow oncoming traffic to pass.

"He's leaving. What do we do now?" asked Ungbar.

"Watch and learn, cadet," she said. Ellie used her holo to take a photo of Ivanov's car, then reached into Ungbar's backpack and pulled out an object resembling a large marble. She pressed an activation button, touched the holo image to the object, then set the object on the ground. As the Senat pulled away on Savushkina Street, the object gained speed and followed underneath the car.

Ungbar was taken aback. "It's very cute, but what was that?"

"That is a Shadow Eye tracker. I imported the image of the car from holo into its memory," Ellie said. "It will now follow the humans anywhere they go."

"But we are stuck here," Ungbar said.

Ellie smiled, then sent a message on her holo as Ungbar watched. "Shadow Eye deployed. Inform Ganplor."

Anton and Margeen were west of the IRA building, and they saw the Senat pass without knowing its cargo. But his holo soon indicated a message had been received. "Acknowledged," he messaged back. He then informed the Chthonic captain, who ordered up an aerial drone. The drone homed in on the Shadow Eye and joined the pursuit.

The driver backtracked into the heart of the city, passing not far from where the Xylodonians had established their base. The Senat eventually slowed and entered the valet lane outside the Belmond Grand Hotel. The driver gave the car keys to a valet, and he and his two passengers entered the hotel. Anton was given the information.

As the driver settled into the hotel restaurant and Nikolai and Olga entered an elevator, the six Xylodonians reconnoitered in the park.

"You four stay here in case Ivanov comes back and we miss him," Anton said. "Just act like you're discussing your professors at the Academy. Message one of us if you run into trouble. Ellie and I will be back soon." *We hope*, he thought.

"Affirmative," Dakkott said.

Anton and Ellie walked to the park taxi stand and hailed a cab.

"*Mesto naznacheniya* (destination)?" asked the cabbie.

"The Belmond Grand," said Anton.

"*Da*."

CHAPTER 34

After the taxi departed from the hotel, its elderly passengers walked carefully into the Belmond's lavishly baroque lobby and found a cushioned sofa to rest upon. The momentary respite added to the illusion of elderly infirmities, while allowing them to scout the room. After a few moments, Anton and Ellie approached the front desk, where a young clerk wearing a suit and a nametag greeted them.

"What can I do for you folks?" asked the clerk.

"You must be Vitaly," said Anton, pointing a finger at the younger man. "It says so right there."

"Yes, that is I. How might I be of service?"

Anton wrapped Ellie's arm in his.

"Today is our fifty-fifth wedding anniversary," Anton said, beaming. "Never thought we would make it this far."

"Congratulations to you both. That is very nice."

Ellie said, "We had our wedding just down the street. The church is gone now. But you should have seen my dress. You should have seen the cake."

Vitaly began to become nervous and confused. He didn't have much experience dealing with *prestarelyy* (the elderly).

"I'm sure you were beautiful."

"Oh, she was. She was," said Anton. "She is still beautiful today. To me, anyway."

"Yes, I agree," said Vitaly, who was looking around for rescue.

"We spent our wedding night in this very hotel," said Anton. He and Ellie chuckled, and she pretended to blush.

"He was my first, you know," said Ellie.

Vitaly cringed.

"My nephew is here now waiting for us. But I don't see him," Anton said.

"He is here? At the hotel?"

"He was supposed to meet us and arrange to obtain the same room we had on our wedding night. He said it was his gift to us," explained Anton.

"Who is your nephew? Perhaps he is here already."

"Nikolai. Nikolai Ivanov. He is an important man," said Anton.

"Let me see." He began tapping on his computer. At this point, Vitaly would have crawled over broken vodka bottles to rid himself of this couple. "Ah, yes. You are in luck. He is already here. Room 424."

"Yes, that's it. That was our room. Remember, three times two is six. That is how we remembered it," said Ellie. "We went in, and we did not come out for two days."

Vitaly began turning red.

Anton pinched Ellie's nose and turned to Vitaly once again.

"Do you know if he has ordered Champagne yet?" asked Anton.

"Let me check with room service," said Vitaly. He hit a number on the phone pad then spoke quickly to whomever answered. "*Du. Du. Spasibo*. Yes, my friends, Champagne has been ordered. A very good bottle."

"Oh, that is so exciting. Thank you very much, young man," said Ellie. She blew Vitaly a kiss. He grew redder.

"Which way are the elevators, Vitaly?" Anton asked. Vitaly didn't answer; he simply pointed. "Thank you, Vitaly."

Anton and Ellie moved toward the elevators; those in the lobby didn't notice that the pace of the two elderly Russians had quickened.

An elevator door opened to beckon them inside, and Ellie hit the button for floor three. The door whooshed open, and they walked quietly down the hall to Room 424. Anton leaned toward the door to pick up any sounds from the room interior, but the door was too thick, too well made.

Ellie held her holo close to the door lock, then twisted the dial. There was a low buzz, and a series of green lights birthed on the display.

Anton entered quickly into the short hallway leading to the central room, with Ellie not far behind. They saw clothes scattered across the floor. A Champagne bottle rested atilt inside a silver bucket amid two half-filled glasses. There was no indication that the two Guardians had been heard. They soon saw why.

On the bed was a blond woman, back toward them, grinding her hips into the mustachioed man beneath her. His eyes were shut, but hands were holding her breasts, a place they seemed to know well. The woman was moaning. "There. Mmmmm. Yes, there. YES," she cried as her ecstasy grew.

Anton stepped forward. "We so hate to interrupt when you're have such fun."

The woman screeched. The man, apparently accustomed to using a command voice, barked, "Who the hell…"

He didn't finish.

A light from Ellie's holo had filled that part of the room.

The two figures on the bed were frozen in place, with the woman astride the man's hips. It was a sight that amused Ellie.

"I never thought of using a holo for that," she said.

"For what?"

She nodded in the couple's direction. "For making you last longer."

"I have never heard you complain about my performance in the past."

"A girl can always dream, can't she?"

Anton just shook his head. "Help me look through these clothes."

After a bit of rummaging, they found the security credentials for both humans, some keys, and a silver-coasted thumb drive. *This could be useful,* thought Anton.

"By the way, Ellie, let me introduce you to Nikolai Ivanov and Olga

Alexandrova," Anton declared, looking at their identity cards. "They both work at the IRA, and Olga here is married, but not to Nikolai."

"Isn't that a surprise. Naughty, naughty, Olga." Ellie examined the woman's face. "Nice Botox job. I wonder how many rubles that cost?"

"Nikolai probably paid for it. Well, we now have our Trojan horse to enter the agency building. What say we change clothes and get on with it," he said. "We can let them enjoy the afternoon, and they can have our old clothes when they're done."

"*Otlichno* (excellent)," she replied in Russian. "Too bad we can't take that Champagne with us."

Anton sent a message to the four cadets, and the two Guardians departed the room—but not before Ellie took some soaps as souvenirs. "Hey, we may never be in a five-star hotel ever again," she said.

Anton paused, turned toward the bed and took a photo with his holo. "You never know," he said.

"Nikolai" and "Olga" walked into the Belmond lobby and were spotted by the Senat driver, who dashed from his café seat to the valet stand and handed over a ticket. The driver opened a rear door for his passengers. In about fifteen minutes, the procedure was repeated in reverse. The Senat pulled up outside 55 Savushskina, the driver jumped out and ran to open a rear door, and the two passengers got out. When Nikolai tried to give the driver a tip, the man seemed surprised. "*Nyet.* Is not necessary, sir," he said.

"I insist." Nikolai stuffed some rubles into the flummoxed driver's shirt pocket then watched him drive away. The four cadets were now approaching on the sidewalk.

"Stay behind us when we go in. We are headed to the fourth floor," Anton told them. "When we get there, you will likely need to spread out. Your job is to holo-freeze anyone who comes in after we enter the room, so keep watch on any doors. I have no idea how long this will take, so be alert."

They all nodded in acknowledgement.

"Nikolai" put on his most imperious official face and strode into the foyer security area. He gave his security credentials to a guard armed with a Kalashnikov. "We have a tour group today. Please let them through. I will take responsibility for them," the director told the guard and his companions.

"Olga" then came to the security turnstiles, which a second guard kept open for the "tour group."

Once they were on the far side of the security area, "Nikolai" bellowed, "They want a picture. All of you turn and look this way, please."

The guards turned as ordered. They were met by a flash of light.

"Dakkott, please go make certain the outer door is secure," Anton said. The double doors past the security checkpoint were locked as well. The Xylodonians proceeded to the elevator. At various points, workers nodded their heads and timidly greeted "Director Ivanov."

The six took an elevator to the fourth floor and entered the expansive room. There were close to one hundred computer workstations—many with double screens—but only twenty or so workers were present, most of them seated together in a middle section. A bank of offices across the way likely accommodated the supervisors, Anton thought. There was what appeared to be a clerical station posed as a lone sentinel near those offices.

The group in the center of the phalanx of workstations—Anton didn't know it at the time, but this was the "SuperMax Squad"—appeared to be in a post-lunch lethargy. A man, dressed better than the others, was standing next to this group, drinking tea. Anton recognized him from the intel provided by the Protectorate as Dmitri Alexandrov, Ivanov's immediate subordinate and weekly cuckold.

Anton gestured for the "tour group" to remain where they were and then, with a worried look, strode purposefully to the central section. He took note of the wall décor. One might call it pre-minimalist at best. *This is the room that makes Earth tremble?* he thought. *What a dump.*

"Mr. Director, is there something we can do for you? We are almost ready to begin our next round of withdrawals," said Alexandrov, part wondering what was so concerning to Ivanov, part wondering why Olga had not gone to her desk, and fully wondering who these other people might be.

"Dmitri, I have just received an urgent communiqué from the

Kremlin. From the very top. It is urgent that we comply," said Anton/Ivanov. "The situation with the United States has taken a turn."

"What does the message say, sir?" asked Alexandrov.

"Olga, show him."

Olga/Ellie raised her left hand. Alexandrov saw what appeared to be light reflected off a piece of metal. His mind began to fade into a deep fog; he could barely control his breathing and movements. He then thought he saw a lightning flash just before the fog enveloped him fully.

"Olga" had directed a compulsion beam at the SuperMax Squad, while Dakkott and Ungbar put the other workers into a freeze state. Julista and Margeen moved to cover the far doors while the two male cadets remained put.

Anton placed a hand on Alexandrov's shoulder. "Dmitri, please tell the team to retrieve all of the funds that were taken, and if you would be so kind, return those funds to their original accounts."

Alexandrov gave the order, and the team began typing furiously. There was actually no need for the order; the Russians were feeling the same effects of the compulsion beam as Dmitri was. It was wonderful teamwork to watch: Without specific direction, some of the team members replenished the coffers for the Hernando banks while several others redirected purloined funds back to Boston and New York.

"Very good, gentlemen. Excellent work. Moscow will be very happy. Now, Dmitri, I have with me a thumb drive. Can you tell me what its contents are?"

Alexandrov put the thumb drive into a computer port. "The device contains the SuperMax program, Mr. Director. It is the program provided by the American, Maxim Everson."

"Thank you, Dmitri. That confirms my suspicions. So, I take it this SuperMax program is still on our system?"

"*Da*, Mr. Director, it is still active. Like a shark in the ocean."

"A colorful description, Dmitri. Please delete the program and destroy all shreds of its existence."

"At once, Mr. Director." Alexandrov clapped his hands, and the team began tapping and hitting delete keys.

"Thank you, Dmitri. The responsibility is on you. All vestiges of the program must be removed from our system."

Alexandrov had the SuperMax Squad do a final check. The cyber terror was gone.

"*Spasibo,* Dmitri. You and your men have done an excellent job. You have saved Mother Russia. There may be commendations forthcoming from our president," he said. "Please, remain here, and in a few moments, you will receive a signal to return to your normal duties."

"*Da*. Thank you, Mr. Director."

Ivanov waved a farewell to Alexandrov, then herded the "tour group" together.

A few minutes later, the Guardians and their cadet companions exited an elevator and walked right out of one of the most secure facilities in Russia.

CHAPTER 35

The return to their dilapidated base was a mere reversal of their journey to Savushkina Street—take the Metro to a bus stop, take a bus to Shpalernaya Street, walk to the rundown restaurant. Anton and Ellie had ducked into Metro restrooms to revert to their elderly Russian personas but with finer attire this time. Anton sent a message to Ganplor, signaling the success of the mission and arranging the return to the Chthonic on the submersibles. He also sent a message with an attachment to Gorthand, instructing him to forward the message to the phone number given in the message thirty minutes later.

About the same time, Ellie halted the holo effects on the Russians within the IRA building—and on the lovers still in *flagrante delicto* in Room 424 of the Belmond Grand Hotel.

Nikolai and Olga both felt that they were emerging from a stuporous haze.

"I don't think I had more than a glass of Champagne. Is that the same vintage you always order, Nikolai?" Olga asked.

Ivanov looked at his watch and felt a tinge of panic. He was an hour late in returning to the office. "C'mon, we must hurry," he said to Olga. "I was expecting a call from Moscow this afternoon."

It was then that he noticed that their clothes were gone; in their place were two piles of cheap, shabby attire.

"Is this some kind of joke?" Ivanov snarled.

"I think we were robbed. Perhaps we were drugged, and someone came into the room," Olga said. "The Champagne! Check the Champagne."

"We don't have time for that now. Let's get back to the office, and then we can investigate."

Ivanov was in such a hurry to put on the clothes that he couldn't pause to appreciate how Olga was struggling to enclose her voluptuous body. He also didn't notice his missing keys, thumb drive, and security credentials.

They rushed through the lobby to the café; the driver was gone. *No surprise the fool wouldn't wait for us,* Ivanov thought. He told the bellman to hail a cab.

The flustered Ivanov was mostly silent on the cab ride back to the Internet Research Agency. He ignored Olga's complaints that she had not had time to repin her hair and fix her makeup. He suggested to her that they tell their co-workers that their meeting had run late. Olga nodded.

After the cab dropped them off, Ivanov and Olga then ran into a gantlet of drama at the security station. He told the guards that they had been mugged, and their credentials had been taken. Fortunately, the guards recognized the IRA director, and his fingerprints matched those on file. The guards let them enter. As the pair left, one guard turned to a companion and asked, "Didn't he just come through here a short while ago?" The other guard shrugged.

Ivanov stormed off the elevator and into the fourth-floor chamber. Dmitri Alexandrov, still drinking tea, was stunned to see the director and his wife in new clothing. "Mr. Director! What has happened?"

"We were robbed, Dmitri. The bandits forced us to strip and took our clothes and valuables. What you see on us is all we could find."

"My dear, that is terrible. Are you injured?" Alexandrov said with rising concern. "Have you called the police? We need to…"

At that moment, Alexandrov's phone buzzed. He knew better than to look at a text from an unfamiliar number, but the portion of the attached that he could see made him curious. He tapped, and the photo expanded. A nude Olga was on top of the director on a canopy bed in an opulent hotel room.

He looked first to his wife, then to Ivanov. Then he held up his phone so that they could see the image.

"Wait, darling, let me explain," Olga shrieked. "The photo must be a fake!"

"It's not what you think, Dmitri," Ivanov stammered. "This must be some type of blackm…"

Ivanov never got the chance to finish the sentence.

Alexandrov pulled a pistol from underneath his suitcoat and shot the director in the forehead. As Olga screamed and began to run, he shot her three times in the back.

Then he sat down and stared at the fading paint on the walls. He closed his eyes, put the gun against his temple, and pulled the trigger.

The Xylodonians entered their hideout in pairs and in quiet jubilation. The cyber ones and zeros that added up to the daily lifelines and retirement dreams of hundreds of humans—and to a certain alien operations fund—had been restored. Anton and Margeen were the first to return, and once ensconced he sent another message to Gorthand. He gave Gorthand the account information for the Xylodonian funds rehoused in Hernando's Sycamore Bank. The funds were to be transferred to a set of ten accounts, set up by the Protectorate at various locations in the Caribbean; better to split up the eggs rather than keep them in one basket.

Ellie and Ungbar were the next arrivals; Ellie, playing mother hen, had stopped for some Russian fast food—*pelmeni* (dumplings) and *chebureki* (minced meat pies)—enough for the group. They were preparing the feast when Dakkott and Julista entered the old restaurant.

"Dig in, everyone. You were great today. I apologize for not having anything stronger than water to offer to celebrate the mission," Ellie said.

Anton concurred. "You four handled yourselves well. You are a credit to the Academy and to the Protectorate." He bit into a *chebureki*. It was warm and flavorful. "Hey, these are good. Thank you, Ellie."

"Yes, thank you, sister," Julista said. "I appreciate your kind words, but really, you and Anton did most of the work."

"We would not have been as successful without you and your fellow cadets. Ungbar spotted the IRA director, and you four kept the Russians at bay while we fulfilled our orders to eliminate that pesky program," Ellie said.

"I wish we had done more," Julista said. Dakkott squeezed her hand supportively. She smiled and, unseen by the others, moved his hand to her thigh, startling the female-shy cadet. Julista giggled at his discomfort.

Anton sent a signal to Ganplor; his reply indicated the submersibles would arrive around midnight.

"We will go to the bridge in pairs as we did when we arrived," Anton said. "Same procedure for embarking on the submersibles and returning to the Chthonic."

Margeen said, "I'm guessing the Russian authorities will be distracted this evening with what happened. That should help us."

"You are likely correct," Anton replied. "I'm sure that Director Ivanov received a surprise when he finally returned."

"I wonder who the woman was," said Ellie. "Olga something."

"Woman?" said Dakkott, Margeen, and Julista in chorus.

"Let's just say the director was entertaining a friend when we dropped in on him at the hotel," Anton replied.

They rested and then made their way to the rendezvous with the submersibles. A half hour later, they were all back aboard the Deep Watch vessel.

"Congratulations!" said a beaming Ganplor. "I am to give you all a 'well done' from the Protectorate."

"Thanks, Ganplor, but we're not quite done as yet," Anton said. "There's one more detail that we need to take care of. Gorthand, I will need your assistance yet again."

The Guardian sat next to the cadet and gave him Ivanov's thumb drive and a document containing a series of numbers. In a matter of minutes, Gorthand, one of the lowest-ranking members of Xylodon's security forces, bled dry the bank accounts of the Russian president and several of his oligarch cronies. The funds were transferred out of the country.

"Well done, Gorthand," said Anton, patting the cadet on the shoulder. Ganplor ordered the Chthonic to get underway.

As the Chthonic began to clear the Gulf of Finland on its return journey, the president of Ukraine sat disconsolately in his secret office in Kyiv. He had just learned that the American president had cut off financial assistance to Ukraine and other foreign recipients—a severe blow to his nation's military operations in the conflict with Russia. The United States had been Ukraine's biggest ally; however, the new president had wanted to build a hotel in Moscow. It was clear which side he favored. Ukraine's friends in NATO might make up some of the loss, but it was a terrible setback. *How will our brave soldiers make do? We are outnumbered and outgunned,* he wondered.

The doors burst open, startling the president. An excited aide rushed in carrying some documents. "Mr. President, you will never believe this. A miracle has occurred! We can now buy what we need."

The aide tried to explain what had transpired, but the president didn't hear much of it. He was too busy weeping.

CHAPTER 36

The undersea journey back to the Xylodonian Atlantic base was quiet for the most part—the crew and passengers managed to view their first squid—with the cadets taking turns making Gorthand envious over the descriptions of their St. Petersburg exploits.

"All I did was hit a few keys. You and the others had all the fun," he said disconsolately to Dakkott.

"Your keystrokes were very important, as it turned out. And there may be more to come, it appears," Dakkott said. "If you were not the best of us for that assignment, Anton would not have put you there. Never underestimate your value in this operation, my friend."

Anton and Ellie spent most of the time resting or trading information with the Protectorate. They did not hear from Korphan directly, but they were told he was elated with the mission's success. His subordinates made sure to emphasize that this "was only phase one," as Korphan had put it.

The return was a bit more eventful for Dakkott and Julista. He had found the pantry, and later, when the crew were about their duties and their companions were sleeping, he asked Julista to join him there.

"Not the most romantic spot, is it?" she teased.

"I'm sorry. There is not much privacy on this ship," he said. "I could try ..."

"Shut up," she said. Then she pulled down his head and kissed him. It was the first for Dakkott, and his insides turned to flame. His lips found her eyes, her nose, her chin, and her lips once again. Julista made soft noises.

"Am I hurting you?" he asked.

"Don't stop. I will let you know when you're hurting me," she said, melting into him.

Instinct triumphed where inexperience failed. Dakkott moved his right hand under Julista's shirt, surprised that she offered no resistance. He lightly grasped her left breast and explored the softness. She began to unloosen his pants snaps.

"GIRGACH! Why is the pantry locked? Who locked the pantry?"

It was Ungbar.

Dakkott and Julista hurriedly fixed their clothing and tried to calm themselves before opening the pantry.

"Hey, Ungbar. We were looking for snacks. Had no idea there was a lock on this side of the door," Dakkott said. "Something you're looking for?"

Ungbar looked at his fellow cadets knowingly. "Uh-huh. You were hungry for something, but I bet it wasn't snacks. Don't worry, I'll never tell."

"Thanks to you, there's nothing to tell," said Julista. "Has anyone ever told you that you have terrible timing?"

"All right now, let's not be waspish," Ungbar countered. "Sexual frustration is not a good look on you."

"Aarrrggghhh. You giant *nimnule,*" she said. Then she stormed away.

The verbal pyrotechnics were much more heated, more explosive miles away above the ocean.

"*Yob tvoyu mat! Blyat!* (Motherfucker! No fucking way!)" screamed the Russian president after learning his accounts had been pilfered.

"I'm sorry, Mr. President," said the military aide who drew the frightening task of being the messenger. "I have also been informed that several of your advisers have reported that they are victims of a similar circumstance. We have not yet determined the scope of the damage."

The Russian leader threw a teacup against a wall. "Get me Ivanov. Get him now!" he bellowed.

"I am sorry again, Mr. President. I have more bad news to report; this time it involves Director Ivanov," said the aide.

"What could be worse than this? Go on," said the president.

"Director Ivanov was shot to death inside the Internet Research Agency this afternoon. His secretary was also killed," the aide said. "Witnesses said the agency's second-in-command, Dmitri Alexandrov, shot them both and then committed suicide. We don't yet know what motivated the attack."

"*Govno, govno, govno!* (Shit, shit, shit!)" said the president. "Who is running the IRA at this moment?"

"Yaroslav Kuznetsov. He was next in line," said the aide.

"Get me Kuznetsov. And then get me Maxim Everson," he ordered.

Kuznetsov attempted to explain what had happened, but he had little more information than the president had. Kuznetsov said he had been on the third floor when the shots were fired. The director and his secretary declared that they had been robbed and were forced to find old clothes to wear. Alexandrov shot them, then shot himself, he said.

"Enough about that. Who took my money? Where did my money go?" shouted the enraged president.

"We are investigating, Mr. President. The SuperMax team is baffled. There is nothing on the security cameras (the cameras had been holo-ed as well) to implicate any of our staff. This must have been an outside attack."

"Outside attack, eh?" said the president, who then shouted at the military aide. "Have we reached Everson yet?"

"Yes, Mr. President. He is holding."

"All right. Thank you, Kuznetsov. Let me know when you learn more." He hung up with the interim IRA director and told the aide to put Everson through.

"Hello there, V-Man. How are things in Vodka-land?" said the billionaire. "Ready for the next round of SuperMax?"

"*Nyet,* you *mudak* (asshole). Where is my money?" screamed the president.

"What do you mean? You have more money tucked into cubby-holes around the world than I do," said Everson.

The Russian president then gave a short, expletive-filled recounting of what had had happened.

"Nikolai's dead?" asked Everson.

"I don't care about Ivanov. Why all this sympathy now for that libidinous prick? I want my money back. Where is it?"

"I assure you, Mr. President, I have no idea. I know nothing about this. But I can get some of my best people on it."

The president sneered. "Your best people. I'm looking right at you, Everson. If my money is not back soon, it will be your head on the pike."

"I rather like my head where it is, Mr. President. Tell me whom to contact at the IRA, and we will try to get to the bottom of this."

"You had better do so and do so very quickly. Even with your billions, there is no place you can hide from us," the Russian leader said before slamming down the phone.

Everson clicked off his "special" phone. *That was uncomfortable,* he thought. *What fresh hell hath been wrought?*

The Chthonic was bearing down on the Caribbean after restocking at Atlantyss Complex. Ganplor was glazing the eyes of the cadets with a discussion of the finer points of Earth's Gulf Stream system when Anton received a message from the Protectorate. Given ALERT status, the message was in regard to some information uncovered recently by Xylodonian operatives working in Texas. The communiqué was thimble brief but offered a magnum of possibilities.

Ganplor gave Anton a curious look. Anton smiled.

"It appears the Russians are not very happy with their 'Benefactor.' "

CHAPTER 37

Ganplor found a deep and convenient location some miles removed from the mouth of the Mississippi to await nightfall, when commercial traffic on the river would slow to a trickle. Ellie would have liked to have taken her sister and the other cadets into New Orleans for a night of hurricanes, gumbo, beignets, and chicory coffee, but the second part of their mission remained.

It was near midnight when the Chthonic halted at its earlier river docking spot. Ganplor bade his passengers farewell as they gathered into their drone ferries. "I am pleased to have met you and glad to have been of service to your mission," he said. "I wish you good fortune with what you have yet to do."

Anton shook his hand. "Thank you, Ganplor. You and your crew are true professionals, and I will say so in my report. Best of luck to you, and may Neptune, the Earth god of the seas, smile on your path."

"I will take all of the smiling sea gods I can muster," said the Chthonic commander. He waved as the seven made their way to the shoreline. The frogs and crickets gave the travelers a victory serenade. Even the gently swaying tree branches seemed to be applauding.

Ellie watched as the drones returned to the Deep Watch ship and then observed with some fascination as the mother vessel slid into the river depths. Anton located the rental van, dusty after several days of sitting under foliage next to a busy river, and he pulled it around. The weary group settled in for the drive back to Hernando, enjoying a short respite when Anton pulled into the same truck stop from the initial journey.

Ellie turned on the van's radio, hoping to find one of the oldies rock stations she had come to love. "A little Queen or Prince would be good for your education, cadets," she told the fivesome behind her. She flipped past a number of country and religious stations, stopping when she heard a female news broadcaster say, "Somewhere in the world, some cyber criminals are not very happy."

Ellie turned up the volume and shushed the cadets, who leaned in to listen.

The broadcaster continued. "In our top story this hour, officials for a number of U.S. banks targeted in recent cyberattacks are reporting that all of the missing funds have been returned. Additionally, bank officials in Mississippi, targeted in an earlier attack, say their funds have been returned as well.

"The bank officials have declined to say how much money was transferred electronically out of U.S. accounts, but it is believed to be in the millions of dollars. U.S. intelligence officials won't say who was behind the attacks, stating only that the incidents are still under investigation.

"However, the White House was quick to claim credit for the return of the bank funds, with an administration spokeswoman stating that the fear of potential sanctions likely had motivated the hackers, who remain at large, to reverse the thefts. The spokeswoman would not say what country would have been hit with those sanctions. The president, meanwhile, blamed 'DEI hires' at the banks for creating lax security that allowed the hackers to accomplish the thefts.

"We will bring you more on this story as information becomes available. Turning now to the weather…"

Ellie turned off the radio. "Can you believe that? That pompous *girgach* is taking credit for what we did. He was probably playing golf the whole time we were gone."

Anton shook his head. "No surprise. And it's not like we can come forward to the human news media and say, 'No, it was us who got your money back.' There is no one who can contest what he says."

"*M'ach sheerok gradakh*! Ellie fumed for most of the ride back. The cadets tried to sleep. For Anton, sleep came only when he desired it.

An excited Gator greeted them all as they entered the house, twirling and wagging his tail. The cadets began filling Roggbach in on what had transpired.

"How is our guest?" Anton asked Roggbach.

"The human is holo-sedated, you might say. I have allowed him to eat, drink water, and use the facilities—all under my supervision, of course," he replied. "This human is very strange. I allowed him to select his food, and all he desired was something called canned chili with beans. He would eat it right out of the can. Oh, yes. And something called Chef Boyardee ravioli as well."

"Cold?"

"Yes, Guardian."

"Just Anton or Michael is fine...depending. Well, I guess there was little meal cleanup to do. So, he was no trouble?"

"No, Anton."

"Good to hear. What about Gator? Any problems?"

"No, Anton. He enjoyed his walks, and he liked to sleep next to me."

"That sounds like him. Can't be away from 'his' people very long. He likes his pack."

Anton walked over and gave Ellie a kiss. "It's good to be home, even if it's for a short time. I am going to report in to the Protectorate and see if there are further instructions. What are you up to?"

"Since we may be gone a few more days, I thought I might teach a couple of these Guardian wannabes how to drive an Earth vehicle. They may need to use the vehicle while we are gone."

"Ooooo. Too bad I'm going to miss that. Who are your first victims?" Anton asked.

"Sister! Dakkott! You're with me." The two cadets followed Ellie outside and to the Tesla. Anton chuckled, then headed to the secret comm chamber. The other cadets turned on the television.

Anton reported their safe return to Hernando, duplicating part of the report already dispatched by Ganplor. He added that the American president was taking credit for the return of the stolen monies, an unexpected development that was met with howls of derision by Sub-Protector Korphan and his aides.

"How did the cadets perform?" Korphan asked at the conclusion of Anton's presentation.

"Spectacularly. They followed orders without complaint and did a stellar job of watching our backsides. Gorthand was particularly useful on the ship's computers. I would think they deserve commendations."

"Commendations? I was thinking of how it would mitigate their punishment. Let me think upon it," Korphan said. "By the way, I have arranged for a refueling for their Dart Lurker at a point when it can be safely performed."

"Sub-protector, I would like to take one of the cadets on the second leg of our assignment. We may need the extra eyes."

"As you see fit, Guardian. But keep them out of danger," Korphan said. "Speaking of the final leg, I want you to rendezvous with two of our Texas operatives, Xylar-17 and Zeequon-5. Their human personas are Charles Loving and George Nelson. They have done surveillance on the property you are targeting."

"Xylar and Zeequon. Got it, sub-protector. Any changes to the mission, sir?"

"No. We don't want any human lives lost, but we can't have this human meddling with our operations ever again."

"Yes, sir. I think I have something in mind, sir."

"Ha. I well know how creative you can be, Guardian," Korphan said. "Too creative sometimes."

"First things first," said Ellie, taking a paper object out of her handbag. It was a bumper sticker. "Teslas have gotten a bad rap of late. You might blame it on managerial misconduct. Anyway, this might provide a cleansing of sorts."

Ellie appended the decal to the rear of the vehicle. *I bought this when*

Teslas were cool, the bumper sticker read. "There now. Much better," she said.

"What is that all about?" her sister asked.

"It's a long story. The maker of this car is about as popular as *geezmar* spit right now. So, you might call it a dose of anti-asshole protection," Ellie replied.

The two cadets looked at one another, shrugged, then got in the car.

Ellie drove Julista and Dakkott to the large parking lot adjacent to the high school football stadium. Luckily, there were few cars in the lot, and most of them were parked near the stadium. She switched places with her sister, putting her in the driver's seat while Dakkott observed from the back. She had the two cadets go through many of the touchscreen options that the car provided. "Many of these features are similar to those on the Dart Lurker, at least in how they operate," Dakkott said. He watched Julista adjust the mirrors, climate controls, sound system, and other functions using the large touchscreen.

"This vehicle is somewhat different from other human transports. For one thing—and this may seem counterintuitive—the car starts when you press the brake," Ellie said, pointing at the pedal.

Julista followed her sister's hint, and the car purred to life.

"Wow," said Julista.

"OK, now, there is a gear selector—kind of a shifter stick—on the right side of the steering column that allows you to change between drive, reverse, and park. Move the shifter to reverse, and let's back up a few feet."

Julista did as asked.

"OK, now put it in drive and press the accelerator pedal," Ellie said. "But be ready to hit the brake if necessary."

Julista was shocked by the jolt from the sudden acceleration. She zoomed nearly 250 feet before Ellie's cries of "Brake! Brake!" sank in.

"*Girgach!* That was amazing. Give it wings, and it could fly," Julista said.

Ellie allowed Julista to circle the parking lot a few times before repeating the instructional exercise with Dakkott. "This would be an exceptional ride out on the plains of Xylodon," he said.

"It might be a little hard explaining how you got it there," Ellie said. "OK, who wants ice cream?"

Anton walked about into the living room and found the other four cadets almost rolling in laughter.

"What did I miss?" he asked.

Gorthand said, "We found a human television program called 'Star Wars.' There are these beings called Jedi Knights who can send out compulsion beams using their minds. And they have talking robots. And spaceships many times larger than ours."

"And they do close combat with something called light sabers," Margeen said. "I could use one of those for those hormonally over-charged first-year Academy *nimnules*. A blue one. Hit the button. *Zooob, zooob*. There goes an arm. *Zooob, zooob*. There goes a leg. *Zooob, zooob*. There goes their…"

Ungbar cut her off. "We get it, Margeen," he said. "Be careful now. I'm beginning to think you have penis on the brain. And here I was thinking you'd use Jedi mind tricks to make your breasts look bigger."

"*Sheerok*. Not that you'd be interested, Ungbar, speaking of penis envy. Anton, I heard a word on another Earth TV program the other day. *Fuckhead*," Margeen said. "Would that apply to Ungbar?"

"Leave me out of this fight. But I'm glad to see you are enjoying the show. Just wait until you see Luke lift a spaceship with only his mind," Anton said. "All right, I have an update. Sub-Protector Korphan has arranged for a refueling ship so we can get you back to Xylodon. But before that occurs, Ellie and I must complete our mission. We need one of you to come with us. Roggbach, since you did not go on the St. Petersburg mission, I am asking you to volunteer for this part. The rest of you can remain here. There are a half dozen or more episodes of 'Star Wars' you can watch. The spinoffs are fairly good as well. Check out 'The Mandalorian.' "

"Indeed, Guardian. Thank you, Anton," Gorthand said.

"Oh, Dakkott? Julista? If you take Gator on a walk, try to stay away from the yellow brick road," Anton advised.

"Yellow brick road? Why avoid that road?" Julista asked.

"Because that's where the dogs of society howl," replied the Guardian.

Julista gave a puzzled look to her sister.

"Never mind him. He's being a *yeepnall,*" said Ellie. "There are no yellow brick roads in Hernando. No brick roads that I know of, either. He's about to learn where the doghouse of society is."

Anton shrugged with an amused look.

Roggbach asked, "Just so I can prepare, what is it you want me to do on this mission, Guardian?"

"I need you to be a guard dog," he replied. "For one Jonnie Barnes Jr."

CHAPTER 38

"Stop. Stop. There it is! There it is!" shouted an exuberant Ellie.

She, Anton, Roggbach, and the still holo-sedated Jonnie Barnes were on the outskirts of Houston, and a treasured landmark for many Xylodonians had come into view: Buc-ee's. In fact, it was the same mega-gas station Ellie and Anton had stopped at months before while driving to New Mexico. At some point in the early days of Operation Silent Vigilance, a Guardian had become so enamored with the Buc-ee's franchise, with its tasty snacks and spotless restrooms, that the name was bequeathed upon Xylodon's Neptune Station. Buc-ee's became a must-stop for Centurion Guardians assigned to the southern United States. Less fortunate Guardians took comfort in learning the franchise was expanding northward.

Anton steered the van into the massive parking area. Ellie began to chant, "Buc-ee Nuggets. Buc-ee Nuggets." Roggbach looked at her in bemused confusion. "Ooooo. You have to try them, Roggbach. Consider that an order," she said.

"Yes, Guardian. What about our passenger?"

"I suppose we can allow him to use the facilities and select refreshments," she said. "Reduce the compulsion level so he can attend to his needs, but don't let him out of your sight."

"As you wish, Guardian."

For Anton and Ellie, it was like a reunion with an old acquaintance. For Roggbach, it was like nothing he had ever seen. He was "ordered" to visit the restrooms to see firsthand what had spawned the nickname for Neptune Station. They bought T-shirts, Nuggets, brisket sandwiches, and cold drinks for themselves and a large bag of beef jerky for Jonnie Barnes. Anton found that appropriate on a couple of levels.

As Anton approached a Buc-ee's checkout lane, an excited Ellie motioned at him. "Come here, come here. You have to see this. You won't believe it."

She led him to a display of wind chimes. "Look at this one." She pointed to a three-foot chime that had a metallic alligator at the center surrounded by five metallic bars. "It's a gator chime. Every time we hear it, it will be like Gator talking to us. This has to come home with us."

Anton gave her a kiss. "Once again, my love, you are a genius."

Once they left the tourist spa, Anton took the central loop around Houston—the sprawling city has three roadway rings—and pointed the rental van west toward Austin, the state capital. They had arranged to rendezvous with Xylar-17 and Zeequon-5 in Elgin, a town of around 12,000 about thirty minutes from Austin and its suburbs. Anton had GPS coordinates to the meeting site, which turned out to be Southside Market & Barbeque, whose "original hot guts" sausage had lured many a traveler from the road. The smoky aroma of the restaurant was its calling card, extending a quarter mile from its point of origin. Many of the decisions that had shaped Elgin's future over the years had been sopped in Southside sauce.

The parking lot was nearly full this late afternoon as Anton pulled in. Roggbach remained in the van with Jonnie Barnes while Anton, who looked over photos of their contacts' human personas once again, and Ellie went inside the building, which was one part restaurant, one part market. Large menu boards adorned one wall of the barnlike interior, demarking the ordering and prep area. Rows of tables and chairs cordoned off much of the large room. Anton fought the pull of smoked delights and scanned the expansive restaurant. Seated at a window table was Xylar-17 (Charles Loving) and Zeequon-5 (George Nelson). Charles was wearing a straw cowboy hat, and George crowned himself with a green and yellow John Deere ballcap. Both had well-attended sausage and brisket plates before them, accompanied by the almost obligatory sweet iced tea. There were no customers at the tables nearest them, protecting their conversation.

"Howdy, Charles. George," said Anton, who took a seat next to Xylar. Ellie sat down next to Zeequon. "Looks like you fellas hit the feedbag mighty hard."

"Howdy your own self," said Xylar. "You cain't beat the barbecue in Central Texas. That's one of the beauties of being stationed between San Antonio and Austin. Nearly every small town has a barbecue joint like this one."

"What about you, George? Where did the Protectorate stick you?" Ellie asked Zeequon.

"Mostly El Paso, but I wander off to Van Horn and Odessa from time to time," he said. "I mostly keep an eye on Fort Bliss and Blue Venture. That's one of the two private space-launch companies trying to buck out here. Xylar's got the other one. There's a lot of energy production out here, so I file reports on that as well."

"We drove through West Texas awhile back. Stopped in Marfa. How do you like it out there?" Ellie inquired.

"Marfa? We flew in over Marfa once. I like it out there. Reminds me quite a bit of home. Hot, Dry. Sandy," Zeequon replied. "The people are friendly and pretty chatty if you buy them a Shiner or Budweiser."

The comment made Ellie reflective. "Yes, Anton and I had a human friend we were quite fond of. He brought us together, actually. Humans are such strange creatures. Capable of incredible feats of bravery and empathy while also capable of terrible acts of cruelty and ignorance."

Xylar and Zeequon nodded, recalling their own unique experiences.

"Here's a new one. You folks had to take up arms yet against the Furries?" Xylar proffered.

Anton raised his eyebrows. "The Furries?"

"Yep. These are people, kids mostly, who dress up like dogs and cats. Hence the name Furries."

Ellie sensed a trap of some kind. "O-kayyyy. Sounds a bit eccentric, but where's the harm?"

"Litter boxes," deadpanned Xylar.

Anton and Ellie replied in unison. "Litter boxes?"

"Yup. Supposedly, kids are assuming the personas of their dress-up characters. They are forcing schools to provide them with litter boxes," Xylar chortled. "That's the story, anyway. What began as a rumor is now a full-fledged landslide of a conspiracy theory. Kind of like that story about the Ohio town where folks were accused of eating dogs and cats and geese. We got a lawmaker from out Smithville way who has introduced a bill to prohibit schools from allowing what he calls 'nonhuman behavior.' Like peeing in a litter box. Naturally, his bill provides an exception for school mascots. Them Cougars and Tigers and Mustangs are all safe for now."

Ellie shook her head. "What about stage productions like 'Cats' and 'The Wizard of Oz'? No more Cowardly Lion?"

"Don't know about that," said Xylar. "Now, mind you, this has all been debunked by the human news media, but who cares about facts when the lie is so much more fun, right? You start with just a seed of truth—a couple of schools apparently got litter boxes in case the campuses were ever on lockdown—and the conspiracy mill just goes epic."

"Wow," remarked Ellie. "And you say the story has been debunked?"

"Several times. But like a virus, it keeps coming back," Xylar said. "That state lawmaker? He claims he was told about schools having litter boxes by a school official during a phone call. But when she was asked about it later, that school official denied ever saying anything like that."

Ellie glanced at Anton. He had that look on his face. *Uh-oh. Here it comes,* she thought. Anton raised an interceding hand. "I bet I know why so many folks wouldn't believe the litter box story had been debunked," he said. "They thought it was yellow journalism."

Xylar and Zeequon just stared at him, then shook their heads. Ellie kicked him under the table.

"What about you, Zeequon?" Ellie inquired. "Got any Earth stories to share?"

"What I can't wrap my head around is all this reliance on religion. We moved away from that centuries ago," Zeequon said. "These humans do a lot of good things in the name of religion, and then they will turn around and go to war with one another because one religion is different than another."

"You're not wrong there, Zeequon. There's a bunch of religions going around, all claiming to be the 'one true path.' I get tickled watching these humans raise holy hell on Friday and Saturday, then they make sure their butt's in a pew on Sunday," Xylar said.

Ellie listened intently. "Yes, hypocrisy abounds. It has been my observation that religion brings out the best—and the worst—in humans. Aren't there still some religious groups on Xylodon?"

"Yes, mostly in the hinterlands, from what I've read. But they are not all that cult-y about it. Their dogma is usually something about personal growth and reshaping attitudes. They don't try to dispute science," Zeequon said. "But you have a point about the hypocrisy of humans, though. I went to one of the humans' churches one Sunday to see what it was like. The sign outside the church said 'Baptist' something or other, but I didn't know what that meant."

"What happened?" asked Ellie.

"It was pretty interesting. Lots of rituals. There was some beautiful singing that made you feel good enough to put some bills in the plate they passed around. Then a feller got up and started shouting about what lowlifes we all are and how we should be ashamed of ourselves and that we all were on the road to some place called Hell. One minute they're lifting you up, and then the next they are tearing you down," Zeequon recalled. "After the service, I talked to a few folks in the parking lot and asked some questions. Got some interesting answers."

He paused for his audience.

"OK, what did you ask and what did they say, Zeequon?" Ellie asked.

"I said to one couple, 'I didn't notice any Black families in here.

Aren't they welcome?' The man says, 'Yes, they are, but they would have to sit on the back row.' I puzzled over that comment. I think he meant that they would need to be kept separate from the white folks at the service. But by my way of thinking, being on the back row puts you closer to the exit when the show is over."

Ellie and Xylar silently attempted to absorb Zeequon's experience.

Anton brought them all back to the moment.

"Speaking of having the spirit move you, are you fellas about done?" Anton asked. "Don't mean to hurry you, but we have an Academy cadet holding the fort outside. And we can chat more safely on the road."

"You have a cadet? Man, those days at the Academy seem like a hundred years ago," said Xylar. "Is this a new program?"

"I'll explain in the van. I assume you brought some equipment with you."

"Sure did. Got some nice little toys," Zeequon said.

Ellie stood. "I will meet you all at the van. I've got something to do first."

Anton figured Ellie's latter comment was code for needing to use the restroom. Xylar and Zeequon led him to a silver Tundra pickup, and the two pulled large black duffel bags from the storage area behind the seats. He guided them to the van, and they placed their gear inside and found some seats.

"Xylar, Zeequon, let me introduce you to Roggbach. Roggbach, this is Xylar and Zeequon. Or Charles and George."

If there had been room, Roggbach would have come to attention. "Greetings, Guardians," he said formally.

"No need for all those protocols. This ain't the Academy," Xylar said. "But back at ya, cadet. Who's the quiet, putrid-lookin' fella back there?"

Roggbach looked to Anton, who replied, "Meet Mr. Jonnie Barnes Jr. He's a little surprise I added to our mission. I think you will appreciate it."

Ellie opened the front passenger door carrying a large plastic bag, which she opened to reveal a variety of smoked edibles from the attached market. "Leave it to Mother to remember to bring snacks," she said. "And a little something to bring home."

Anton leaned over and gave her a kiss. "I knew there was a reason why I love you."

The van pulled out and headed toward Austin.

"OK, let's talk. How much did Korphan tell you?" Anton asked.

"Just the broad strokes," Xylar said. "That Everson was the architect behind a cyberattack that hurt our Earth operations. And that he involved the Russians in some way."

Zeequon snorted. "I'm glad Everson is in your surveillance area and not mine. I read about him all the time. What a *girgach* asshole."

"Yeah, he's an attention whore, all right," Xylar chuckled. "So, what does the Protectorate have in mind for Mr. Everson?"

"We were able to remove Everson's new software off of the Russian computers," Anton said. "But it's dangerous, and we need to know if he has copies. Korphan wants that program to never be used again. He said the order comes from the highest levels. The Presidium."

"The Presidium? Wow, ol' Max sure pissed some people off," Zeequon said. "This should be fun."

Ellie offered some beef jerky to Roggbach, Anton, and their new companions. "Where are you two from on Xylodon, and how long have you been on Earth?"

Xylar looked at Zeequon, who nodded to him to go first.

"I'm from the Xylodonian sticks. Out near Denthos. Been in the Security Service for twelve years and on Earth for eight. I've only been stationed in Texas, but I travel around when I can. Got to see the big Hollywood sign in Los Angeles last year."

Zeequon picked up when Xylar paused. "I'm from the capital. Xylos. So, I'm a city brat. Been in the service almost fifteen years. Spent some time on Neptune Base. Then I was part of our China team. That was up until that other American billionaire started launching rockets into space. One thing's for certain: not much Chinese food in West Texas."

"I bet. Not much in Mississippi either," said Ellie.

"OK, let's get back to the mission," Anton said. Ellie stuck her tongue out at him. "You're no fun," she said, winking at the two Guardians.

"I think it best we pay Mr. Everson a visit at night. But how will we know he's home?" Anton asked.

Xylar placed his arm where both Anton and Ellie could see his holo-biotrometer. "Everson has homes all over the world, right? One of the perks of being Earth's richest man. One of those homes is outside Austin, where we're headed. I figured he'd be one human the Protectorate would be interested in keeping track of. So, I managed to put trackers on his plane and his primary vehicle. Now, that's not proof that he's inside the residence, but that has always been the case so far. Right now, his plane is at a private Austin airfield, and his car is at his Austin mansion."

"Excellent. We're in luck then. Let me know if that changes," Anton said.

"How do you intend to get inside?" asked Zeequon. "He's got a perimeter fence. Guards. Probably security cameras out the wazoo."

Anton smiled. "I've thought about that. When you have to get into Troy, you might need a Trojan horse."

CHAPTER 39

If you thought five cadets who had traveled across half a galaxy to find Earth were going to stay confined to a two-bedroom house in Hernando, Mississippi, you would be…naïve.

On the first day after the two Guardians and Roggbach had left, the cadets contented themselves with making popcorn and watching reruns of "My Favorite Martian," "Lost in Space," and "Star Trek." They were impressed that Spock didn't need a holo to do his mind tricks, while the robot accompanying the Robinsons reminded them of some Xylodonian museum pieces. Ungbar became overly enamored with the phrase, "DANGER. DANGER, Will Robinson," almost to the point of exile.

But the cadets began to grow restless behind the curtains. At first it was simple ventures. They would take Gator on walks by themselves or in pairs. Initially, they assumed the personas of Anton and Ellie, but after having not experienced any human encounters, they decided any human persona would suffice as long as Gator walked point.

Julista and Dakkott enjoyed walking the canine, what with his tail wagging and his sniffing of the world's wonders. The sojourns also gave them time to talk.

Julista reached for Dakkott's hand. "Everything is so green here. I can see why Ellie enjoys Earth so. I can also see why the Protectorate sees Earth as dangerous," she said.

"Yes. From what I have been reading, it seems like every time the humans pass a law, another group of humans finds ways to get around that law," Dakkott said. "Their system of health care also puzzles me. They let other humans die simply because of money. Life should have no price tag."

"Indeed. Heal the person, then see what they can contribute to society," she said. "Oh, well, if they only would put us in charge…"

Dakkott chuckled. "If only…"

Gator began sniffing at a fire ant mound. Julista tugged on his leash just as a paw crushed part of the mound. Ants began pouring out.

"No, Gator. Get back from there," she said sternly. Then she looked at Dakkott. "Changing the subject, we have not had an opportunity to finish the conversation we started on the Chthonic," Julista said, adopting a naughty tone.

"I have been looking for such a moment, but there have been too many eyes. And just when I thought some privacy was possible, then that Barnes human showed up."

"Yes. Even while holo-ed his presence was unsettling. Did little for the mood, one might say."

Dakkott nodded. "Hey, we are almost to that...what do they call it? Convenience store. Want something to drink?"

Ellie had left the cadets with some cash and a credit card. "That sounds good. I bet Gator is thirsty, too," Julista replied.

As Dakkott and Julista neared the store, they spotted three older boys in the side parking lot surrounding a smaller Black boy.

"Leave me alone," the small boy said.

The tallest of the trio said, "Curtis Moooooooo-ton. C'mon, moo like a cow. That mean you are full of bullshit? Moooooooo!"

"Bite me," spat Curtis. "I ain't mooing for nobody."

One of the other boys stuck a leg behind Curtis, and the tallest boy pushed Curtis over that leg, sending him to the pavement. His arm began bleeding from the scrapes.

The third boy kicked Curtis. "Stay down, you little punk. Your kind ain't nothin' but punks."

Rage fired Curtis, but before he could stand, one of his antagonists tripped him again.

Gator began barking. Dakkott then yelled, “Hey! Stop it.”

Julista touched her “watch” and a small beam of light, barely visible in the brilliant sunshine, was emitted.

The three older boys suddenly could not move their legs.

“What the hail?” one of them said.

Curtis stood. Then he smiled. And then he kicked each of the antagonists in the crotch.

Julista touched her holo again, and the three boys crumpled to the ground in agony. Then they half writhed, half stumbled away as Curtis watched.

“I doan know what yous did, but thanky, y’all,” the boy said.

“Not a problem. I think they must have gotten scared stiff when they saw us,” Dakkott said. “We’re glad you’re all right. You are all right, right? And what’s your name, young fella?”

“Curtis. Curtis Mouton. I was headed over to the school to shoot some hoops when those fools jumped me.”

“Hi, Curtis. I’m...Julie. And this is my friend David. We’re here visiting my aunt and uncle. She’s Ellie Atkinson. He’s An...Michael Gort.”

Curtis’ eyes widened. “You-all related to Coach Gort? He’s the best. He’s my favorite teacher, and I don’t even have his class.”

“That’s good to hear,” Dakkott said. "Say, are you thirsty? We were headed to the store for something cold to drink. Our treat.”

“Man, yous folks is nice. Not ever’body like that ’round here.”

“We noticed,” Julista said. “Curtis, meet Gator. Gator, meet Curtis.”

Dakkott procured the drinks while Julista and Curtis waited outside. Curtis gave them a wave as they parted. “Bye, Gator,” he shouted.

Gator’s tail wagged.

Dakkott and Julista smiled as they walked back. “More humans saved from other humans,” Dakkott said.

Julista turned to him with an excited expression. “Hey, let’s celebrate our victory with some pizza!”

Dakkott nodded his approval. “You better do the driving, though.”

About thirty minutes later, the five cadets were seated around a table with three large pizzas before them. The pies never stood a chance.

"I wish we had restaurants like this on Xylodon," Margeen said. "This is amazing."

"Where are we going to get the sausage and the pepperoni and the beef from?" Gorthand countered.

"Well, that's a problem. Maybe we can make them artificially. Or maybe we use our own ingredients. Nebula berries, *mannug* peppers, and *jarm* algae might be good with sauce and cheese," Margeen replied. "Can you imagine operating a pizza place next to the Academy? We'd be rich!"

"Isn't that just like a female? I thought you wanted to serve our planet," Ungbar said, ladling his comment in sarcasm. "Dangle a little coin in front of a girl, and look what happens."

"Ppfffftttt. *Nimnule,*" Margeen spat.

Julista tossed her napkin onto the table. "Anyone up for ice cream?"

The query was met by unanimous consent. Fortunately for the cadets, Dell's Frozen Treats was just a door down from the pizza joint.

The five sat outside eating cones of various flavors and pastels.

"I wonder how Anton, Ellie, and Roggbach are doing," Margeen mused between licks.

"I'm sure they are doing fine," Julista said. "Look at all they have done on Earth so far without being detected."

"I wonder how Jonnie Barnes is doing," Ungbar said. "He's kind of cute in the right light."

Gorthand elbowed him. "You are one disgusting individual, Ungbar. You know that, don't you?"

Ungbar blew him a kiss.

Dakkott then shared the story about the encounter with the young Black human. "No wonder the Protectorate sends Guardians to watch Earth. These humans learn cruelty at an early age," he said.

"I wouldn't mind being stationed here," Margeen said. "As long as I can have pizza. And ice cream."

They all laughed then finished up and went back to the house for more "Star Trek."

Obtaining bathroom time wasn't easy in a house with five beings, much less eight. But Dakkott managed to grab a shower while the others watched the USS Enterprise become overrun by tribbles.

Afterward, wearing only a towel, he walked into the garage and its secret comm room to get some fresh clothes. In the dim light, he saw Julista's head and bare shoulder under the quilt on his cot. She lifted the covers to reveal much more.

"Ready to finish that conversation?"

Dakkott said nothing. The towel dropped.

CHAPTER 40

In Greek lore, the Trojan horse that procured the end of the ten-year war between Greece and Troy was a monstrous wooden edifice that secretly held, according to various accounts, thirty to forty Greek warriors inside its bowels, including Ithaca's king, Odysseus. It was the Trojans themselves, celebrating their presumed triumph, who sealed their doom by pulling the massive horse within their gates.

Such a horse was not needed to get inside Maxim Everson's gates. It took only a Cybertruck.

It was nearly closing time when "Charles" was dropped off at the Cybertruck rental facility in Austin. The transaction took almost twenty minutes, but Zeequon eventually had the satisfaction of knowing he was reducing his carbon footprint and feeling the thrill of all-wheel drive, all while enclosed in state-of-the-art features including advanced safety technology. He had no intention of being safe, however.

Zeequon followed the van to a liquor store—the Guardians' Trojan horse needed a modern-day twist to the ruse—then to a wooded area the operatives had selected earlier. Xylar took one look at the Cybertruck and shook his head. "This thing looks like a half-blind shade tree mechanic ran out of tin foil before they finished it."

"Yes, it is hideous. But its acceleration ability far surpasses its looks. You would love driving it over the hills of Denthos," Zeequon said.

"Let's get ready," Anton said. "It's time to put one of your toys to use."

"The drone?" Xylar asked. Anton nodded. Xylar then pulled a hawk-shaped device from his duffel bag. "It's my own variation," he said. He motioned Roggbach to stand beside him and learn how to use the drone controller. Handling the drone and watching for unwanted passersby would be the cadet's primary duties during the operation—that and watching Jonnie Barnes. The other three Guardians tested their communications and other equipment.

The hawk-drone was equipped with a high-resolution camera and heat sensors that were more cutting edge than the Cybertruck's features. Even at a half mile altitude and with the sun not yet completely down, the hawk was able to detect the body-heat signatures of various humans within the villa and around the pool area. The hawk had a sound-detection feature as well.

"OK, it's working fine. Let's bring it back for when we really need it," Xylar told Roggbach.

Fortress Everson was a 14,400-square-foot villa within a walled compound located in the hilly outskirts of Austin. Adjoining properties within the compound gave residence to the consenting wombs that had produced Maxim Everson's growing number of babies. The villa itself had six bedrooms, to which Maxim's concubines had access only according to his discretion and mood. An extravagant pool and hot tub rested at the foot of the villa, itself largely walled as was the exterior of the property. There were multiple fireplaces and three cupolas, one substantially larger than its brothers, standing vigil along the roofline. The entire compound was bedecked in rancid opulence.

The four Guardians and Roggbach watched as evening changed into deep nightfall. The lights that had earlier shone brightly from the villa and from neighboring homes went out one by one. The voices and music that could be heard earlier were now quiet. A coolness settled quietly over the enclave, as if lulling it to sleep.

Anton felt an unexpected twinge of anticipation, something he had not felt when he stood before Congress or faced off with white supremacist human traffickers. Those humans had not posed a possible threat to his planet. Everson and his software did.

It was almost 2 a.m. when Anton signaled Roggbach to send the hawk-drone over Everson's compound. Roggbach put on a pair of headphones and peered at the images relayed from the drone to the controller screen. There had been no road traffic for nearly an hour. All was quiet except for the occasional dog bark.

After about ten minutes of aerial patrolling, the drone had located three heat signatures—one near the main gate, one near the main entrance and one in an upstairs room. "The two signatures outside the main house move from time to time," Roggbach said. "The signature upstairs remains still."

Roggbach maneuvered the hawk-drone slowly over the compound's exterior, detecting numerous motion sensors and motion-activated lights amid the trees and gauche statuary. "Fortunately, these all are powered from a central energy source," he told Anton and Ellie. "There," Roggbach said as the drone cut the power supply. "So much for that. I can't do anything about the power to the cameras without outing all power to the house."

"That's OK. We can deal with that once we get inside. Any change in the humans' movements?"

"No, Guardian. No change."

"It's too bad we don't have the American rock star Jim Morrison with us on this mission," Anton said.

Oh, no, thought Ellie.

The other three Xylodonians looked at him curiously. "Why, Guardian?" asked Xylar.

"He could find all the Doors."

Ellie shook her head. The other two Guardians just looked at one another in silent disbelief. Roggbach remained as puzzled as before.

"Why can't we recruit this Morrison?" he asked. "We could use our holos."

"Well, he's dead, so that's a problem. OK, then. Let's move out," Anton said.

Xylar and Zeequon took the lead in the Cybertruck. Anton and Ellie followed slowly at a short distance, without headlights, and with

Roggbach and Jonnie Barnes in the back. They watched as the Cybertruck advanced up the road alongside Everson's compound. The Cybertruck virtually roared with sudden acceleration then veered left into the compound. Second later, there was a thunderous crash and the screech of metal on metal. The twin gates were now little more than twisted wreckage. The Cybertruck came to a halt about fifteen yards past the gate, angled partly on the grass along the driveway, lights still on. From the van, Roggbach could detect two figures running toward the vehicle.

The first guard rapped his knuckles on the driver's side window. "Charles" rolled down the window, then was almost blinded by a flashlight glare in his eyes. "Wass up, partner? Get that damn light outta my eyes," he slurred toward the guard. The vehicle's interior reeked of bourbon. "Wass you doin' at my house? You doan live here."

"This isn't your house, you fucking idiot," the guard said. "You just crashed into the wrong damn place." The guard pointed his flashlight toward the passenger seat. The male passenger, wearing a cowboy hat, appeared to have passed out, head against the window.

The second guard ran up to join his comrade. "Goddamn, Daron. What happened? We're fucked if Mr. Everson wakes up. You know how he is about his sleep," said the second man.

"Keep your voice down, Tucker. These two drunk sonsabitches just ran through the front gate. Fucked it all up," Daron said. "Think we should call the cops? That'd wake the prick up for sure."

"I don't know. You know the cheap bastard won't want to pay for the gate," said Tucker. "Maybe we can get some IDs and insurance info off these A-holes. Doesn't look like they are in any shape to drive."

The two security men each opened a car door and began searching for wallets.

"Charles" held up his left arm as an offering to Daron. "Wouldja call my wife? Ro-Ro-Ro-berta ser name. She's gonna be peee-issed," he said.

Daron returned to his guard voice. "I ain't calling no-…"

Before he could finish, there were twin flashes of light.

"Charles" and "George" got out of the vehicle and moved the holo-frozen guards into some thick bushes. They adjusted their body shapes to accommodate the guards' clothing and took on their appearance. Zeequon pointed a flashlight into the sky, a signal to the drone and the van. Anton and Ellie arrived moments later.

Like the Earps and Doc Holliday at the OK Corral, the four Guardians marched up the driveway to Everson's villa.

CHAPTER 41

"OK, Maxie Waxy. Time to wakey-wakey."

Maxim Everson stirred. Was that a real voice he heard? He noticed that his headphones had been removed as he pulled down his blindfold. Although his vision was still fuzzy, he made out a figure seated in one of the two wingback chairs near the window.

"Who the hell are you?" Everson said in a slumberous bark.

"We can save the introductions for later. As Ricky may or may not have said to Lucy: Max, you've got some 'splainin' to do," said Anton.

Everson rose to the side of the bed. There was a quick flash of light from his right.

"And who the fuck are you?" Everson said to the dark-clad figure in the shadows of his sanctum sanctorum.

"Who, me? I'm just the backup singer," Ellie said.

"GUARDS! DARON! HELP!" Everson screamed.

"Shut up, you *sheerok girgach*. No one is going to hear you whimpering, you fucking asshole. It's time for you to listen and not speak," Anton said, leaning forward in the chair.

About fifteen minutes before Everson was roused from a dream about a sixteen-year-old girl who had asked for his autograph,

"Daron" and "Tucker" had entered the mansion to look around, and the pair quickly determined the first floor was clear. Roggbach messaged Anton that the sleeping figure upstairs had not moved despite all the commotion at the gate.

"Good. Recall the drone and bring Mr. Barnes to the house," Anton said.

Xylar waited for Roggbach while Zeequon searched for any room that might be a control site for the external security cameras. It didn't take long for Zeequon to locate the mansion's first-floor "surveillance center." There were almost four dozen screens monitoring various areas of the property as well as a handful of computer servers. He began killing the feeds but then had to chuckle—Everson was spying on the residences that were housing his various "baby mamas" and offspring. *I wonder if they know,* he thought. He noticed there were cameras placed in several bathrooms and showers as well. *Welcome to Perv Central,* Zeequon thought. He then began erasing the night's image recordings on all hard drives in the room.

Anton and Ellie had crept quietly upstairs and down a long hallway until they found the room that Roggbach had indicated was holding the third human heat signature. Ellie silently turned the doorknob, and the two Guardians entered the expansive chamber. A truck-size Persian rug stretched across the polished wooden floor. A floor-to-ceiling fireplace, adorned with a variety of what appeared to be medieval carvings and crests, stared back at them as the two advanced. A half down impressionist paintings—Monet? Manet? Degas? Pizzaro? It was hard to determine in the dark—flanked the fireplace. There were doors to their right, perhaps leading to closets, a bathroom or some adjoining room.

To the left was an oversize four-poster bed, possibly made of cherry or walnut. A figure in navy blue silk pajamas was lying on his left side upon the bed's covers, facing the windows. He was wearing a night mask and had an air pod in his right ear. His right hand seemed to be entertaining his crotch.

Anton sat down while Ellie kept a watch position at the foot of the bed.

Now awakened, Everson rose to sit on the edge of the bed,

steadying himself by grasping the bedpost with his right hand. That was as far as he could move. His face, hands, and feet were almost albino white in the moonlight.

"Max, Max, Max. Can I call you Max?" Anton asked. "Oh, that's right. You can't talk. That's fine; I wanted you to listen anyway. Well, Max, you've been a very bad boy."

"Mmm-mm-mmmm-mmm," said Everson in the best reply he could muster.

"It appears you have created a bit of software that endangers the interests of some folks who are much higher on the food chain than you are. Much higher. They are concerned, Max."

"Mm-mmmm-mm-mmmm."

"What do you call this software? Have a name for it?" asked Anton, who gave a nod to Ellie. She twisted a dial on her holo, allowing Everson to speak.

"We named it SuperMax."

"Oh, I bet you did. And I bet there wasn't a 'we' involved either. Well, you should know that my friends and I removed all traces of SuperMax from the devices of your Russian friends. It appears that they aren't too happy about that. Some of them think you are responsible for its disappearance. You might have a target on your back, Max."

Ellie smiled. "You'd better watch out for needles and pointed umbrellas."

Anton continued. "What we'd like to know now is if there are any copies of the software. What is it? SuperMax?"

"No. There are no copies. I sold it to the Russians, as you noted."

"Max, Max, Max. Now, that just doesn't seem to be very likely, does it? I mean, you named this child after yourself. Why would you just abandon it?" Anton nodded at Ellie once again, and she pressed her holo. A reddish light was emitted, one that activated the compliance sections of the human brain.

"There's no…no…copies …" Everson struggled to say. "Except for the flash drive."

"And where is this flash drive?"

"It's in my safe."

Anton almost chuckled at Everson's attempt at resistance. "Where is the safe, Max?"

"In this room."

"Thank you, Max. Where in this room?"

"Behind the painting."

Anton and Ellie both rolled their eyes.

"Which painting, and what is the combination?"

"Behind 'The Water Lily Pond' painting by Monet," said Everson, who then blurted a series of numbers.

Ellie went over to the painting and noticed its frame had a hinge on the right side. She moved the "Lily Pond," revealing the safe behind it. She punched in the numbers Everson provided, and the safe door opened. She nodded at Anton and began rummaging through the safe's contents. There was a large amount of cash, various jewelry pieces, a number of documents, and three flash drives. "There's more than one in here. What do you want to do?"

"Let's take them all. No telling what else Max has been up to," Anton said. Ellie put the drives in a jacket pocket and returned to her shadowy position.

"What are you going to do with me? Don't hurt me. You can have the money and the jewels," Everson blubbered.

"If it was up to me, I'd put you in your fireplace and add some logs. Make a real ash of yourself. But you've kind of done that already," Anton said. Ellie covered her mouth with a hand to hide her smile.

Everson just stared.

"Here you are, the richest man on the planet, and what have you done for the benefit of your fellow human beings? Nothing. No schools are named for you. No libraries. No charities. Nothing. Do you remember back in school when teachers talked about three forms of conflict? Man against nature. Man against man. Man against himself. You're oh for three, Max," Anton said in stern ridicule. "You know, there was a great line in a television series that I just watched that applies to you. One of the characters said to another, 'You are a parasite that eats joy and shits destruction.' That's you, Max. A parasite who lives to suck money from others, no matter how many it hurts."

"I don't know what you're talking about," said Everson.

"Tell me, Max, what's it like to go through life looking at people as mere dollar signs?"

"Shut up. Shut your mouth. You don't know anything about me. Do you have any idea how expansive my intellect is? You people are nothing but insects. Serfs. Dirt. Serf and turf." A hideously maniacal laugh followed.

"Serf and turf. Oh, you're hilarious. You really are the smartest man on the planet, aren't you Max?" said Anton. "I know plenty about you, Max. Too much, actually. But have you ever heard of Bobby Clay? Miriam Pederson? Everett Washington? Those are some of the people you hurt when you and your Russian friends robbed the banks in Hernando, Mississippi."

"They weren't really hurt that much. Maybe in the beginning. The FDIC would have paid them back."

"Maybe. Maybe not. There's a new wind blowing in Washington these days."

Ellie whispered to Anton. ("And blowing hard, too.")

"The dictionary is filled with appropriate adjectives for you, Max. Odious. Reprehensible. Detestable. Execrable. Flagitious…"

"Flagitious. Ooo, that's a good one," Ellie said.

"Yes, and I know of some old sailors who would have their own terminology, likely with a lot fewer syllables," Anton said. "The bottom line is, Max, with all you have accomplished and with all the money you've made, not many people on this planet would miss you if you weren't here. Not even your kids, I suspect. Well, we're going to change that."

Anton gave another nod to Ellie, who then spoke softly into her holo's comm feature, "Bring him up."

"Bring him up? Bring who up? What are you doing?" said Everson, struggling in vain to move.

Anton simply stared at Everson.

"Who's here? One of the Russians? Please, no. I can give you whatever amount of money you want. Don't forget the jewels. Even the paintings," Everson said. "Take what you want."

Anton then noticed a dark stain growing in the crotch of the billionaire's pajama bottoms.

Out of Everson's line of sight, Roggbach arrived at the bedroom door with Jonnie Barnes Jr. Ellie greeted the cadet and told him to return downstairs. She then led Jonnie Barnes to where Anton was seated.

"Who is this? He looks like something skid row rejected for being too rancid," spit Everson.

"You and he are going to get to know one another quite well. Tomorrow, Max, you are going to call a news conference. Invite all of the national media to attend," Anton said, leaning forward. "And this is what you're going to say..."

CHAPTER 42

The entire alphabet of the modern news universe—ABC, CBS, NBC, CNN, MSNBC, BBC, OAN, Fox, and dozens of their journalistic cousins from broadcast, print, and online—scrambled into action when word was received that Maxim Everson, the world's wealthiest man, was calling a news conference for 4 p.m. that day. News executives appreciated the start time; the event would make nearly all East Coast cable and network broadcasts. Everson had given little clue as to the subject matter, just that he planned a "huge" announcement.

Everson's news conference was to be held in the Rotunda of the Texas Capitol in the heart of Austin. Under most circumstances, use of the Rotunda for such an occasion would have been forbidden, but there was too much Everson money in too many pockets to turn him down. News trucks were soon lining Lavaca and Guadalupe streets, as well as their various tributaries.

Everson, clad in his signature all-black couture with black pearl sunglasses as an accessory, was seated on a small stage bearing a lectern and microphone. Seated with him was his usual coterie of aides, along with an unknown guest who was gathering murmurs from the news folk filling the first two floors of the Rotunda. Everson's guards, Daron and Tucker, stood behind the stage with their arms crossed.

A large blue banner above the stage, the ends attached to second-floor railings, vowed "A NEW BEGINNING" in all-cap silver letters.

Everson checked his watch, approached the lectern, and tapped the microphone.

"Good afternoon, everyone. Thank you very much for making your way here. I know it's a busy time around the news world, but I hope to make it worth your efforts on getting here.

"If you take note of the sign above me, you will see that it signals a new beginning. For me, it's a new venture, one that may be of benefit to millions of people. You folks with the notebooks and microphones and recorders have often referred to me as 'the world's richest man.' Perhaps I am, perhaps not. But for the record, let's just say, according to the last time I checked, I'm worth roughly 380 billion dollars."

The number drew some mild gasps, even from some of the more bark-skinned journalists.

"That's right. Billion with a B. I have been very fortunate. This country has made me a wealthy man. I have come far from my days in Estonia," Everson said. "And as my bank account has grown, so has my family."

The remark brought a few chuckles.

"For too long I have concentrated my life on my business interests, my companies. But life is more than business. Family is more important than companies. We will all face a day of reckoning at some point. That day has come for me.

"So, today I am announcing the formation of a project that will change America. Maybe change the world. I am forming a nationwide health care system that will be affordable to every American. No American will be turned away. Let me repeat that. Not one single American will be turned away. Pre-existing condition or no pre-existing condition.

"How serious am I? I will be investing 300 billion dollars in a range of investments and annuities to fund this health care system. That's right, 300 billion dollars. This system will be named SuperMax, and it will be headquartered right here in Austin. Yes, I thought of the name myself. We will take and screen applicants on a website that will soon launch. To avoid fraud, I will contract with teams of health professionals across the country to make home visits with all applicants. Only those truly in need of SuperMax health care will receive it."

The news conference was broadcast on all news channels of the television in the room adjoining the White House's Oval Office. The president threw his diet soda at the wall when he heard "300 billion dollars."

"What the fuck? WHAT THE FUCK!?!?" he bellowed. "He can't do that!"

"We are in the early stages of forming SuperMax, but I hope to have care providers recruited and the website launched by the end of the year. There may be some rough patches in the beginning, but let me assure you: Every man, woman, and child in America who needs health care will receive our help. While I hope to make SuperMax a primary health insurance system, I see it as a possible supplement to the various incarnations of Medicare. Since much of the health insurance in this country is paid for by employers, I am hoping to enroll U.S. companies and corporations under the SuperMax umbrella. I might say SuperMax is a version of nationalized health care, but it will be nationalized by a businessman and not the government.

"And now, keeping in mind that I am in the early stages on this endeavor, I will take some of your questions. My team has prepared and will be passing out packets that provide some of the details I did not go over. Now, to your questions."

The Fox News correspondent raised her hand.

"You said you are putting 300 billion dollars into this project. That means you will have only 80 billion dollars after that," she said.

Everson stared. "Is there a question in there? Suffice to say that I think I can live a full and meaningful life with 80 billion dollars. Next question, and, please, make it a question this time."

The CBS reporter was then acknowledged.

"You said no American will be turned away, no matter their pre-existing condition. Health insurance companies now turn people away all the time because they can't make it work financially. How are you going to make a profit?"

"I am happy to see that you are concerned about my welfare," Everson said to more smirks and chuckles. "Making a profit is not my first priority in this venture. If it happens, so be it. But I am very tired of seeing small children suffer. And I can assure you that the doctors and nurses employed by SuperMax will be well compensated. Next question."

Everson nodded to a reporter from the Associated Press.

"Will those who are covered under your plan...what is it? Super-Max, right? Will those covered by SuperMax have to pay anything?"

"This is explained in your packets. I am asking that our low-income applicants pay 10 dollars a month for SuperMax. Those who are doing a little better are asked to pay 20 dollars a month. Those funds will be blended into our investments to help pay for the overall plan. Let me add that if some applicants are so destitute that even 10 dollars a month is a burden, then they will pay nothing. You heard correctly. Nothing. If their situation improves, then they may be moved into the 10-dollar-a-month category. There are a number of tables in the packets, but I am trying to keep it simple. Next question, please."

A reporter for the Huffington Post raised her hand.

"How will you handle patients who might be seeking an abortion or abortion medication?"

"Ah. I am so glad you asked. I almost forgot. Forgive me for being a stupid man," Everson said, pointing to his head. "Any woman in need of such care will receive such care. I will pay for their transportation to any state of their choice that allows abortions."

The president jumped from his chair.

"What the fuck? WHAT THE EVER-LIVING, EVER-LOVING FUCK!?!?" he screamed. "Get Everson on the phone. Now!"

Everson continued. "In fact, SuperMax will operate a legal defense fund to address any legal ramifications from any state attorneys general who wish to make a name for themselves by getting in our way. I will also set aside an undetermined amount of money for a political fund to assist the opponents of any AG, any state lawmaker, or any congressman who takes a stand against us. Let's see who is ready to die on the hill of abortion now."

As the gathered newspeople sat in stunned silence, Everson's phone vibrated in his coat pocket. He pulled it out, glanced at the number, then silenced the phone and returned it to his jacket.

A *Houston Chronicle* reporter raised his hand. "Mr. Everson, when you refer to attorneys general, do you include the Texas attorney general? You said your headquarters will be in Texas, and he is a long-time abortion opponent."

"Yes, that includes him," Everson replied. "He may be in jail before any legal drama emerges, so it may be a moot point. I neglected to add that I will be contacting a number of pharmaceutical companies regarding drug-pricing issues and the abortion drug as well.

"Now, most of you know that I made much of my fortune from wind and solar power, so you may think this idea is nothing but hot air. But I can assure you it's not. Any more questions? Time is starting to run out."

The U.S. correspondent for the BBC was given the next query.

"I must say that this is a bold and audacious path you have set yourself upon."

"Thank you. Let me add that if SuperMax works here in the United States, we will look at expanding into other countries. Go ahead, ask your question."

"Thank YOU, Mr. Everson. I'm not sure if this is health care related or not, but there is one gentleman in your entourage whom I do not recognize. Can you tell us who this is?"

Everson smacked his head. "I am getting more forgetful every day. Let me introduce you all to Jonnie Barnes Jr. I have placed Jonnie in charge of my new counter-cyber unit. We don't have a name for it yet —maybe you folks can come up with something—but Jonnie and his team have been instructed to work with Silicon Valley and the National Security Agency to strengthen America's antivirus infrastructure to prevent any future attacks like the encroachment that occurred earlier this year. America's financial systems will soon be encased in a digital fortress."

The president of Russia had been watching Everson's news conference as well. He slammed his fists on his desk.

"*Какого черта?* What the hell? Who does this double-crossing fuck think he is!" he screamed at an aide. "Get me the GRU on the phone."

Everson waved an arm at Jonnie Barnes. "Jonnie, why don't you come up and say a few words to the nation."

Jonnie Barnes Jr., freshly shaven, with a new haircut and wearing an ill-fitting suit, a hand-me-down from Everson, rose from his seat and joined the billionaire at the lectern. He appeared shy and uneasy.

"Any questions for Jonnie?" Everson asked.

"Where are you from, Jonnie?" asked the Politico reporter.

"I'm from Eudora, Mississippi."

"Where did you go to school?" asked The New York Times reporter.

"I almost finished Hernando High School."

A low tremor of confusion rumbled through the journalists.

"What is your background in the cyber world?" said the Times reporter, grabbing a second question.

"Ain't got none except for playin' 'Call Of Duty.' Mr. Everson said he would pay for any trainin' I need." He's even puttin' me up at his mansion for the time bein'."

Not to be outdone by the Times, The Washington Post reporter asked, "Have you ever confronted a cyberattack?"

"Don't think so," said Jonnie. "I had a panic attack once, though."

More glances were exchanged about the Rotunda. The Newsmax reporter jumped in. "This sounds like a pretty important position. Just what are your qualifications?"

Barnes looked at Everson, who looked at his watch. "I'm afraid that is all the time we have now. Don't forget to pick up your packets. We will send out a news release tomorrow on Mr. Barnes and the cyber unit. Good day, all. Thank you again for showing up."

And then the two men turned and walked away amid questions dangling in the air.

CHAPTER 43

Anton, Ellie, and Roggbach had almost reached Interstate 55 in Mississippi by the time Everson had concluded his news conference. Xylar and Zeequon had already returned to their separate stations in Texas. The Cybertruck—rented under the name and persona of someone who does not exist—remained a mystery to police investigating the Everson mansion gate crash. Why there was no security footage of the incident, despite the 122 cameras about the compound, was also a mystery.

After a few hours, the van pulled into 1287 Beauvoir Drive in Hernando. An excited Gator jumped atop the sofa to herald the return of his pack leaders.

The two Guardians and Roggbach were greeted with hugs from Gorthand, Ungbar, and Margeen.

"Where's my sister?" Ellie asked.

Margeen shrugged, then quickly looked away. Ellie didn't need her empathic abilities to sense a conspiracy was afoot.

Anton, despite having holo-coached Everson, was still surprised to see Jonnie Barnes' countenance on the television as a newscaster attempted to summarize the news conference. He placed their luggage and equipment in the master bedroom then headed to the comm room to report to the Protectorate. As he formulated the message in his head, he was startled when both Dakkott and Julista exited the comm room. He looked at one, then the other. Neither would meet his gaze.

"Well, now, this is a surprise. But since I don't know either one of you that well, maybe not," said Anton.

Dakkott said, "I'm sorry Guardian. I didn't mean to..."

"It's fine, Dakkott. And it's still Anton. No judgment on my part. I just hope you both were...careful...if you want to finish up at the Academy."

The two cadets nodded.

"Now, if you'll both can excuse me, I need to send a report to our overlords," Anton said. "Julista, you might want to talk with your sister. I'm little help when it comes to these matters. That's one of the reasons I celebrate my coupling with Ellie."

Anton watched Dakkott and Julista go into the house, then he went into the comm room. He noticed a silky bit of black apparel on the cot; it was a pair of women's panties. A pair Ellie had loaned to her sister, to be specific. He shook his head and smiled.

He sat down and composed a communiqué to Sub-Protector Korphan. He indicated that the human billionaire Maxim Everson had been "persuaded" to avoid cyber activities going forth, and that he and Ellie had procured three flash drives from Everson's residence. At least one of them held the blueprint for the SuperMax virus. He made no mention of Jonnie Barnes Jr.

"It is my understanding that a supply ship will be dispatched to Earth to refuel the Dart Lurker used by the cadets. I will give the flash drives to the captain of that ship so they may be brought to Xylodon for analysis," he said in the report.

Anton also noted the roles played by Guardians Xylar and Zeequon, and the contributions of cadet Roggbach, in the success of the Austin mission. "If these six cadets are an indicator of what the Academy is producing, then the Protectorate training staff should be quite proud," he wrote.

He sent the message, then waited for any reply. He was surprised when one came quickly. "Message acknowledged. Mississippi Station should be aware that a supply vessel has already been dispatched.

After making some repairs at the moon sub-base, it will head to Earth. It should be at the coordinates provided earlier tomorrow night."

Tomorrow night. That's not a long time to say our goodbyes, Anton thought.

He returned to the house to find five of the cadets in the kitchen rummaging through the remaining treats from Elgin's Southside Market. Ellie and Julista were not among them; however, the door to the master bedroom was now closed, and he could hear voices on the other side.

He didn't need to raise his voice, but he wanted to make sure he had the cadets' attention.

"If you all could listen up for a moment. I guess it's a good thing I got back today because I just learned that a refueling ship will be arriving tomorrow night. I was planning on returning the van tomorrow, but it looks like we will need it for another day to get you all out there," he said.

"You mean we have to leave?" Ungbar asked.

"I think there are some folks at the Protectorate and the Academy who want to talk to you. I would suggest being as forthright as possible."

"I want to thank you, Guardian, for all you have done for us," Gorthand said. "We learned much more under your tutelage than we ever would at the Academy."

"Save your thanks for tomorrow. You should start preparing for the return trip—what you will wear, what gear you need. It should not take long to refuel a Dart Lurker, but we will still have to be cautious."

Margeen raised a hand to be acknowledged. "Anton, is there any chance we can take a pizza back with us?"

Anton looked at the cadets with puzzled surprise.

"Don't ask," said Gorthand.

"I won't say yes, and I won't say no right at the moment. Isn't that something else you would have to carry to where your ship is located? And I guess it will depend much on what you get accomplished tonight."

Margeen smiled, then stuck out her tongue at Gorthand.

The bedroom door opened, and two laughing women—one appearing to be a younger version of the other—emerged arm in arm.

Anton and the other cadets gave looks that begged for a report.

Ellie just stared back. "What? Did you think I was going to yell at my baby sister because she had sex for the first time?"

Roggbach choked on some surviving Buc-ee's jerky. Dakkott retreated hastily out the back door.

Ellie continued. "I just wanted to know if she did it right."

"Oh, my gawd," Ungbar said. "Honey, you need to come back to Xylodon and have your own show."

"Can't leave Gator and this guy behind," she said, pointing a thumb in Anton's direction. "Gator might never get fed. Or they might end up eating the same thing."

Margeen looked at Julista. "Anything you want to share with the group?"

"Nope," she said. "But I will take some of that barbecue."

Anton then told Ellie about his communications with the Protectorate.

"Oh, wow. Only one more night with my family."

"We're your family, too," Anton said.

"You know what I mean."

"While our guests are getting ready, you and I can put together a plan for tomorrow night. We'll still have the van, so that helps," he said. "We can have pizza delivered tonight, if that is OK with you. Margeen wants to take one back to Xylodon for scientific study or some such."

Margeen gave two thumbs up.

Ellie looked at Julista. "Don't you just love it when a man takes charge? Makes you want to jump all over him."

Now it was Julista's turn to walk out the back door.

"Roggbach, my young friend," Anton said to the cadet, who looked up from licking his fingers. "It looks like you will have to find a new place to sleep tonight."

And on the last day of the cadets' three weeks on Earth, let there be pancakes. And coffee.

The next morning, Anton and Ellie took their houseguests to a Hernando diner to gird themselves for the long trip home. There was much debate over what syrup was best, maple or blueberry.

"These pancakes are a wonder. So warm and fluffy," Margeen said. "The flavor balance between butter and syrup is sheer perfection. These humans may be savages in many ways, but you have to give them this. And then there's the coffee. *Deeznosh!*"

Ungbar goaded her. "So, Margeen. What's it going to be? A pizza parlor? A pancake house? Or both? There goes your long, distinguished career as a Guardian."

"At least I will have a career of some kind, you *nimnule,*" she fired back.

Ellie sipped from her mug. "You know, Michael," she said, using Anton's human persona, "I was starting to get used to the noise around the house. Now I think I will enjoy the quiet again."

Julista made a hand gesture she had learned from television.

Ellie feigned shock, then glanced at Anton. "You dress them up, take them places around the world, feed them well, and look what you get."

"Yes, a good thing we always followed the rules and never dipped into sarcasm," he said.

He received his own hand gesture in reply.

As Anton was paying the check, a woman, who many humans would charitably describe as "healthy," walked by their table wearing a T-shirt emblazoned with "Momma's Milk Bar" across the front. The cadets smothered their chuckles into their hands.

Anton started his best Bob Hope impression, "Thanks for the mam—"

Ellie put her hand over his mouth. "Stop. Don't. Just don't. Nope, nope, nope."

Ungbar preened, "I just have to get one of those shirts."

Dakkott raised a hand to garner Anton's attention. "Guardian, I…"

He was cut off by a chorus of shushes.

Dakkott continued. "Sorry. I have a request to fulfill before we return...," He pointed upward. "My cousin, who provided the vessel that brought us here, would like for us to bring something back."

"What would that be?" Anton asked.

"Some Earth coffee. Any brand will suffice."

"I think we can handle that," said Anton as his receipt arrived. Ellie gathered the group and drove them to a nearby grocery store.

"Just wait until you see this," said Ellie.

They entered the store, and the Guardians led the cadets to aisle 12. Before them was arranged shelf upon shelf of caffeinated enticements, with scores of coffee supplements as well.

Ellie gestured. "Have at it, kids."

The six cadets filled a shopping cart to almost overflowing. At the checkout line, a store worker rang up the items with a bemused eye. "What, no doughnuts to go with your coffee?"

"Maybe next time," replied Anton.

Back at the house after the long breakfast and store trip, Anton pardoned himself to go to the comm room. One by one, he placed the flash drives removed from Emerson's safe into his computer. The first held the origin code for SuperMax, the digital bug that had created mischief on multiple continents and fomented galactic consternation.

The second drive was also interesting—it held the names of humans across the planet who were paid various amounts by Maxim Everson. What was paid for was unclear, but beside each name there was an account number, sometimes more than one. Many of the names appeared to be in the American and Russian governments, but those were hardly the only countries.

I think I'll make a copy of this, just in case, Anton decided. He downloaded the information into a file on his computer desktop.

The third flash drive took him aback. It was filled with video files. From Everson's bedroom and other locations. Anton had only to glance at one to get the general idea. He started to toss the drive but then thought better of it. *This will make Korphan spit up his coffee when he sees it.*

While Anton was on the computer, Ellie and Julista began their parting dance.

"Will I ever see you again?" Julista asked.

"Yes, sister, I'm sure of it. As you know, my stay here was extended, but at some point, the Protectorate will allow us to return," Ellie said. "You have just two more years to go at the Academy, so who knows? The Protectorate could send you to Earth."

"Two years seems so long. But I guess it is pretty short considering we had not seen one another in a decade," Julista said. "I know the Protectorate does not allow new Guardians to pick their assignments, but perhaps I can emphasize my experience on Earth."

The pair began to tear up. They hugged and sobbed. Gator whimpered.

"I will miss little Gator. I would like a companion like him," Julista said.

"Speaking of companions, you must promise to let me know if any ceremonies are forthcoming," Ellie said, with a nod in Dakkott's direction.

Julista wept once more.

Ungbar cleared his throat. "OK, you two. That's enough tears. Let's get some pictures before we go. Gather 'round, everybody."

Dakkott retrieved Anton, setting off a carnival of photographic memories. Everyone was allowed to take whatever group or individual shots that they desired. Gator managed to get into more than a few; Dakkott and Julista had Ellie take pictures of themselves behind the wheel of the Tesla.

As late afternoon approached, the four male cadets loaded the van with their gear, including the pizza for Margeen. Anton opened a bottle of red wine and filled glasses for all.

He raised his glass in a toast. "Here's to new friends, renewed relationships, brave actions, and to safe journeys. And here's to Xylodon."

"Hear, hear," the others said in unison.

As the light began to fade, the eight Xylodonians piled into the van. Ellie carried Gator on her lap as the vehicle headed into the Mississippi countryside. As the inevitable parting neared, a somber silence overtook the camaraderie.

The van's headlights provided solitary illumination on the road after the vehicle passed the service station first encountered by the cadets. Anton pulled the van onto the road's shoulder. He checked his holo comms. "The supply vessel is ready to rendezvous. I guess we should be on our way."

Anton grabbed a large flashlight as the cadets collected their belongings. Ellie stood outside the van holding Gator.

"Aren't you coming with us?" Julista said.

"No, sister. Someone has to stay with the van in case human authorities happen to come along. Besides, I might not be able to stand watching you fly away."

They hugged once more.

"Go now, sister. Join your friends."

A red-eyed Julista nodded her head. She turned and crossed the fence into the empty field. After about ten paces, she turned and waved at her sister. Ellie waved back then entered the van.

After a short march, the group found the Dart Lurker. The commander of the supply ship was waiting for them; his crew had begun the refueling operation. A couple of cows stood nearby watching.

"Are those the same cows we saw when we landed?" Margeen asked.

"Who knows? Maybe. How can you tell?" said Roggbach. "It would be appropriate if it were them. They greeted us after we landed. They might as well see us off."

Anton handed the three flash drives to the supply captain. "Make sure Korphan gets these immediately. The Protectorate's cyber unit will be most interested in at least one of these."

"Yes, Guardian," the commander replied.

The cadets and Anton gathered for a group hug. "Send word when you arrive safely," he told them. "It has been an honor serving Xylodon with you."

The cadets began boarding the Dart Lurker. Julista held back. She hugged Anton once more. "Please take care of my sister. She's all I have."

"That's not entirely true," he said, looking toward Dakkott. "But I promise you I will do my best."

Julista wiped some tears then joined her companions.

Anton moved to a safe distance to watch. Even in stealth mode, one could make out the edge of the ships as they lifted off; first the supply ship, then the Dart Lurker. Within seconds, they were gone in a whoosh. Soon, Anton heard only crickets and a few startled cows.

The adventure born at an Academy café table had drawn to a close in a Mississippi field.

Anton returned to the van and found Ellie sobbing. He put his arms around her and kissed her forehead.

"I have a feeling we will see her again. And sooner than you may think," he said.

Ellie nodded and wiped her cheeks. "Perhaps. I hope so. I would like that." The last word ended with a choking sound. Finally, she said, "Let's go home."

EPILOGUE

"Well, look who's back," said a beaming Kendall Guthrie. She made a bowing gesture. "The Gurls will be so happy you're back."

Their return to Hernando Elementary seemed somewhat anticlimactic to Michael Gort and Ellen Atkinson, but it brought a welcome reduction in stress as well. And it was not without a few rewards—Michael received a high five from little Curtis Mouton in the hallway.

Kendall's welcome brought Principal Helene Appleberry out of her office.

"Am I ever glad to see you two. I can't tell you how many shades of Hades it was getting substitutes for your classes," Helene said. "Well, was whatever it was you did worth losing all your sick days and leave till next fall?"

Ellie thought, *Wouldn't you like to know*. She answered for them both. "Yes, indeed. I hadn't seen my sister in a long time, so showing her the sights was a joy."

"Good morning, Helene. Kendall. Who are these strangers and what sights are we referring to?" said Chadwick Cartwright, dropping off some documents to Kendall.

Ellie had readied her cover story. "We gave Memphis a good look-see, and we went over to Tupelo for a bit. There's a nice B&B there. My sister is a big Elvis fan. Didn't she tell you that when you went out?"

"No, actually. We talked about other things," Chadwick said.

"You didn't tell her your 'elephant woman' story, did you?" Michael asked.

"No, I did not. That would certainly not have been gentlemanly of me," he replied. "But Ellie, how is your sister? I was hoping I might hear from her again. I thought we had a lovely time."

"She told me she had a wonderful time, Chad. But sorry, I wouldn't wait too long by the phone for her," Ellie said. "She plans on touring Europe for a year before going to graduate school. She's already gone, actually."

"Well, that's certainly my loss. I want you to know I would have made a remarkable brother-in-law."

Michael coughed.

"Shame on you, Michael. You know it's true. Think about all the summertime cookouts you'll be missing. Aperitifs on the veranda," Chadwick said.

Michael and Ellie looked at one another. "I think it's time to get to class," Michael said.

They held hands as they walked down the elementary school hallway until they found their respective corridors. Michael gave Ellie a kiss.

"And we have found it yet again," he said as they broke hands.

"Found what?"

"Normalcy. Whatever that is."

Three months later…

Thomas Dettwiler slowly retrieved the crankbait attached to his new fishing rod, a gift from his colleagues after retiring from the FBI. He was hoping for even a small explosion as the bait formed a vee on the water as it returned toward him. No such luck. He cast again, and the lure puh-looped below the surface.

Standing on the shore of his lakeside property in the sticks of northern Mississippi, Dettwiler considered how fishing mirrored his career. *You keep searching and keep casting until you finally get a bite,* he thought. *You can't catch if you don't throw. And sometimes you hook a big one.*

He cast again, about thirty degrees away from his previous attempt. *Life is certainly much easier now,* he thought. No bank thefts to investigate. No school shooters to chase. No more office politics. But sometimes Dettwiler would remember a few of those "big ones" that got away. Roy McDonald. Radley Duvall.

Dettwiler kept his hand in the law enforcement game a bit, doing some consulting on old cases. Agent David Broadscale would call occasionally to check on him and to "shoot the shit" about Washington. What a mess. Broadscale. for whom venting was becoming a medical necessity, described the management style of the new director, a conspiracy theorist with Marty Feldman eyes, as "barely controlled chaos." Dettwiler didn't miss it—the powers that be in Washington appeared more interesting in freeing criminals than catching them.

He reeled in his bait and headed to the cabin's kitchen for a sandwich and a fresh beer. Dettwiler did instinctively what most American men do when they enter a room with a television: He turned it on but with the audio muted. He could not recognize the well-coiffed, well-dressed man on the screen, but the crawler type under the picture identified him as Jonnie Barnes Jr., CEO of so-and-so tech company in Texas. Apparently, the company had made some antivirus software breakthrough.

Dettwiler didn't think much of it as he slathered mustard on two slices of bread. Then he stopped. Jonnie Barnes. Jonnies Barnes Jr. *Where have I heard that name?*

Like a small fish at the end of his line, the thought kept tugging at him. *Maybe the answer is in my files. Damn it, I stashed them all in the basement.*

He started to walk away from the half-made sandwich but stopped after a couple of steps.

Nah. I'm retired. It can wait.

"I can't wait any longer. This is fucking ridiculous," the president told his hand-picked FBI director. "It's been months."

"But, dear leader, please tell me what has been missing for months. I know nothing about this," the director replied.

"That damn freeze gun. The one that guy used to paralyze everyone in Congress. I want one," said the president, now playing with a model airplane. "Zoom. Zoom."

The director looked at video of the incident the president had described. His eyes, surprisingly, got wider. "Mr. President, I don't see a gun."

"It's got to be there somewhere. I want you to put one hundred agents on this, and I want results."

"Yes, sir, Mr. President. I'm not sure I have one hundred agents left after all the cutbacks, but I will see what I can do," the director said. "Can I ask what you will use this freeze gun, or whatever it is, for?"

"All these people with French names. There's too many of them. And some of them aren't even in France. Got to do something about that," the president said. "Whatever happened to those great Polish names? Like Schlotzky."

The director pulled at his eyebrows. "All right, sir. Let me get right on this. Find a mysterious freeze gun that no one can describe. Got it, sir."

"Oh, and Mr. Director?"

"Yes, Mr. President."

"Do you know what will happen if you can't find it?"

"No, sir. Tell me."

"You're fired."

"Fuck me," said Jonnie Barnes Jr. Once again, he had run out of guesses playing Wordle. He pulled at his shirt collar. Wearing shirts and ties every day aggravated the pimples and ingrown hairs on his neck.

The intercom buzzed. "Mr. Barnes, you have a call on line four," said his secretary.

He hit the blinking button.

"Woooooooo-weeeee. Look at you, sonny boy. You have a secretary. I always knew you'd make good somehow."

"Good morning, Dad. Thanks. What do you want now?" said Jonnie Jr., who had already bestowed a new truck and big-screen television on his father.

"Dad now, is it? Used to be Pop. Anyway, me and Shonea are going to be passing through Austin next week. You up for lunch?"

Jonnie knew that meant he would have to pick up the tab.

"Sure, Dad, just let me know when you get in. I gotta go. Got a call holdin'."

"Wooooo-weeee. A call holdin'. Big, important man, you are. Working for Max Everson hisself. All right, son, see ya next week."

Click. There was no other call.

He hit the intercom.

"Hey, Sherrie."

"Yes, Mr. Barnes?"

"Can you show me how to get on Facebook again?"

Isabella Muñoz had been working at her *tia*'s restaurant, Rio Grande Cocina, for only a few weeks. The hours were long, but the tips were good. Some customers got a bit handsy, giving her momentary flashbacks to her captivity with the Aryans—but one pleading look to her aunt, a razor-tongued Mayan matriarch, would result in the offender being put in the street.

Isabella was on break in the kitchen and watched one of her fellow waitresses deliver a Modelo to a solitary male customer at a corner table. It was a less well-lit section of the dining room, but the man's physique seemed familiar. Isabella looked away, trying to place him, then looked again. She couldn't get a clear look at his face from this vantage point.

Her coworker then entered through the kitchen's swinging doors, snared a plate of beef enchiladas, and headed back out into the dining room. Isabella moved to the doors; its windows offered a better view of the corner table.

She put her hand to her mouth and gasped.

The man in the corner was the coyote who had led her family through the tunnel and into El Paso. He was also the *gran hijo de puta* who had sold her to the Aryans. He had shaved his beard, but she knew it was him. She bit her hand as the man bit into his enchiladas.

Isabella hurried to the employee restroom, locked herself in a stall, pulled out her cellphone, and called her contact at the El Paso FBI office. Special Agent Damian Cruz, one of the last Hispanics still employed by the FBI, answered.

"Cruz here."

"Agent Cruz, I don't know if you will remember me, but this is Isabella Muñoz. I led the police to that tunnel in the warehouse that had been filled in."

"Yes, Isabella, of course I remember you. What can I do for you?"

"The leader of the coyotes—I can't remember his name—is in my restaurant. Right now. He's here. Sitting like nothing happened."

"I believe the man's name is Ernesto Cabrillo. He is high on our Most Wanted list. Are you in a safe place?" Cruz asked.

"Yes. For now. I am hiding in a restroom."

"What is your restaurant's address?" She texted the information.

"Good," said Cruz. "Stay where you are. We will have some agents there in a few minutes."

Isabella sat on the floor, her face in her hands, occasionally trembling, and waited. The bustling sound of her chattering co-workers outside the restroom did nothing to relieve her trepidation. *He's out there.* She was unable to measure time amid her fear. *When will the police get here? This is taking too long. What if he…*

The restroom door opened, and then the stall door rattled. Isabella almost screamed.

"Isabella, it's Agent Cruz. I'm here with your aunt. It's OK to come out."

Cruz led her to the dining room. "He was sitting over there?" he asked. The table was now empty, but the plate and beer bottle were still there.

"Yes, that is where I saw him. Where is he now?"

"We don't know," said Cruz. "He was gone by the time we got here. Didn't finish his dinner." Cruz signaled to another agent, who placed the beer bottle in a plastic bag. That agent then began dusting that side of the table for prints.

"This should let us know if it really was Cabrillo. If it is, that's a bit worrisome to know he's operating on this side of the river," Cruz said. "Isabella, do you know if he saw you?"

"I don't think so. I was in the kitchen on break."

"Good to know. Thanks again, Isabella, we'll take it from here. I will let you know of any developments. I promise," said Cruz. *"Te lo prometo."*

After the agents left the restaurant, Isabella's aunt asked her if she wanted the rest of the night off.

"No, *tia*. If it is all the same to you, I want to stay right here for now."

She sank into her aunt's embrace and wept.

The six cadets were hailed as heroes upon their return by their fellow Academy enrollees. No cadet had ever flown off-planet before, unless with special Presidium or Protectorate permission, much less six of them. The Academy directors had created special commendations for Dakkott, Julista, Margeen, Ungbar, and Gorthand for their assistance to the St. Petersburg mission, and Roggbach was given a similar commendation for his actions in Austin, Texas.

But the commendations came with strings. The cadets would have to make up all assignments that they had missed, and they would have to devise a collective presentation on what they had experienced. That presentation would be given to the entire Academy and to any members of the Protectorate and Presidium who requested it. In short, they would be dancing at the behest of all who desired it.

Sub-Protector Korphan added yet another string. "You young fools," he called them. The six couldn't tell, but behind those words was a smile. He ordered the cadets to spend the next twelve weekends washing and cleaning all Xylodonian vessels. Some of the ships were not housed in facilities; they were parked outside in Xylodon's heat.

Ungbar huffed and puffed. "What is it they say on Earth? 'To the victor belong the spoils'? Well, this victory is spoiling my complexion."

"Oh, hush, Ungbar. You know you had a good time on Earth. This is the price you pay. That we all pay," Dakkott said. "It's not like we didn't know it was coming."

Gorthand put some suds on a hull and began to wipe. "I miss little Gator."

"I miss my sister," said Julista.

"I miss pizza. And ice cream. And pancakes," said Margeen.

Roggbach asked, "Hey, Margeen, what happened to that pizza you brought back with you?"

"I took it to the Academy research department. They are going to see if they can replicate it."

"Interesting. Then what?"

"Then, who knows?" she said. "Maybe I will open up a café someday, especially if I don't get the assignment I want. Have Earth food on the menu. And different coffees."

Dakkott reminded her, "You know you are obligated to the Protectorate for at least eight years."

"We'll see," Margeen replied. She splashed some water at Dakkott, who tried to duck but failed. *Splat!* The others laughed. "All right, Julista, tell us what you want to do after the Academy. Where do you want to serve?"

Julista never looked up.

"Earth."

And then she threw down her rag and walked away.

Lurkon-4 sat at his desk staring at the flash drive that had once belonged to Maxim Everson. He and his team had analyzed the code for days. It was simple for trained Xylodonians to take apart, but it was more sophisticated than any other software they had seen humans produce. *They are getting dangerous, these humans,* he thought. He put the flash drive in his own safe.

It was almost as if Jenklor-9, the chief engineer on the Protectorate's cyber unit, had the same thought at the same time as Lurkon. Actually, that wasn't quite true. Jenklor and his fellow engineers had developed rising concern the more they explored SuperMax. One of his colleagues posed an idea; it seemed ludicrous at first. But the more Jenklor thought about, given what had happened on the SuperMax mission, the less crazy the idea seemed.

He worked up the nerve to pose it to Lurkon. Perhaps a more seasoned Guardian could sprinkle some sanity on the plot.

"Enter," Lurkon said to the knock at his door. In stepped Jenklor.

"Sir, I was wondering if I you had some time. I would like to speak to you about an idea that I and the other engineers have been discussing."

Lurkon pointed to a chair. "Please, have a seat, Jenklor. Now, tell me. What is this idea?"

"This SuperMax program indicates that the humans are reaching a level of deviousness that we never expected. Don't you agree?"

Lurkon nodded. "Yes, and what they did with this software was most alarming. There was no conscience, no empathy attached to the human's use of this software."

"Yes, sir, and it came close to ending our operations on Earth."

"Perhaps not that serious, but serious indeed. I have forwarded your findings and my recommendations in a report to Sub-Protector Korphan and the Presidium. I have not yet heard back from them, but it's early, so I'm not surprised," Lurkon said.

"Forgive me, commander. Not knowing what your recommendations include, let me share with you what my colleagues are suggesting. I was unconvinced at first, but now I find it somewhat intriguing."

Lurkon noticed that Jenklor appeared to be hedging his words. *He doesn't want to put himself too far out there.*

"We had reviewed Anton's action report, how he had taken the persona of the Russian cyber commander."

"Yes, go on."

"We were curious to know if anyone in the Protectorate had considered taking Anton's actions a step further?"

"What do you mean?" said Lurkon, eyebrow raised.

"What if we replaced the leader of a human nation with a Xylodonian operative? Have the operative take the persona of a president or king or chancellor," said Jenklor. "If you control the leader, you control the government. If you control the government, you control the country. Put the right operative in the right position, and we would never have to worry about any more SuperMaxes. Ever again. And think of the other human problems we might avoid or correct as well."

Lurkon stared at Jenklor for a hard half minute. "You haven't put any of this down in writing, have you?"

"No, commander, I wanted to speak with you first. We are just computer engineers, not field operatives. But the idea is interesting, is it not?" he said. "If not for an actual operation, perhaps it could make a good book, at least."

"Hmmm. A book. Books are interesting, but you might want to weigh what you put down on paper. Paper leaves a trail. You never know who will read it and what they might do that could affect a budding career. Do you understand my meaning?" Lurkon said. "And you do know the Protectorate has a strict prohibition against interfering with other life forms, don't you? This case was an exception. The humans attacked us, even though they didn't know it."

"Yes, commander. Noninterference. I remember that principle from the Academy."

"It's good that you do. Well, this is all very interesting. You and your colleagues are quite creative. But let's put this idea on the shelf and keep you fellows out of trouble," said Lurkon, gesturing toward his office door.

"Thank you, commander. I just needed to hear a voice of reason." Jenklor left.

Lurkon sat for a moment, stewing in his internal disquiet. Then he stared at his safe.

Replacing a human leader with a Xylodonian agent...that could never work, Lurkon mused.

Could it…?

ACKNOWLEDGEMENTS

My knowledge of the cyber world is limited, so a big shout out goes to my son, Brian McGrath, who is a president at a Texas information technology firm. He pointed me in the direction of the NSO Group and its brainchild, Pegasus, which is the inspirational genesis for SuperMax. He also provided the broad strokes of how a cyber theft could be attempted and how the thieves might be tracked down via the activities between crypto exchanges and "cyber wallets." The website for Chainalysis, a firm that tracks global crypto crime, also assisted with supplying information on the scope and nature of such activity; the $24 billion figure quoted by Lurkon-4 comes from that company's website. The information about the hack of the U.S. Treasury comes from a December 31, 2024, article by CNN.

The website CSO assisted with defining "zero-day bugs" and related terminology, and it provided some of the examples given in this book.

Details on the activities of Russia's Internet Research Agency were provided by a 2019 Wired article by Andy Greenberg and the 2024 book "Interference" by Aaron Zebley, James Quarles, and Andrew Goldstein. The trio were part of the Mueller team that investigated Russian meddling in the 2016 presidential election. Additional details came from a 2015 New York Times Magazine article by Adrian Chen, appropriately titled "The Agency," and a 2017 NBC News interview and story with Russian tell-all troll Vitaly Bespalov, who penned an exposé of the troll farm under a pseudonym. A 2018 article by Charles Maynes for The World website and a 2017 article by Louise Boyle for the Daily Mail broadened the details in Bespalov's account. Amazingly, Bespalov is still alive and residing in St. Petersburg. The material on

Russian propaganda attacks on Moldova was reported by NewsGuard. The subsequent failures of attempted Russian election interference in France and Moldova were widely reported by various news services.

The incidents and references of a political nature described or commented upon by the characters come from an assortment of news media accounts. Any resemblance to actual events or human inhabitants of Earth is entirely satirical.

A huge thank you goes to my former Houston Chronicle colleague Suzanne Garofalo, who used her +4 sword of editing to whip this story into shape. She corrected my predilections for dropping question marks and messing up Xylodonian names. Suzanne, you did a great job.

And, as always, thanks to those at Stoney Creek Publishing who have kept this novel dream alive.

ABOUT THE AUTHOR

Paul McGrath is an award-winning journalist and educator whose career spans five decades. He spent thirty-seven years working at the *Houston Chronicle* after stints in Conroe, Lubbock, and Lockhart, Texas. His debut novel, *Left*, won the fall 2025 PenCraft Award for Literary Excellence in science fiction.

McGrath graduated from Texas A&M University and earned a master's degree from Marist College. He and his wife, Liz, live on a tranquil fish-filled lake near Houston, Texas.

Think the saga of Anton and Ellie is over? Don't be a *nimnule*.
Look for our space visitors to fashion together an encore performance in *All That's Left*, coming soon!

Scan the QR code for 20% off for other installments in the Terran Incognita Series, as well as other award-winning titles

Stoney Creek Publishing
A Member of the Texas Book Consortium

www.ingramcontent.com/pod-product-compliance
Lightning Source LLC
Jackson TN
JSHW081219140826
106542JS00005B/1
9781965766811